The BADNESS

The BADNESS

NANE QUARTAY

A
SBI
PUBLICATION

A STREBOR BOOKS INTERNATIONAL LLC PUBLICATION
DISTRIBUTED BY SIMON & SCHUSTER, INC.

Published by

Strebor Books International LLC
P.O. Box 6505
Largo, MD 20792
http://www.streborbooks.com

ISBN 13: 978-1-59309-037-1   ISBN: 1-59309-037-4
LCCN 2004118327

Distributed by Simon & Schuster, Inc.
1230 Avenue of the Americas
New York, NY 10020
1-800-223-2336

Cover Design: www.mariondesigns.com

First Printing May 2005
Manufactured and Printed in the United States

10 9 8 7 6 5 4 3 2 1

ACKNOWLEDGMENTS

Sometimes a journey can begin without your knowledge. It may come to you disguised as an artistic spark of imagination or it may be lit by the fuse of a muse unspoken. I've been fortunate in my travels, encountering many people who have come into my life and helped me touch flame, igniting the fire that has enlightened my path. I wish to thank them here.

To Teresa Sterrett, for having my back and believing in my talent. I'll never forget the way you looked at me when I was trying to be creative and asked, "What got into you?" Your support and affection have kept my light burning. Luv you, gurl!

Much love to all my friends who lent me those all-important words of encouragement when the weather got rough. There are so many...and I'm trying to name them all!

To Stephanie Kelly for a love that transcends and lasts with a strength beyond separation. Remember: "Creation is between prayer and fasting; between burning and blasting!" I sincerely hope that you find the true artist inside you.

To a few unsung readers who let me invade their intellectual space and that took the time to read my novel...and gave me some dap when I needed it. Norma Chapman, Bernard Moseby, Cheryl King, Darlene Roberts, Pam Shepard, Jennifer Moak, Hugh Matson, David Perez, Jennifer Hong, Keith Sowell, Georgia (Lorraine) Burdett, Pat Cook, and Crystal Taylor.

I also got mad love from new acquaintances that welcomed me with open arms after my move back to the East Coast. Group hug! Group hug! To my Dank Brothers who I often got lifted with: Adryann Glenn (looking for you on the airwaves, uhhh!), Jason Ferebee (I am not angry, I am anger!), and Erik Reid (ATL!!! ATL!!!). To my ex-Smart Tee's (I'm laughing!): Jackie Penn, Rajjae Brown, Richard Smith (I'm still shredding papers); and Ken Blount (who still owes me money).

Writing can be a lonely occupation but the kinship of fellow scribes often helps take the edge off the solitary journey. First off, I'd like to thank Zane (Publisher, Strebor Books), a mentor by her actions and a fearless lady. My forever gratitude for taking a chance on me and allowing my flights of fancy to get some wind underneath them—they gain altitude with every page. (And let me take a moment to holla at Wayne for being my mudda-fudda!!!) Big Up to Charmaine Parker for the thankless and stressful job that you do and for always having a moment to answer my many questions no matter how mundane they might be. Many, many thanks. To JD Mason, thanks for pointing me in the right direction and sending me on my way. To my fellow Strebor authors who have shown me that there is strength in numbers: D.V. Bernard, Harold L. Turley II, Tina Brooks McKinney, Allison Hobbs, Rique Johnson, Jonathan Luckett, Shonell Bacon, Michael Baptiste, Laurinda D. Brown, Shonda Cheeks, JDaniels, J. Marie Darden, Shelley Halima, Laurel Handfield, Keith Lee Johnson and Darrien Lee.

Like many writers before me, when I first embarked on this writing journey, I traveled on the Internet Highway. Many websites granted me access to their spaces and I would like to acknowledge them here. Memphis Vaughn at Timbooktu, Tee C. Royal at RAWSISTAZ, NEB Publishing, LooseLeaves, MystNoir, Shades of Romance (SORMAG), Blackrefer, Powell's Books,

The Sista Circle, Ebony Pages, A Place Of Our Own (APOOO), Nubian Goddess Publishing, Cushcity and Nubian Sistas.

I would also like to extend a big "Thank You" to the many bookstores that have been gracious enough to allow me the opportunity to host book signings at their place of business. Finally, I would like to give much love to the many readers that have turned out to lend me their support and good-will. It has been my pleasure to meet and greet each and every one of you.

Peace!
Nane Q

PROLOGUE

The cornfield glowed with a soft yellow light that pulsed gently, illuminating a rugged, wooden shotgun house that stood at the field's edge. The building was a weatherbeaten gray that appeared haunted in the ethereal cast of light, and a large porch enclosed by a handrail, protruded out into the yard. The banister stood with strength despite the years-old cracks and crevices designed by nature's hot and cold mood swings ingrained in its design. There was no lawn in front of the house, just ancient, war-torn dirt, stomped and stained with the spilled blood of soldiers from the Civil War that had just freed the slaves from bondage. A busted-up wagon lay crippled on the side of the house pining for a wheel repair, languishing crookedly and looking forward to better, more useful days. Several cords of wood were stacked neatly in front of the wagon, drying out in the heat, aging and priming for eventual burning in the hearth that would provide heat for the house in the coming winter months.

A family gathered in the front yard, having an "old-fashioned hoedown," dancing and kicking up dust in a joyful cloud. Grandmother and grandfather sat at an old, rough-hewn table with content smiles spread across their faces as they acknowledged the respectful, loving hugs and kisses that were rained upon them. Daisy Mae and Lam-Lam had given birth to thirteen children who had, in turn, sired the brood of grandchildren that were now whooping and hollering, running around the yard, jumping up and down on the old busted wagon, causing playful havoc with the unbridled joy of youth.

Daisy Mae and Lam-Lam seemed to have had their children in pairs; like *matching sets in a genetic game of chess. Some of them had skin of deep, dark chocolate like their mother, while others shared Lam Lam's steep, sloping forehead and piercing eyes. They all shared genetic similarities indicative of their clan; all except for the first-born son they named Jefferson Browne.*

Jefferson differed from the others in much more than the physical attributes that marked his other siblings. From his towering air of superiority down to his stoic demeanor, Jefferson Browne always seemed to be a hair's breadth away from his brothers and sisters, a tiny step removed from inclusion in the family circle. He kept to himself, seeming to make an effort to stay contrary to the family consensus. If his brothers went left, he went right. If they jumped up, he sat down. While his family planned on tending the land and tilling the soil, Jefferson Browne placed his stake in the tenets of education. He was rumored to be a highfalutin' man, stuck on book learning and fanciful notions bred by the white man. He ridiculed his family's primitive customs, boldly dismissing their silly superstitions as ignorant blindness, a darkness descended from tribal memory. The power of bags of bones and witches' concoctions held no threat or meaning to Jefferson, so he openly scoffed at the credibility that his family gave to the supernatural. For every unexplained occurrence—from lightning strikes to floods to sickness and even stomachaches—his kinfolk would attribute the misfortune to the madness of the devil. To demon bones that rattled in the night. Jefferson pitied their stupidity.

Three generations of the family tree milled around the yard, enjoying distant relatives that might soon be distant for years to come. A steady hum of family talk could be heard in snatches of conversations when the dark shadow of Daisy Mae's sister, Ruby-Ruby, wobbled into view. Ruby-Ruby was an old witch who practiced roots. She was a fearful old woman who carried a jaded whisper in her cowl, a slight curse in her shoes and blight's madness on her lips. A wide path automatically opened whenever Ruby-Ruby walked by; tales of her dark work preceded her. She was root-woman, darkened voodoo with eyes peering into the spirit world, eyes that translated evil mojo into guttural syllables. Ruby-Ruby was a painstaking woman and sensible folks avoided her misery at all costs. They had seen her spill guts in the dirt and twist minds into addled spins and dips. They had watched from the corners of their eyes as an angry man had once stormed into her hut only to emerge, minutes later, with a permanent crook in his neck. Years before, they had seen a pregnant girl go in to see Ruby-Ruby and emerge a short while later, childless, her previously swollen belly as flat as a board, while she fled, sobbing hysterically. Ruby-Ruby caused a light tread, an easy step from the average person...but Jefferson Browne was far from the average man.

Ruby-Ruby stopped at the table with a loud exclamation and opened her arms invitingly as she greeted her sister and brother-in-law. They exchanged wide grins; the warmth of their embrace was as real and deep as the midday sunshine and as radiant as the beautiful day that surrounded them. They shared a sisterly bond that, for a brief moment, gave Ruby a reflection of normalcy, a step just outside of the surreal world she claimed to reign over. But all too soon that moment passed. Her body went rigid and she turned, eyes widened, as she gazed out at the people in the yard. Ruby-Ruby took two steps forward and let loose a wild, yipping yell.

"I-I-I, E-E-E, I-I-I, E-E-E, I-I-I..."

People moved as one to form a circle around her as she sucked her skinny, wiry frame to its full height. Her features took on an otherworldly-type quality as her forehead bulged, then flattened; bulged, then flattened in an eerie syncopation. With eyes as big as saucers, the pupils shifting from dark black to a translucent gray and back again, her bony arms dangled at her side, twitching and bumping against her tiny waist. She shrieked again.

"I-I-I-, E-E-E, I-I-I, E-E-E, I-I-I..."

Suddenly the back door of the house banged open and out stepped Jefferson Browne.

Jefferson Browne was a big man. He wore cotton pants that were held in place by a pair of suspenders made of thin, hard rope. His boots were made of some kind of animal skin with waxed stitches running across his ankles. Big, bald and large with a wide African nose, Jefferson was intimidating. His eyes were unrelenting and his features wore anger and violence like a skin tone. His very presence could sometimes dissuade opposition.

Jefferson muscled his way past his cousins in the yard. They were frozen in place, afraid to move lest they draw Ruby-Ruby's attention; none of them wanted that, so they watched in horrified fascination as Jefferson stalked right up to his aunt and glared at her. Silence descended upon the yard, sight and sound became immobile in the face of the oncoming cataclysm—even the wind stilled when Ruby-Ruby's eyes darkened to scarlet red orbs of fire. Jefferson stood firm.

3

Ruby-Ruby trembled and shuddered. It was an evil undulation with dark implications.

"You mixed yo' seed, boy! For that you suffer."

"Ruby-Ruby," Jefferson said calmly. "I suffer every time I see your back-country, root-totin' ass."

Ruby-Ruby shrieked. Jefferson talked over her.

"I mean roots and voodoo and black magic and devil bones and all that…ain't never got you a thing…yet it's your god. Your deity, for chrissakes!"

"Yeahya." Ruby's voice was deep, its timbre resonant with the quality of a dark pit. "Yeahya. Chrise. For chrissake. That's dem white folks' god. Yo'sen too, now that you done gone and mixed seed wid 'em."

Jefferson's jaw dropped. How did his aunt know about his trips over to the Wheatleys' farm, his wild romps out in the cotton fields with the young white girl! It had only been a couple of times since he had been sexing with her. Janie Wheatley was a country girl. Her body was thick and hefty, her figure solid and hewn from the hard work that farm life demanded. She was stern of hip and her body was strong enough for Jefferson Browne to buck up between her legs with all the force and rage that he felt he owed her. Janie would take the pounding that he gave her and breathe heavily as she reached for more. She would cry out like a cat when he took her from behind, especially when he curled a handful of her blond hair in his fist and pulled her head back to meet his thrusts. He would buck up into her until she pushed her face into the hay and screamed. He knew she loved it. She wasn't nothing.

They were as secretive as spies—but as careful as he had been, he hadn't been cautious enough and now this root woman had found him out.

"Now, I gots to do sumptin' to ya'," Ruby-Ruby finished as her body began to dance a macabre jig.

Jefferson cursed her. "You ain't doing a gotdamn thing to me, devil woman." He spun on his heel and stormed back toward the house. He was nearing the foot of the stairs when a sharp pain stung him with a dizzying force that felled him. His hand flew to the side of his head, clasping his ear as he cried out in anguish.

"What in hell," he roared.

"You are cursed," Ruby-Ruby danced.

"No in hell." Jefferson struggled to his feet.

"Yes! You! Your first born! The males! You are cursed!"

Jefferson started toward her when the pain flared anew, bringing him down again.

"But I shall mark you," Ruby-Ruby continued, pointing a long, bony finger at him. "I shall! You are cursed."

Jefferson struggled to his feet, fighting the pain. Rage was strewn across his face and he couldn't move. A spiral of heat was burning into the side of his head.

Ruby-Ruby chanted as she danced.

"You mixed your seed with chrissakes! You bring bad back with you. You don't fear the mojo. But now you fear. You fear and you see."

Ruby-Ruby raised her hand in the air, and made an angry, twisting motion. Jefferson did a painful pirouette, spinning on his toes and shuddering uncontrollably.

His right earlobe began to separate into worm-like tentacles of flesh. They wriggled violently, synchronized trembling in a macabre cadence, dancing in time to the nerve-racking, high pitch of Jefferson's screams. They banged against each other, frenzied, as if looking for an escape from the keening wail that reverberated across the countryside. The faster his flesh moved, the higher Jefferson's anguished cries rang out. Finally, the writhing tentacles suddenly dove inside of what could only be described as his ear hole, accompanied by a sickening slurp as the flesh jammed into the narrow opening. Abruptly Jefferson's screams subsided; he collapsed in a heap by the porch.

Jefferson Browne was begotten by a curse that day. A curse that was passed down through the generations to the first-born males of each family and manifested by the mutilated ear. From Jefferson Browne to his son Robert Abraham to Robert William and, finally, to the reflection of Alias.

CHAPTER 1
In The Flame

Doin watched as his life danced in the fire. Watched as the hot licks of flame's consequence and pain jumped higher with each kernel, fueled by deeds both hidden and exposed. The spectrum of heat ran the gamut—from demented to sinister, and, in the flame, there was a distorted reflection of the peaks and valleys of his soul's landscape. From lukewarm to hot, each episode carried the fiery brand of hell stamped indelibly on his psyche, imbedded forever. Dysfunctional tattoos.

He remembered the first feel of flame as it burned across his memory.

He was ten years old, huddled in fear next to his mother on the living room couch. They were still living in the projects, a five-bedroom of darkness. His drunken stepfather was embarking on one of his ranting, ghetto horror stories. Doin sat there listening but he never comprehended the full extent of the degrading insults that his drunken stepfather spat out.

"You and that bastard son of yours," he yelled at Doin's mother, through red eyes and spittle. "You know who your daddy is, boy? One of them slick-talkin' niggas! Talked her right into opening them legs and fucked her. Tha's right." His stepfather looked like Super-Bad-Nigga and Doin had learned the hard way that it didn't pay to fuck around with the SBN. The SBN lived inside of anger and menace and was more than willing to share his pain with all eight of his children; at any given time, in any given mood.

Doin looked to his mother with tears in his eyes—he knew that this was something bad just from the harsh tone of his stepfather's voice—but she simply looked straight ahead, eyes blank.

His stepfather railed on. "Then she gonna try to act like you mine! Skinny little, peanut head nigga! You can't be from me. You too stupid for that! How? Shit." He shifted his gaze back to Doin's mother. "I betcha she just threw them legs up. It ain't never been that hard though. Just like a slut. And then, here you come." Doin's stepfather was a big man, surly and violent...especially when spurred on by alcohol and anger. He towered over Doin and his mother with clenched fists; his body tense and poised in his drunken rant. His next sentence was a hiss. "I'll run this whore in the river down there...and she can take her bastard, too."

Ninth grade in high school.

Another memory and the flame licked higher. Doin's life was full of the abrupt feedback of combustion which lit the darkness of his youth.

A growth spurt had shot him up to five feet eleven inches in height, transforming him into a lanky one hundred and fifty pounds. The scar on his face was still fresh, and he carried it with a sense of sad novelty, an object of curiosity and wonder. When he returned to school after the bandages had been removed, his classmates weren't exactly tactful with their questions.

"How did you get that?"

"Don't that shit hurt?"

"Damn! Man! How?"

Questions. Questions all. They stared at him like he was a rocky horror picture freak, some openly, some with disgust but Doin soon learned to file all of them in the "fuck 'em" category and leave them there for life. They didn't matter to him anyway. No one did.

Until he met Bonita.

She was a small, beautiful girl who had just moved to town and she had captured him with one gesture. He had first seen Bonita leaning against the wall outside of the school by the football field. Hudson High School had acres of land attached to it, including two football fields, a soccer field and a baseball diamond. Everybody played ball at lunchtime and the sounds of kids running, clashing and straining against each other manifested itself as the hum of laughter and joy. One of the football fields stretched out about thirty yards away from where Bonita stood and a bunch of jocks had a game going. Doin could hear the star quarterback, Rosand Babjack, yelling at his teammate for dropping a pass. "You are a fucking retard. A moron, too!" Rosand was a doo-doo hole. Doin spit in his direction.

When he saw Bonita standing by the wall, Doin slowly inched his way toward her until he was close enough to see her face clearly. She was staring out over the fields toward the perimeter of lush foliage in the distance. She looked just like someone who was lost and friendless on her first day at a new school. Her eyes were pretty, and her hair was pulled back in a ponytail and a thick, curly strand was hanging down over her eye. Doin watched her.

"Go deep! Go deep!"

On the football field, Rosand backpedaled into the pocket and set his body to throw the pass. He looked to his left, then to his right, reset his body and threw a bomb, straight up into the air in a high graceful arc, perfectly leading the receiver. The tall, gangly kid was flying full speed down the sidelines with the defender a half-step behind him. The football came down to earth and landed thirty yards down the field…a full five yards short of its target, bounced over the head of the defender and into the arms of the exasperated receiver.

"You got a rag arm, man," he screamed before he angrily reared back and dropkicked the ball. It slanted off the side of his foot and sailed toward the wall where Doin stood watching Bonita. The football rolled to a stop at his feet.

"We ain't got a chance tonight," the kid screamed. "You ain't shit!"

"Fuck you, man!" Rosand yelled back. "Your mother!"

"Throw the ball," the receiver yelled at Doin from the far side of the field. Doin never took his eyes off Bonita, who was still lost in the woods, oblivious to the football game. "Throw the ball back, dickhead!" Doin turned sharply to see who had said that word; it was Rosand Babjack. Then he quickly turned to see if Bonita had heard. She turned toward him and Doin half-smiled at her. She smiled back.

"Hey," screamed the kicker. "Throw it back, punk!"

The smile faded from Doin's face. He bent down and picked up the ball, slowly turning it over in his hands. He turned to face the guy who had yelled him punk. He stood about fifty yards away.

"Throw it to me, superstar," the kicker jeered. Doin stepped up and heaved the football down the field as far as he could. A hush fell over the entire field. The players all looked up to watch the flight of the ball, open-mouthed, as it sailed up into the air and came down in the kicker's hands. All heads turned to Doin.

Doin turned to Bonita.

"Hi," he said, smiling. Bonita darkened a bit and shyly looked at the ground. When she raised her eyes to meet his, there was a worldly silence, because his world had stopped turning, and it seemed to last an eternity. Doin pinned his hopes on her smile.

"Hi," she said.

A hand clapped onto Doin's shoulder and spun him around.

"Hey!" The wide receiver stood before him with the ball in his hand. "You play football?"

Doin became the new starting quarterback of the football team and Bonita became his girlfriend. If there had ever been a period in his life that Doin could call blissful, it was at that perfect moment. He was a natural at football and after his first game he became the starting quarterback, mostly due to the strength of his arm and his elusive quickness. Bonita was his dream come true. She was his joyful escape from the madness at home that he lived with every day. He never talked about that. They went to movies, played pinball games and darts and sometimes they went on long walks together. She even let Doin put his arm around her when they were alone in the park.

For once, his stepfather even eased up on the terror treatment for a few nights. He spent most of his time over at The Hole, a drinking spot where all the serious alcoholics hung out. His new routine consisted of stumbling into the house in the wee hours of the morning with a tired, dull roar of profanity, falling asleep on the couch and waking up early in the morning, cursing at Doin to get up out of the bed. This was an improvement over the regular pattern of abuse and, for once, Doin was sailing along with no worries. That peaceful respite was short-lived. It ended that fateful day when the flame blazed to life, as brilliantly as an inferno, and the fire had come raging with the ferocity of an arsonist putting out a flame…with gasoline. The heat would change Doin forever.

It started on the night when Doin and his younger brother were fighting in the living room. Doin had him in a headlock and was twisting his brother's neck with all the strength he could muster. His mother heard the commotion and charged into the room. She immediately ran to Doin and began slapping him in the face—each blow landing with enough strength to force him backward. *Slap!* He felt the screen door push open behind him. *Slap!* His face was on fire and the heat pushed him back. *Slap!* Finally, with one foot out the backdoor, Doin reached up and caught his mother's arm in mid-air.

"Stop," he said.

His mother got hysterical. She started yelling and crying.

"Go tell your father that Doin in here trying to hit me," she cried. His brother sprinted out the door in a mad dash up to The Hole.

Doin yelled, "I didn't try to hit you, Ma!" He stepped back into the house, ran upstairs and flopped down on his bed. He didn't understand his mother. Didn't understand why she always took his brother's side against him. It was like she had something personal against him. He pulled a pillow up to his face and resigned himself to the punishment that was sure to come. The SBN would be home soon.

It wasn't long before he heard the front door bang shut, followed by heated conversation.

"What's going on in here?"

"He tried to beat on me."

"Where he at?"

"Upstairs."

"Doin! Get yo' ass down here! Now, boy!"

Doin rose from the bed and walked over to the stairs. His stepfather was waiting on the landing with eyes as red as fire. "Get here!" Doin took the stairs warily. In his fourteen-year-old mind he had decided that it was time to escape the insanity of this household. He was leaving. He sauntered down the final two steps. When he was within an arm's length, his stepfather reached up and grabbed a fistful of shirt. "Is you in here hitting your mother, boy?"

His stepfather held Doin close enough for them to touch noses, and Doin's feet dangled a few feet from the floor. He was a ragdoll in the big man's paws and due to their proximity, the smell of liquor was intoxicating. Doin turned his face to the side and said, "Look, just let me go, man, and I'll leave."

"Who the fuck..." His stepfather took a step back and threw two hundred and sixty pounds worth of power into a punch that caught Doin on the side of his head and sent him flying across the room. Doin blacked out for a second but when his vision returned, his stepfather was straddling him with one hand around his throat and the other cocked to deliver another blow.

"Da! No!" His oldest brother burst through the front door and grabbed the drunken man's arm, preventing a possible deathblow. His stepfather pulled back and looked down at Doin for a long second before letting him up. Doin scooted off the couch and stomped toward the front door. He opened it and turned to face the man who had just beaten him. "You ain't my father. In fact...you ain't shit! You just a raggedy muthafucka! Muthafucka." A tear rolled down his rapidly swelling cheek.

With that, he stormed out the door...and straight into a horrified Bonita.

CHAPTER 2
Much Too Much

She possessed the deadly yet beautiful soul of a bitch. She was too much really. Much too much. She was a terror with personal flaws; imperfections that were revealed only to her son, D.Wayne. He had long ago given up hope that his mother would take a look at herself…and it would have to be one big look because she would have caught a wicked reflection.

Yet she had become his queen. She really was much too much! In fact, from her throne, which sat up above D.Wayne's life, she had made him a man. She had left her mark on him, indelible and deep, left him on the precipice of his sanity, peeking over the ledge as thought escaped him, as time passed for him, yet strangely stood still. The mists of his childhood settled over him in mad wetness as he looked back on his time spent under the gentle hand of his mother. Joselle. She had that effect.

She had taken control of him the moment that she had given birth and, months later, D.Wayne's father had gone to the liquor store, gotten himself a bottle of vodka and headed off into the sunset…never to return. In his entire lifetime, D.Wayne had never heard Joselle mention his father's name. Not once! Not that D.Wayne was mad at the asshole bitch for leaving; he could understand the need and the motive. Joselle had that effect.

She always loved D.Wayne! At least that was her mantra whenever she was sloppy drunk and deep in the throes of inebriated free thought. But she only loved to control him. Her physical and emotional tyranny was a rule of life that reached back as far as D.Wayne's first conscious thought. Every attempt at normal growth, any stretch toward childish bravado, any thoughts of independent expression on his part was crushed down by the will of his mother. She controlled every aspect of his life except for his breathing, and he tried not to do that too loudly.

Joselle was also a vibrant woman; many men flocked to her sexuality like bees drawn by the sweetest, most irresistible of nectars. Joselle had that effect, too. Her body was framed to perfection by the tight clothes that she wore, which only served to heighten the visual effect of her flesh. Joselle wore her body; she moved it with imagination and skill…and she loved every minute of attention that she drew.

Gradually, over the years as D.Wayne grew into his teenage years and played the role of spectator to a parade of weak-willed men, Joselle's perfection soured and she turned her emotions inward, toward her son.

On his first day at Hudson High School, he got into a fight. D.Wayne made his way home and slammed through the front door. There was a deep gash, smeared with caked-up blood, slightly above his right eye. He stomped his way through the living room, vaguely registering the sound of the television before making his way directly to the bathroom. Joselle was sitting in her chair and spotted him rushing by.

"Hey, boy!"

He turned his head to look at her but he kept on walking. Joselle was wearing a dark, blue mini-skirt that stopped slightly below her thighs; it was one of her "fuck-em" outfits. The sheer, soft fabric molded to her body like a tiger's skin and she moved with a cat-like sexuality. She followed D.Wayne into the bathroom with a drink in her hand. *Vodka probably*, D.Wayne took note. Joselle was nothing if not a creature of habit. She must have just lost one of her men. Another lust-driven guy who had gotten tired of her bullshit, finally figuring out that the temporary sexual satisfaction wasn't worth the permanent hell of Joselle. D.Wayne couldn't figure Joselle out; she treated men as if they were her enemy, yet she acted like she couldn't live without a man around. That shit was stupid. Yet here she was again, as usual, sitting around with her "fuck-'em" dress on, chugging the juice. In a while she would put on some records, some slow, broke-my-heart, no-good-ass-man, he-wasn't-man-enough-for-me music. She would drink some more vodka and then head out the front door to the club to find herself another man. Never failed. But sometimes she would get stupid, too.

"What happened to you?" She leaned against the doorframe and sipped her drink. It wasn't like she cared.

D.Wayne glared at her. He didn't care either. On his way home after school he had gotten into a fight with a kid named Sanford. D.Wayne had taken a straight right to his grille. When Sanford's knuckles slammed into his forehead, D.Wayne thought the world was black. After a few kicks to the ribs, that notion was cleared up.

"Who punched yo' bitch ass?" Joselle demanded over the rim of her glass. D.Wayne turned to the faucet and twisted the knob for the hot water, gingerly leaning forward to look in the mirror at the cut on his face. His ribs screamed in protest when he stretched forward but the sharp pain soon subsided into a steady, manageable throb. While he waited for the water to get hot, he reached up to snatch a washrag before he began to gingerly pull his shirt up over his head. His ribs felt like there was a sharp stick poking into his side every time he took a breath, but he knew that he had been lucky. After Sanford punched him in the face, D.Wayne had landed awkwardly with his ribs exposed. He quickly curled up defensively and Sanford had been in such a hurry to hit him that the brunt of his blows that made contact with D.Wayne's chest had been glancing kicks without full impact. He was glad when Sanford finally stopped.

He dropped his shirt to the floor and put the washrag under the running water to test the temperature. Warm.

"You getting too big to be getting your ass beat!" Joselle was standing in the doorway now, watching him. She was drinking from one of her "'good" glasses—which meant a different kind of drunk—and her eyes traveled up and down his body. "Yeah. You getting big now." She paused a moment before she exclaimed, "Look at them pants, boy!"

D.Wayne looked down. There was a small tear along the seam of the pant leg. "So what, Joselle," he answered, annoyed. The gash above his eye looked much more gruesome in the light, and he wasn't looking forward to washing the clotted blood out of it. Maybe he could get Joselle to take him to the hospital so that it could be cleaned properly. *Shit!* D.Wayne reasoned. Joselle would probably punch him in the other eye at the mere mention of such a thing. A steady throb was beginning to pulse above his eye with a life of its own, as if a sharp nail was pushing against a painful, exposed nerve.

"So what!" Joselle shouted. "So take those pants off and get in that shower and wash your ass! Clean up your act! That's 'so what!'"

I really do not want to hear this shit! D.Wayne watched Joselle in the mirror and gritted his teeth.

"Take them pants off," Joselle barked. "Now!" D.Wayne mumbled something under his breath but then a stabbing pain shot through his ribs. He winced again when he took off his pants. Turning back to the sink, he put the washrag under the water, which had finally turned hot, and held it there until the cloth steamed. He wrung out the rag and started dabbing at the cut above his eye, tapping around the edges of the puckered skin in order to test his threshold. He stared at his reflection for a moment, resigned himself to the fact that he was about to experience pain, and pressed the hot compress to his wound.

"Yaahhhh!" D.Wayne danced with the shock of pain but he held the rag in place.

"Hah!" Joselle gave a loud hoot before she turned and went back to her chair in the front room. She collapsed into the cushions, crossed her legs and watched him with undisguised interest. D.Wayne ignored her, choosing instead to focus on cleaning out the cut over his eye. He washed it until there was no more blood leaking into the open wound, and then he turned and closed the bathroom door. He stripped out of his underwear, turned on the shower, waited a few seconds until the water warmed up and stepped under the gentle spray, adjusting the water until his body began to relax under the heated streams.

"I wish Sanford would die!" D.Wayne groaned as he pulled the knob back, which increased the water pressure, and let the hot water blast into his face, stinging him as the water doused the cut above his eye. Leaning back against the wall, he let the water massage his body and he closed his eyes. Joselle was right. He was too big to be getting his ass waxed all the time; though Joselle sometimes did the waxing herself.

Joselle was a trip. As many men wanted her, as delicate and feminine as she appeared to be, she could run any man straight up out of the county. She could fight 'em, fuck 'em or fuck with 'em, but eventually each man in turn would get the message and get to stepping. There were a few occasions in which Joselle's authority was questioned by a few of her men, causing her to pull out Flo Jigga, her special hook-handled knife which she kept hidden on her body at all times. After many years of practice, she was pretty quick with Flo Jigga.

"Yeah!" D.Wayne warmed to his subject. "That's why she got on that 'fuck 'em' dress. Joselle done ran another one of her men outta town and now she going down to the 'fuck 'em' dance." He reached for the soap and began washing himself, lathering himself, along with his attitude, in the solitude of the shower. "Fuck 'em dance! Fuck 'em dance! Fuck 'em dance!"

D.Wayne was so wrapped up in his pointless bravado that he didn't notice the bathroom door as it inched open. Nor did he notice the shadow of Joselle on the other side of the shower curtain, listening.

He started singing and dancing, snapping his fingers in time. "Fuck 'em, girl! Fuck 'em! Fuck 'em, girl! Fuck 'em!" He ducked his head under the stream of the hot water, letting it wash over his face once again before he continued with his mad tirade. "Yet she wanna do is talk shit about me! I come in here bleeding and shit and all my perfect mother wanna talk shit like I just ate her favorite drink! Shee-it! Can't mess with Joselle's drink water though! Better not! 'Cause that's her ho juice. My mother the ho. Drunk ho, too. I bet like sometimes, like sometimes, like, there'll be some man talking to his friends. He'll point at me and be like 'yo' fine ass momma got some of the finest, goodest pussy in the land. Shit!"

Suddenly the shower curtain was ripped back to reveal a drunken, pissed-off Joselle. She glared at her son with a malice that shook him and he felt himself involuntarily shrink away. His heart thumped when he noticed the full glass of vodka in one hand…and Flo Jigga in the other.

CHAPTER 3
Flo Jigga

D.Wayne lay on his bed, staring at the ceiling. He had a comic book spread open on his chest, happily lost in a world of his own creation, when he heard her voice break the barrier.

"Come here, boy!"

He groaned out loud and turned over on his side, facing the wall and closing his eyes in an attempt to ignore his mother. He pretended to sleep.

"Don't make me get up and come up in there, D.Wayne. If I come up there, you know that I'm gonna whoop 'em ass! I know you hear me, boy!" The drunken timbre of Joselle's speech warned him that she may have been deep inside of that bottle of vodka so it was best to go ahead and get the alcohol tricks over with. Sometimes Joselle would get really juiced up and her mind would conjure up all manner of twisted, stupid brain teasers. Games like, "who hid my bra" or "scrape the gum off the floor with a fork," and once they had played a game called "get my earring, I dropped it down the toilet." D.Wayne especially hated that one.

At other times Joselle could be real ornery and scary. Her aggressive nature sometimes burst to the fore and she would take the stance of a defiant woman against a world of manly confrontations. It was during these episodes that she would bring out the knife, her friend, Flo Jigga—bent flat and curved for a nigga. Joselle sometimes conversed with the knife as if Flo Jigga was a lifelong buddy.

"Shit!" D.Wayne groaned as he rose from his bed. His ribs were feeling much better. All that remained was a dull throb, and that was only when he moved suddenly, but the cut over his eye still felt fresh. The insistent pain hovered near the edge of his mind, steady and bothersome. He didn't bother to put his undershirt on as he plodded over to Joselle's room to see why her drunk ass was calling him.

D.Wayne wished fervently that he could have a mother that acted like a regular mother. Like the mothers he saw picking up the other kids from school, the ones he saw at football games and at the malls. He longed for the serenity that he saw everywhere...laughter, hugs, harmony...everywhere except where it mattered most—home, the place where he lay his head.

So he was an outsider. He couldn't relate to the cliques and other little groups of kids his age because he had no common interests; in essence he had no commonality at all. He often told himself that he was above the need for that particular type of group therapy, that he was strong enough to be alone, that he was a tempered steel mandingo and nothing could hurt him.

Until he met Alicia.

Alicia was special. She made him "stir" the first time that he saw her. *I wanna do that porno movie-type shit with her.* That was how he knew that he liked her...more than liked her. He casually followed her, hoping to catch her alone so that he could look at her up close. She was pretty; he could tell that from afar, but there was something there that was much better than pretty. She wore her hair short, close cropped to her skull and brushed back into finger waves. Her burnished copper skin reflected the intensity of her eyes showing hints of daring that radiated from her. D.Wayne fidgeted with fear. He couldn't wait.

As fate would have it, he didn't have to wait at all. Alicia was a loner just like he was. She was always alone, away from the crowds, separated from the mixed-up girls who were always so worried about their hair and clothes and other kiddy shit. She chose the outside. And that's just where D.Wayne resided.

They eyed each other warily—each suspicious of the invasion of their solitude, yet each open to the possibility of a loneliness shared. D.Wayne was drawn to her. Pulled by an attraction that forced him to cast his inhibitions aside, he had to investigate that stir that she had awakened in him. She was a step beyond the other girls, those silly girls who would often stop and stare at her as she walked by. She shied away from others and apparently seemed oblivious to their cold, penetrating stares.

She and D.Wayne had been moved from subtle glances to more meaningful eye contact. It signaled an attraction that would lead to its resultant physicality, and soon he found himself on the precipice. He was having magnets in his dreams. He dreamed of Alicia, imagined her flying through the air, naked and willing, with him on her tail, more than willing and ecstatic in the throes of the virginal flushes of lust. He saw her with the clarity of realness as she landed on her back in a soft field of cotton flowers. The space between her legs, her center, glistened with wetness and beckoned to the urges that engorged his suddenly swollen member. When his lips touched her softly rounded breasts he felt sensations that sent currents throughout his body and sent them to *his* center. And he heard her make sounds! A combination of breathing and moaning right next to his ear as she pulled him by the back of his head and pulled him...pulled him...pulled him. He felt liquid pleasure coming down the center of his body. Like ragged iron filings that scraped the inside of his core; only each ragged piece of metal sent molten sparks of pleasure clattering down his shaft; and Alicia controlled his polarity. He was having magnets in his dreams!

They passed each other often in the hallways at school and when their eyes met, D.Wayne would feel his heart pick up its pace. Soon he began to imagine that maybe, just maybe, he might have a chance with Alicia. But his courage would fade with the remembrance of her pretty brown eyes and her soft, full lips. *She is just too pretty*, D.Wayne rationalized.

But one day, Alicia set D.Wayne's world on fire. He was sitting outside the school, with his back against the wall during his lunch break reading a comic book. D.Wayne was caught up in the cartoon world of daredevil dandies that were saving the world from evil. He was spaced-out, oblivious to the raucous laughter of kids at play on the sprawling, well-kept fields. The school was shaped like a humpbacked "U" and there were athletic fields on every side of the building: football fields, soccer fields and baseball diamonds, each lined perfectly for play. A soft voice spoke to D.Wayne, rousing him from his favorite superhero's dilemma.

"What you reading?" Alicia stood before him. She had on a pair of blue jeans and a pleated pink shirt. She had the prettiest eyes that D.Wayne had ever seen.

"Comics," he finally managed to gasp.

"You read them a lot, huh?"

D.Wayne fidgeted. "Yeah. They good."

An awkward moment of silence stretched out between them as D.Wayne looked at her. Alicia shifted nervously and, without a word, sat down next to him. D.Wayne's heart pounded in his chest as the warmth of her nearness heated the space between them. His mouth went dry as his mind worked furiously in an attempt to conjure up something magical to say to her. He looked over at her when she turned to face him and the sight took his breath away. His blood pounded down through his veins and he felt the distinct sensation of an erection blossoming to life. He pulled his knees up to his chest and dropped the comic book on the ground in front of him.

"I see you all the time," Alicia began. "By yourself."

"I see you, too," D.Wayne answered. "Hey, Alicia?"

She looked up at him. "You know my name?"

"Yeah. I saw you, too."

She took D.Wayne's hand and intertwined their fingers. She looked into his eyes and then suddenly bent his fingers backwards. D.Wayne yelped out in pain just in time to hear the school bell go off, signaling the end of the lunch period. It was time to go to his next class. Alicia was watching him with a wicked grin on her face.

D.Wayne was puzzled. "Why you do that?"

"Let's cut class," Alicia whispered. "Let's go over there." She pointed to the woods that were beyond the edge of the school property. "Nobody won't know. Let's go! We can have some fun."

D.Wayne looked back at the school and then at Alicia. "Come on," she urged. He jumped to his feet and they ran together to the woods. They spent the rest of the school day out there, exploring the open, deserted fields; playing semi-erotic games of hide-and-go-get, freeze touch and red-light-green-light. They found a patch of thick, plush grass surrounded by a copse of trees and they stripped down to their underwear, lying down side by side with their arms folded behind their heads while they looked up at the blazing sun. Alicea reached over and tickled D.Wayne's nose and he tickled her back, giggling. Their horseplay soon took on a more serious tone and they started on a journey of exploration, beginning with their lips, fumbling in the daytime against each other in clumsy attempts to find intimacy. D.Wayne moved over her and conjured up every image that he had memorized from the nasty books that he had hidden under the bottom of his stack of comics in his closet. He moved her bra up over the slight swell of her breast and took her nipple in his mouth. He rolled it on his tongue, marveling when he felt the small bud grow rigid as he began to suck and lick. Her moans barely reached his ears as he ran his tongue around the perimeter of her tiny breasts and then paused to look at her face. He wanted to see if she liked what he was doing. He couldn't tell. He spread her legs and wedged himself between them so that the only impediment to penetration was the fabric of the underwear that they both still wore. D.Wayne felt his hardness swell to the biggest degree that he had ever felt and he dipped his hips into her, grinding until he felt a warm friction building in his shaft. Alicia put both hands on his chest and pushed him off her and onto his back. She leaned up on one elbow, reached over and began to trace the outline of D.Wayne's raging hard-on with her fingers. She looked up at him and smiled.

"We can't do that!" she said, watching him. "But one day?" She began squeezing him through his underwear and his breath caught in his throat.

"Get here, boy!" Joselle's gruff voice snatched him away from his soft memory of Alicia's touch and right back to his present, unpleasant situation. He couldn't escape his mother; she even intruded on his memories. He stepped over to her bedroom doorway.

"What, Joselle?"

She was laid out on her stomach on the bed. She wore a skimpy pair of black underwear that barely concealed the roundness of her fat ass while she watched herself in the mirrored headboard and put on her lipstick. Joselle was so nasty. She needed to cover herself up; D.Wayne could see the imprint of her privacy through her flimsy panties. She turned toward D.Wayne and he couldn't help but notice the fullness of her bra as it strained to contain her healthy titties. She opened her mouth to say something but caught herself. Her eyes traveled downward and a wicked expression came across her face. D.Wayne followed her obvious stare and looked down to see that his cock was quite noticeably swollen, jutting against his underwear in a rage. He moved to shield himself with his hands and jumped behind the doorway to hide his shame.

"Get in here, boy!" Joselle commanded. "At least something about your ass is growing into manhood! Now get here!"

D.Wayne hesitated. He was still hard, even though he wished it to go down. It was like Little Petey had a mind of its own; some volition to exercise and the circumstances were irrelevant. Joselle was waiting.

D.Wayne stepped from behind the doorway. There was a drink on the nightstand next to Joselle's bed. A tall bottle of vodka also sat on the table next to her knife, Flo Jigga. The sharp edge of the blade gleamed in the lamplight, its menace intrusive and deep.

D.Wayne started whining. "What, Joselle? I need to get some sleep! Dag!"

Joselle rose from her bed. She shot a quick glance at Flo Jigga before turning to stare at D.Wayne. "Nigga, who you talkin' to like that? Try it again and I'll fold you." She walked over and stood in front of him, looking down at his hardness that was still jutting out. A knowing smirk crossed her face before she looked up at him. When she shifted her body, her titties strained, trying to escape the lacy bra that she wore. D.Wayne's eyes were drawn to the enticing movement of the twin mounds of flesh. Guilt clouded his vision and he quickly looked away. Joselle grunted and stretched her body to its full height and posed seductively. It was a practiced undulation that had moved many men into actions that they would later regret.

"Ma," D.Wayne exclaimed and instantly regretted it. Joselle's hand balled into a fist and he instinctively flinched from her violent reaction. Joselle had beaten him once before for calling her out of her name. Joselle had power in her fists—she had given up on using the belt on D.Wayne when he was in the seventh grade—and she had pummeled him about the chest and ribs, all the while repeating her name to him. So it had been "Joselle" from that day forward. It had been a rough beating. D.Wayne closed his eyes and waited for this one to commence.

"Say that again," Joselle commanded. "Say it!" D.Wayne opened his eyes, surprised to still be upright, and stood stock-still.

"You better not!" Joselle's eyes blazed. "Sho' nuff! Now go in the bathroom and get me that cocoa butter and bring it here."

D.Wayne scrambled into the bathroom and gratefully retrieved the lotion. When he stepped back into her bedroom Joselle was bent over, going through her dresser. Turning back to face D.Wayne, she had a full drink in her hand and the early warning signs of drunkenness were on his mother's face. Her liquored-up eyes were starting to look like bloodshot devil's orbs, and there was always evil shit in the night when Joselle got drunk up.

She stared at D.Wayne and held him motionless. "You see this." She held the glass of vodka in the air. "This," she paused for a quick sip. "This is my ho juice!" She looked at D.Wayne and mocked him, throwing his own words back at him in an off-key imitation. "Ho juice! Ho juice!" She paused to stand directly over him. D.Wayne was not a big kid; he was almost average size, but Joselle towered over him. She bought fear from up above—with a temper to match.

"You called your own mother a ho!" Her lips were mere inches from his face.

There was nothing that D.Wayne could say to defend himself. Joselle had caught him at point-blank range, on the other side of the shower curtain, so there was really no denying. He did not intend to give Joselle any further ammunition so he was definitely keeping quiet and riding this one out.

"If I'm a ho, a damn good ho! Sexy enough to be a ho if I want to," she demanded.

D.Wayne didn't know the answer to that one. He didn't know that hos had to be sexy. *But there are some sexy hos though*, he reasoned. *Some of them girls be wearin' that real sexy shit, too!* D.Wayne's nature twirled at the memory as he pulled up the images of a few of the working girls that he would see on his way home from school. He fixed them in his mental Rolodex and began to replay their fleshy movements, practiced to enticing perfection. His imagination caught on one fine-ass woman with an ass that he could only describe as perfect flesh. She liked to wear tiny mini-skirts but she didn't particularly care for underwear. D.Wayne liked to watch her walk and as her hips caught his lust in an uproar, he thought that he spied the roundness of her mound, swaying with the openness of pleasure. D.Wayne was a virgin but instinct screamed for him to put his manhood inside of her and once that mission was accomplished there would be no better place on earth. He felt his cock stiffen with the anticipation.

Joselle looked down at D.Wayne's hard-on and then back at his face.

"Look at you." She indicated his erection. "You talk that shit…but look at you!" She quickly reached down and grabbed his dick through his underwear. "That! That is the same shit that men do! Then they wanna call you a ho! You seen ho juice, boy, and look at you! You just another motha fucka." Joselle released D.Wayne and walked over to her dresser with her drink in her hand. D.Wayne fell to the floor, his knees weak with shock. Joselle had touched his privates! "Joselle," he screamed. "That's nasty! You can't touch me there! No! You can't!" Joselle turned to look at him. She tilted the drink and drained the rest of her vodka before she slammed the empty glass down and picked up her knife, Flo Jigga.

She walked back over to D.Wayne. "Get in my bed." It was a simple command spoken without question and with a quality that he had never heard before. But he was not going to get in Joselle's bed. She had to be fucking kidding.

"But Joselle…" D.Wayne began. Joselle reached down and he felt her fingers dig firmly into the flesh of his throat.

"You better not lose that hard, boy," she snarled. "Now get. In. That. Bed!" She yanked him to his feet and threw him toward the bed. D.Wayne tumbled forward. When he regained his balance he turned back toward Joselle and was met by Flo Jigga, inches away from his throat.

"Take them draws off." Joselle had a mad glint in her eye. D.Wayne shook his head "no" furiously. In desperation he grasped the band of his underwear with both hands and pulled upwards as far as he could. He stretched them over his stomach while trying to back away from Joselle.

She wrapped her hand around his throat again, squeezed and pulled, nearly lifting D.Wayne off the floor. She swung him around by his neck and slammed him on the bed. D.Wayne could smell the stink of the vodka as it rolled over his face. Suddenly, Joselle raised Flo Jigga in the air and D.Wayne froze. She reached out and grasped the band of his underwear, pulled it toward her and slashed down with the knife. She cut them straight down the middle and suddenly D.Wayne found himself naked, exposed to his mother.

"Lay on the bed!" Joselle commanded. "And you better get back that hard! Lay on the bed...and don't move!" He did as she commanded, lay there on the bed, motionless, as Joselle moved over to her dresser, poured herself another drink and tossed half of it down in one gulp. She let out a loud gasp as the liquor hit home and then she stepped out of her underwear. It was the first, real cooty cat that D.Wayne had ever seen! And it was his mother's! He closed his eyes against the sickness he felt building in his brain, his mental rejecting the transpiring reality. His eyes popped open when he felt the cold touch of Flo Jigga pressed to his neck. His erection went instantly soft. Joselle looked down.

"Oh no, nigga," she exclaimed. She took Flo Jigga and nestled the flat curve of the blade against the base of D.Wayne's cock. "Perform, nigga. Now!"

D.Wayne felt the cold, flat blade of steel press against him and tears began to well up in the back of his eyes. He willed his erection to stand tall. He envisioned all of the erotic women he had seen in his magazines. He imagined that it was his cock going in and out of their pussies and mouths, and he felt his hips try to buck in response. His fear intensified.

Joselle sat astride him and began to grind her nakedness against his thickening penis. She moved and moved...but it wasn't working. D.Wayne felt fear mounting inside of him. He knew that Joselle would cut him...she was crazy when she got all liquored up. *I gotta do this. I gotta!* He made his mind a blank. Phased out every sickening thought that threatened to invade his consciousness. Ignored the feel of the cold knife-edge that was pressed to his balls. Denied the hate that he felt for Joselle as she sat astride him, doing the bad thing that a mother is supposed to protect her child from. Focus. He felt the pressure of Joselle's weight as her sex pressed down on him. Felt the fat moistness of her pussy lips as they caught the tip of his dick. Blood flowed up inside of his cock, engorging it, and D.Wayne felt the guilty hell of pleasure as his manhood began to grow. He was invading his mother's warmth; and it was nasty. He felt the suction of her lips pulling at him and he became fully aroused. Her sex enveloped him like a fetish, an agonizing dark penchant, and a yearning heartbeat that went deeper and deeper inside of her. He felt her inner walls clench around his shaft. Joselle moaned. D.Wayne separated his mind from his body…and felt a dark stain expanding across his soul as he lost his virginity…to his mother.

CHAPTER 4
A Badness

Doin was frozen with anger, the rage in his eyes deepened by the fright that he saw in Bonita's. He stepped toward her. She shrank away from him.

"No! No! No!" Doin jumped up and down in an angry tantrum. Bonita looked back over her shoulder as she ran away from him toward Front Street. He calmed himself, facing the realization that she would never see him with the same eyes again; maybe she never had.

His stepfather stood in the doorway, watching. His face was etched with regret. All traces of alcohol seemed vacant from his red-rimmed eyes. He stepped halfway through the screen door and stood silently with an outstretched hand. A single tear rolled down his face.

Doin didn't see that drop of sorrow trail down the dark-skinned cheek. All Doin saw was the menacing devil of pain. The maker of scars. The giver of life marks. He ran his fingers across his disfiguration, the scar that tore a swath across his face, the mark of the devil who stood before him. The blotted soul who had come for Doin one cold day and altered his life forever.

Memories. Sometimes they felt like yesterday.

His stepfather kept his demon in a bottle, trapped in the watery grave called vodka. It was a thirsty little devil that couldn't be slaked, absorbing mothers and fathers, sisters and brothers, dollars and dollars until entire paychecks were consumed. Alcoholics never made enough money.

They never make good providers either so at the tender age of twelve, Doin found himself working on a farm alongside migrant workers, picking apples in order to buy his own clothes. He had managed to save over twenty-five dollars in a savings account for a pair of sneakers that had caught his eye and, with a few more dollars, they would soon be on his feet.

Doin walked into the house one evening to find his stepfather in a rage. He had been gambling and, poor gambler that he was, lost all of his drinking money. He was cursing up a storm when Doin walked in the door. He angrily summoned Doin to the kitchen.

"Boy!" he thundered and pointed at an opened letter laying on the kitchen table. It was Doin's bank statement.

"You got some money in the bank, nigga," his stepfather commanded. "We goin' to get all of that shit!"

Doin's heart sank.

"Come on!" His stepfather bustled out the front door. Doin straggled behind him, angry and scared, with unformed tears stinging his eyes. They piled into the car and his stepfather raced to the bank trying to beat the closing time.

"I know you don't like this shit, nigga!" The car roared around the corner onto Warren Street. They had ten minutes left before the doors at the bank were locked. Doin prayed that they wouldn't make it. Maybe a cop would pull them over for speeding.

"How you think I feel when you wanna eat eva' day? I got to go down in my pocket eva' time yo' black ass wanna eat!" They pulled up in front of the bank and screeched to a stop in the handicapped parking space.

His stepfather turned to him. "Now gone! Get up in there, nigga!"

Doin crawled out of the car, his heart aching, and slowly trod into the bank.

"And how much are you depositing today, young man?" The teller was a kind, gray-haired lady who always smiled at Doin when he made his weekly visits to deposit money into his account.

"I'm taking it all out," Doin said.

"Well, you'll build it back up in no time." She took his withdrawal slip.

Shortly, he emerged with a closed-out bankbook in one hand, twenty-five dollars in the other. He climbed into the front seat and held the money out to his stepfather, who snatched the cash from his grasp and stomped the gas, making a beeline to the nearest liquor store.

They pulled up to a glass storefront. His stepfather hopped out and vanished through the front door. Doin waited in the car and watched him through the store window as he strode up to the counter to pay for his drinks. Doin cursed the devil and wiped away a tear, wishing to God that he had never met this drunk-assed man. Muthafucka.

The front door swung open and his stepfather came bustling out of the package store like he had hit the number, carrying a brown bag in each hand. He tossed one back through the open window into the backseat, snatched the door open and eased his considerable bulk behind the wheel. He pulled the other bottle out of the bag he was holding—the word "vodka" was printed on the label in large letters—and twisted it open. He paused to look at Doin.

"From you to me," he cheered and raised the bottle to his lips. Huge gulps of air rushed toward the bottom of the bottle as the devil tilted the quart to the sky and toasted his demon. When the bottle came down…it was empty. Doin stared, open mouthed, as his stepfather tossed the drained bottle into the backseat and started the car. It didn't seem possible that a human being could drink that much liquor, that fast.

"That ain't nothin' but water," the devil belched before he pulled away from the curb. "Count your blessings," he sang as he stomped on the gas, burning rubber before he pulled out into traffic. "Count them one by one."

The car squealed around the corner onto Columbia Street, tires screeching, and right then, Doin knew that the devil had dues to pay.

"Count your blessings," his stepfather sang drunkenly as he swung the car onto Third Street. The tail swung out from under them, sending them into a spin. Doin screamed and tried to find something to hold onto.

"See what I have done." His stepfather's voice was tight as he battled the wheel, straightened the car out and pulled around the next corner onto Second Street. When the wheels caught traction he pressed his foot on the accelerator again. The car shot forward with such velocity that they were both thrown back in their seats. They went barreling toward Warren Street, the busiest intersection in the city, and the light facing them was red—but the devil never hesitated.

A huge, black SUV reached the crossing slightly ahead of them. His stepfather yanked the wheel to the right, avoiding impact by mere inches but he was unable to maintain control of the vehicle. The car rammed headfirst into a street lamp on the corner of Warren and Second Streets. The force of the crash flung Doin face-first through the windshield and fifteen feet through the air, crashing through the glass window of Mardell's Sporting Goods store. Baseball bats, footballs, basketballs and soccer balls came crashing back into the store with the force of the breaking glass. Doin was thrown into a sneaker display and crashed into the store counter. The pair of shoes that he had been saving to buy landed on his chest. And then...darkness.

His stepfather stumbled out of the wreckage and staggered three blocks down Warren Street and pulled the lever on a fire alarm box. He told the police that he had seen an accident and that someone may have been hurt.

Doin awoke the next day in the hospital staring into the darkness, assuming that he was dead and that this was what death looked like. He was blinded by the bandages that were wrapped around his face to cover the deep and vicious cuts that would later scar him.

The devil...his stepfather, suffered a broken hand.

That was the curse of the demon that had hit him, the one standing in the doorway, reaching out. The one who was responsible for Bonita trembling in fear from Doin's touch. The origin of misery, the pain of daily existence was the tall, dark inferno that ruined everything with his touch.

"Fuck you!" Doin felt a tear roll down his cheek. "You the bastard."

Memories of childhood held no joy for Doin. Any happiness that he might find was simply a harbinger of disaster, the yin and yang of dysfunctionality. More than anyone, his dark stepfather had colored Doin's life, shaped his development into a hard, distant thing. An entity that couldn't be reached by caring, emotion or compassion. A badness is what it was. A badness that spread through his inner self and separated him from the most basic human desire; to love someone passionately...and to be loved the same in return.

Memories.

CHAPTER 5
Soul's Moisture

D.Wayne hid in his mother's closet with a baseball bat resting against his thigh. He was waiting for Joselle. He had to kill her for what she had done to him—rubbing and grinding her sexuals into his private parts the way she did. His mother. But she had made a mistake when she pushed her friction upon him…because D.Wayne didn't have a dick anymore. He had grown from pubescence to manhood; synchronized to the time of Joselle's rhythmic bumps and grinds. He had manhood now—and it felt like a baseball bat upside his mother's head.

A tear slid down his face in the darkness of the closet and D.Wayne didn't move to wipe it away. He stood, motionless, waiting for his mother to walk through her bedroom door. This was her tear. Her emotional sculpture. He counted the cost of his soul's moisture, its value increasing with each beat of his heart, its worth blossoming. Soon, its creator, the artist of this torture, would be executed. Judged and sentenced by her subject, her son, brandishing his brand-new manhood.

"She needs to die!" D.Wayne gasped. His breath was taken away every time the pronouncement hit him with its cold realization. *Only dead people do the shit that she does*, his mind ranted. *I ain't do nothin' to her! Nothin'!*

The tear slid further down his face.

D.Wayne had missed his childhood. He didn't remember diapers, didn't recollect his first step or his first words. His earliest memory was waking up one morning and belonging to Joselle. His only sin was being born into the world…and that seemed to be enough of a crime to Joselle. She had told "mommy" bye-bye quite a long time ago.

D.Wayne peeked out between the slats of the closet door at his mother's bedroom. The closet sat directly across from the door, which meant that he would see her face the second she walked in. She would probably be drunk when she came back from the bar—he hoped that she would be blasted out of her skull; that would make his task that much easier. Joselle's big, king-sized bed stood off to the right side of the room—and she loved mirrors. She had a mirrored headboard and there were reflective surfaces placed strategically on the walls around the room. She had a beveled mirror on the ceiling that lent a surreal, sexual vibe to her bedroom escapades. A long, wooden dresser was pushed up against the wall next to the bed. D.Wayne didn't know much about furniture, but he knew that there had to be serious money spent on that dresser. It was made of solid wood—oak or something—and it was so heavy that he couldn't move it by himself. He had tried to slide it away from the wall so that he could hide behind it and wait for Joselle to come home, but the dresser hadn't budged.

Bottles of perfume lined a good portion of the dresser, along with body lotions, oils and other toiletries, but on the far end lay Joselle's collection. She didn't try to hide her assortment of vibrators, dildos and other little toys from D.Wayne. Most of the time she stood them pointing straight up into the air so that she could salute them on her way out the door.

I hate her!

As the tear made its final descent, D.Wayne's soul danced on its fire, on the heated tendrils of moisture that snaked its way down his cheek and fell to the floor. D.Wayne himself did a mad tango with the blaze of insanity. He was warm all over with the thrill of madness; and in that instant he decided to feel no more pain. To feel nothing. He dedicated himself to killing her.

Her mark on him was indelible. Reflexively, his hand went to the scar tissue that was forming in a slightly curved pattern on his neck. Joselle had cut him there. She had held her knife—she called it Flo Jigga, curved and pressed for a nigga—and scarred his throat while she raped him. D.Wayne had been oblivious to the small trail of blood that leaked down his neck when Flo Jigga bit into his soft flesh. The violent force of Joselle bucking wildly atop him had pushed the blade deeper and deeper into the side of his neck in tiny degrees, little by little, marking him, permanently, with her incestuous violation.

His hatred grew tenfold with the memory. It surged in intensity until he was delirious with the madness of his lost innocence, his childhood that had been ripped from him.

"Yeah, bitch!" D.Wayne screamed in the darkness. "Come in that fucking door! Come on in!"

The front door squeaked open and the sound of muted voices could be heard through the closet door. D.Wayne stood motionless as he listened.

"You don't come up in here demandin' shit!" That was Joselle.

"I ain't demanding nothing, baby," a man's deep voice answered. "My nature is making all the demands! Demanding that sweet, chocolate body of yours."

D.Wayne looked through the slats of the closet door. A strange man stood inside the doorway, holding Joselle in a passionate embrace.

"And you know this would be some good loving, girl."

Joselle looked up at him. "You do, huh?"

"Yeah," he continued smoothly. "You got all that pretty, chocolate skin wrapped around you...I like skin." He paused to kiss her. "And lips." D.Wayne saw the man smile before he continued. "Long as you ain't got no big-assed soup coolers."

"Shee-it!" Joselle exclaimed as she stepped from his embrace and posed seductively. "I could be a white girl named Shanequa and you still gonna be tryin' to hit this!"

The man laughed and pulled Joselle to him again. His voice was heavy with lust when he spoke. "Your lips are to kiss. But we can go deeper if you want to. I can go deep. We can kiss and we can touch. But when I touch that coochie spot...I'll touch that with me."

He kissed Joselle softly. "Come on." He led her to the bed.

Damn! D.Wayne swore under his breath. *Now they gonna do it.* He closed his eyes to the scene taking place in front of him. He ignored the sounds that emanated from the other side of the closet door. The rhythmic squeak of sex, the unmistakable sound of flesh slapping flesh, the thump of the mattress pounding against the headboard—sexy noises that reached his ears in staccato echoes. First slow. Then faster and harder. The man began to groan louder, losing his breath slightly before the pounding slap of their bodies met in a hot clash. He let out an odd-sounding noise; it was like a soprano wail escaping a deep, bass vocal chord.

"Hold up!" Joselle's voice rang out. "Stop, I said! Get up off me!" She spoke so forcefully that D. Wayne's eyes popped open in the closet. All he could see was the man's face looking down at Joselle underneath him. A puzzled expression passed over his face, quickly replaced by a look of determination as he resumed trying to sex her up, thrusting himself further inside of her.

"Hold up, I said!" Joselle pushed her hands against the man's chest. His eyes were bulged in disbelief as he sputtered. "Wh...wh...what?" He paused to clear his throat and get himself back under control. He rocked his hips gently before he spoke with as much conviction as he could muster.

"Ain't no need to stop, baby! I can feel your walls. Feel it? Right. Right there," his voice trailed off.

"Stop movin', nigga!" Joselle pushed the man off of her.

"What's wrong?" he said as he rolled over on his side.

"I'm thirsty," Joselle replied. "I need a glass of water." Without another word she pushed him aside, sprang from the bed and walked out of the bedroom. The man sat on the edge of the bed, slumped over in dejection.

"I thought we was fucking?" he yelled.

"Be quiet with that shit," Joselle hollered. "My son is sleeping." She turned on the water and began opening cabinet doors in the kitchen.

"You want something to drink?" she asked him.

"Fuck no, I don't want nothing to drink! I want some ass!" He reached for his underwear and pulled them on. By the time Joselle came back to the bedroom with the drink in her hand, he was fully dressed, sitting on the edge of the bed and tying his shoes.

Joselle stated the obvious. "You leavin'."

"Yeah. Getting the fuck up out!"

"Why?"

"Because you'd rather have a glass of water than take my magic carpet ride… so I hope that drink can keep you wet, lady." The man straightened up and stepped over to the door. Joselle moved in front of him, blocking his exit.

"Wait a minute!"

The man looked down at her. Joselle's eyes were solemn as she held the glass in front of her. "Would it help if I told you that this was water…and vodka?" Her mocking laughter rang out even before he slammed the door shut.

"Bitch!" she hissed as she flopped down on the bed, careful not to spill her drink. "I hate a sensitive motha fucka." She took a long pull on her drink. Her collection of sex toys beckoned to her from the dresser. She spoke to her favorite: a big, golden-colored vibrator.

"You ain't soft like that though, huh, Goldie?" She walked over and picked the long device up, holding it as if it were a golden, prized possession. It was thick and round with little bumps on the business end and dark, black stripes ran over its length.

"Naw, Goldie," she slurred. "You up in there! You ain't power charged like men is. All you need is batteries…and I know you got some of them, 'cause I bought them muthafuckas!"

She paused to slosh down the rest of her drink.

Boy! D.Wayne looked out from the closet. *That woman know she can drink a lot of liquor.*

Joselle smiled in her nakedness. She paused to pick up a lighter from the dresser and started lighting the many candles that she had placed all around the room. She danced over to the stereo, popped in a tape and pressed play. A slow groove emanated from the speakers.

"Don't you say no tonight,

Don't you say no toniigghttt!"

Joselle floated over to the light switch and flicked it off. Suddenly the room was illuminated with hundreds of reflected candles, the result of the many mirrors that Joselle had lining the walls and ceiling. She walked over and retrieved Goldie before heading back to the bed. She lay down, spread her legs and flipped the switch. The soft, electric hum of Goldie was quickly joined by the moans of Joselle as, together, they got moist.

D.Wayne leaned back and closed his eyes in the darkness of the closet. This was a scene he could have lived without. He was able to close his eyes but he wished that he could block out the sounds...Joselle thrashing and moving on the bed, Joselle panting and calling out men's names, Odis, Calvin, Ray-Ray...so he was relieved when the noises stopped. He leaned forward to spy her through the slats. Joselle was laid out on her bed; her breath coming in short, panting rhythms with her eyes closed. Her ragged, rasping breathing slowly returned to normal and soon the bass of her snore could be heard throughout the room. When he looked out between the slats, Goldie was sticking out between her legs. D.Wayne sat back and waited.

In the darkness of the closet, he knew that this was his only chance. It was now or never and he had to get her. *Joselle is the devil and she gots to go!* Joselle. His mother.

Images of Joselle thrashing on top of him flashed through his mind once again. The memory had tortured him every waking moment since it happened. Joselle bucking and lurching on top of him. Flo Jigga digging into his neck. His blood dripping onto the sheets...D.Wayne felt the rage surge anew. He felt the clock he could never turn back. He felt the blood go dry in his veins and he succumbed to the desire to spill some in return. In the darkness of the closet, D.Wayne leaned back and gripped his Louisville Slugger...and cried.

His soul moisture came at a price. The price of passage. The cost of never. D.Wayne burst through the closet door and rushed toward his unconscious mother with the bat raised high over his head. In that instant, when Joselle opened her eyes, a shocking glimpse of realization flashed before her. A heartbeat before he brought the bat down with all his strength, a tear fell from his soul and hatred hardened his heart. Forever.

2000 — PRESENT

CHAPTER 6
The Curse

The smoke rushed up the pipe past the dead spider's legs, crushed maggots and ganja, pausing to invade Alias' lungs, expanding his spirit and taking his life. He felt the "curse" inside him, growing with the swelling of the acrid smoke, burgeoning with each beat of his heart, dancing amongst the whispers of his ancestors as they chanted in mind music.

Alias closed his eyes and exhaled.

More than once, he had questioned why this curse was put upon him. More times than he cared to remember, he had cursed the fates for placing this burden at his feet. He had learned, quite quickly, that his curses had no power. His utterances were mere words, mere exclamations that resulted in the tiniest of cosmic ripples; while the blight that afflicted him was real, solid, tangible and the harbinger of pain and sadness.

Alias put the pipe to his lips and inhaled.

The bitter, caustic smoke tore angrily at the lining of his throat, which constricted in response. It caused him to cough and hack violently.

"You a filthy vampire, me man! Easy with that smoke, brah."

Alias looked up at his younger brother who was making his way across the yard. Tyrone was carrying a small oval of plastic in his hand. The small container was filled with more of the ghastly concoction that Alias was compelled to inhale. Dead spiders' legs, crushed maggots and reefer! That was a recipe that had to have been brewed up in hell with no real concern of its effect on the human body.

In his other hand, Tyrone carried what Alias could only describe as an urn because he had never seen any other piece of pottery quite like it. It was shaped like a wide-mouthed pitcher with a good-sized, bulbous body but it had two small handles—one at its base and the other up toward its neck. The opening itself was wide enough for Alias' hand to fit inside. Protruding from the base of the bowl, directly across from the handle was a tiny, hollow, metal tube that extended outward nearly three inches. Alias assumed that the stem's purpose was to allow air inside to feed the burning contents of the urn, but for a bowl of such size the tube appeared to be much too small. The outside of the urn was stained a dark, coarse black with streaks of red that slashed like living blood around the entire surface. The colors seemed to move and pulse whenever the urn was seen from a different angle.

"Urn" was the proper name for that vessel of evil. Devil's ashes, death's ashes…neither could find a more appropriate place to reside than at the bottom of that unknown pit.

Tyrone paused to look at him.

Alias was seated at an old, ragged armchair that their mother had discarded months ago. He had dragged a small dresser he found in an alley in front of the chair to use for a table. There were three dollar bills laid out on the dresser, all waiting to take part in the hell-bound incantation now underway.

Alias took a ritual drag from the pipe and pondered his fate.

It was Hell. Had to be. When he thought about what he had to do…and the ease with which it was made possible! The devil had to have had a hand in this drastic game.

Gathering the reefer had been no problem, after all, weed was always just a toke away, but accumulating the spider's legs had been a daunting task. He had been out searching for spiders, wondering how in the world he was going to catch even one spider, much less dozens of them, because he hadn't even spotted so much as a spider's web. He looked everywhere that he could remember seeing spiders hang out…in abandoned houses, in forgotten areas of neglect. He even ventured deep into the woods…and he still hadn't seen one single, solitary, creeping crawler. He had plopped down, disgusted and angry, on a huge rock facing the mountainous cliffs that overlooked the Hudson River. He looked up at the caves that were carved into the side of the mountain. He remembered back when he was younger, the times he and his friends would hide out in those dark recesses, defying their mothers who had warned them against playing up there. He also remembered seeing spiders inside the cave. Well, he remembered feeling the little critters scampering across his skin when he had been hiding out in the caves. So Alias climbed the once familiar rock face to what used to be their favorite hideout and stepped inside.

A rotting, putrid odor assaulted his senses as soon as he stepped through the cave's mouth, and when his eyes adjusted to the sudden darkness, he saw the source of the rotten stench. There was a dead, decaying corpse lying on the floor of the cave with a mass of maggots that moved and hummed and slurped and slivered over the remains of the body. A long axe handle protruded from the corpse's chest, a maggoty heart beating in lieu of its rotting one. The dead head was turned toward Alias, looking toward the mouth of the cave through an empty eye socket that twitched back and forth in a lump of vermin. Alias jumped backwards, a gag forming in his throat, when the realization hit him that he would need to collect some of the maggots from the body. He would have to fight his revulsion. When he thought about the devil and how demons operate, it all made sense.

He had a brought a coffee can with him for the spiders' legs. He figured dead maggots would fit in there just as well, so he began looking for a stick to scrape the nasty things into the can. No way was he going to touch them with his bare hands.

He saw a flat piece of wood under an outcropping of rock and bent over to retrieve it. That was when he saw the spiders. They came marching toward him in military formations from all sides and some of them were pretty big. Alias spun back toward the entrance of the cave but a few troops of spiders quickly cut off that avenue of escape.

Alias grabbed the stick and raised it defiantly.

"Y'all are devil bastards. Pure bastards." The spider troops continued to close in on him. "But some of you are gonna die with me. Fuck that!"

Alias started pounding and flailing wildly with the stick, splattering the spiders in all directions, moving in a frenetic frenzy. He felt tiny legs on the nape of his neck but he ignored them, closed his eyes and swung harder. The stick flailed up and down, back and forth until his arms fatigued, and the only sound heard in the hollow of the cave was his labored breathing. Exhausted, he opened his eyes…and the spiders were gone. The dead remains of hundreds of them were scattered about the cave. He had slung them far and wide, a silent testament to his primal fear amongst the unnatural silence of the cave.

"Devil shit," Alias panted. He walked around the cave and began plucking the spiders' legs from their bodies—he had gotten quite a few big ones—and piling them up in the coffee can. When he had gathered enough for the ritual, he went to the back of the cave. He scraped a glob of the mass of maggots away from the body with the stick and smashed them on the ground before scooping them into the can on top of the spiders' legs.

"Could'a been me, you know."

Alias shook his head as he awoke from his nightmarish memory. His little brother stood in front of him with a serious expression on his face.

"Could'a been me," he repeated. "Steada you."

Alias reached up and touched his younger brother's ear. Tyrone was as solemn as a kid his age could get. He was fully aware of the gesture and its meaning.

It seemed as if Alias and Tyrone had been bred from different stock, opposite blood; but life together had pushed them close and their bond had become unbreakable. Tyrone wore his hair in tight little naps that he refused to let any comb get into, and he wore a smile that hid a joke he was about to tell. Alias wore dreadlocks and serious expressions everywhere he went. Where Alias was tall and solid, Tyrone was small and slim. Alias' face had a stern, unyielding demeanor that put most people at a distance. Tyrone was impishly handsome and openly inviting, hinting at the kindness of his heart, still young enough to think that life was fun…and funny.

Alias squinted at his brother, his mind pulsing with a glowing buzz and suddenly amazed by the differences in their physical makeup. Though four years separated them, Alias knew no other peer. His younger brother had a life to live, and Alias would brook no interference in its natural progression.

A ritual drag from the pipe and Alias felt a stinging sensation in his eyes. Behind his pupils he heard something burning.

"Tyrone."

His younger brother looked at him defiantly. Alias paused before blowing out a stream of blue-gray smoke.

"All right, man! All right?" Alias was escalating to the high spots. His concentration was wavering under a slow haze that was descending like a curtain on his mind. He felt through the fog and pulled out a memory. He remembered. He remembered.

He remembered when Tyrone was going through one of his mercurial changes…this one, a name change. He had wanted everyone to call him by his new, more meaningful name…Tyree. Tyrone was naturally and notoriously stubborn, so when he decided that he would not answer to anything but his new name, he stuck to his guns for days. He could hold out forever until he got his way.

Alias remembered. Yeah. He remembered.

He remembered the time when Tyrone—spoiled and pampered Tyrone—had gotten so angry that he announced to the family that he would hold his breath until he died. The response was a family chorus.

"Go on then, old crazy boy."

"You Stoopid McNoopid!"

"Go ahead, boy!"

So Tyrone did it. He held his breath until he fainted. He awoke on the couch to condescending stares and knowing smirks.

"You so hardheaded boy," Mama told him.

Tyrone was defiant. "Umma do it again."

"Do what? Pass out again?"

"Hold my breath! Umma do it again!"

"Go ahead then."

Tyrone got up and walked to the door. "All right then. I will."

"Where you goin', Tyrone?" Mama demanded.

"This time…" Tyrone paused. "Umma try it underwater."

Tyrone always got what he wanted.

"Tyree." Alias struggled with clarity but he was slowly bringing his high back down. He was adapting. He just needed a moment to pull himself together. A moment that he didn't have. He held the pipe out to his brother.

"Fill it up," Alias rasped. "It's empty."

"That's like prophetic words." Tyrone looked worried. "I learned that word in school today. Prophetic. It means …"

"Quit brickin'! Let's finish this."

"Fuck no. I ain't giving you shit! This is crazy, Alias! You should see your eyes man! You look like a serious zombie and shit! Worser than a …"

"Stop cussing!"

"Worser than a crackhead. You high!" Tyrone laid the pipe on the table.

"Tyrone." Alias' voice was raw. "You my brother…and you know I gotta do this." Tyrone watched him, uncertainty knitting his brow. "Come on," Alias said. "Let's finish this."

Tyrone unscrewed the top half of the bowl, emptied the ashes on the ground and then re-filled half of it with the mixture. He stopped to study Alias' face with a sincerity that reflected the regard that only a big brother inspired.

"It coulda been me, you know," he whispered and handed Alias the replenished bowl. "Steada you."

Alias put the pipe to his lips. "But it wasn't." He pulled out a lighter and flicked a flame to life. He puffed on the pipe until an amber core burned and crackled, sending plumes of smoke up the stem and directly into his lungs. He puffed and puffed, pulling and sucking smoke until his lungs felt as if they were about to explode. Wisps of it escaped from the corners of Alias' mouth, but he kept on puffing on the pipe.

Tyrone picked up the dollar bills from the dresser and stuffed them inside of the urn. He turned to Alias just in time to see him slump back into the chair, smoke seeming to escape from every orifice. The depleted pipe fell from Alias' fingers and clattered to the ground as his chest began to heave and his lungs began to cry for pristine oxygen. Tyrone grabbed Alias by the hand and jammed it into the mouth of the urn as he had been instructed… and waited.

The urn began to heat up. Heavy, gray smoke began to flutter up from the vessel around Alias' hand. It glowed and pulsed a faint yet deep, churlish red and a thin stream of dark air began pouring out of the small stem that poked out from the side of the urn. Alias' body shot forward. He sat erect in the chair with his hand firmly implanted in the urn and his eyes closed. Moisture began to form on his fingertips; he felt it drizzle from his pores onto the papers. It had the consistency of sweaty blood...only darker. Like devil's ink churning from within his body. Somewhere inside of himself the voice of sanity reminded Alias that he was under the influence, that he was beyond the typical high and that his mind was playing imaginary tricks with the physical world. The roar of the dark, crashing liquid that cascaded through his veins and pulsed toward his fingertips drowned that wayward voice out. Alias felt it and went liquid with its fiery flow as it escaped his body. He gasped...and gasped from the sensory overload as he faded from consciousness and collapsed in a heap to the ground, unaware of the demonic messages that were now clearly written, in deep, dark letters on the three dollar bills inside of the urn. Blood flowed from his fingertips to the devil's ear.

CHAPTER 7
Mourning Papers

It was well past midnight before Alias finally succumbed to sleep. His body was exhausted from his chemical ordeal but he was still wired, restless and alert. The pains of abuse ravaged him physically; his head pounded and he was nauseous, but rest still eluded him. He cringed inwardly when he thought about the concoction that he had inhaled in such great amounts.

The three dollar bills lay on the stand next to his bed with messages scrawled across them. Alias stared at the foreign scribbles, struggling with the realization that the words weren't written by his hand. The loops and curlicues belied a penmanship that was spawned from hellfire, both blood red and evil black simultaneously. The ancient curse was strong…and Alias was lost in its incantations.

The ominous words had power. Alias stared in curious wonder, and struggled to decipher their meaning, their origins. He drew a blank, unable to recall various portions of what had transpired only hours earlier. Closing his eyes, searching for sleep, he laid his head back on the pillow and rummaged around in the darkness, concentrating, meandering in the space between sleep and consciousness, on the edge of an incubus. From the depths, just behind his eyelids, a vision of the previous hours emerged.

Alias sat at the table in his yard with his hand inside of the urn. The demon smoke of cannabis, spiders' legs and crushed maggots, curled around his head and billowed from his lungs. His fingers inside the urn became engorged, turning fat and numb as the smoke took his brain and sent it on a warped ride to the far side. Smoking blood began to spurt from his fingertips onto the dollar bills that were laying on the bottom of the urn, spattering in a seemingly random pattern. The bills seemed to thump rhythmically with each pumping of dark fluid shooting from Alias' fingertips, but slowly words began to take shape on each surface. Alias saw it clearly in his nightmare. Blood-red words that were born in the abyss, legible to the world and destined to wreak a tumult of pain. Each bill shuddered once and then lay still.

Alias gasped and bolted awake from his vision. Sometimes he still had to convince himself that these events were really happening, that the facts were actual, that this Curse was a real entity, a blot on his life. One look at the bills on his nightstand and his doubts were all answered. He was cursed. He was destined to take those bills, those mourning papers, and pass them on to some poor, unsuspecting soul. To wait for the curse to manifest itself. There was no alternative for him, no way out…and the inevitability of his fate infuriated him.

The mourning papers cried for him from his bedside. His brain felt melted and chilled, shaken—not stirred—and served like lamented wine. Myriad visions nagged at the edge of his drowsiness, dancing like insipid rays of light that fought against his depleted body. Burying his face in the pillow, Alias screamed helplessly and closed his eyes, feeling around inside his head for elusive sleep. He glimpsed it, sneaking around a corner, tantalizing and flirty, and he quickly gave chase. He just wanted to sleep and forget, toss his troubles aside and never wake up. But he would awaken…that much was certain. Easy answers had never been a part of his life.

Not that the questions had been of his choosing! Only that fate had been his main interrogator, grilling him, sizing him up and then slicing his soul wide open. Laying his insides bare, exposing an inhumane jigsaw puzzle from which the most jaded colors and schemes were formulated…and the sinister scenery blackened his spirit.

Alias fought the wave of guilt and self-pity that threatened to wash over him but his feelings ran over him like hot water running in the river of morality. His fate, fouling the waters, bringing steam from a temperate stream that, ideally, ran a course of mutuality. Not too hot. Not too cold. Yet water is life…in form as well as in substance and his fate produced swirling steam, dipping its toes in the rapids and causing turmoil. Bubbling lust, boiling greed or simmering vanity—no matter! It was a river, its course fixed, its power gained from the strength of its creator.

Alias looked over at the mourning papers and wondered…what claim had morality over fate? What design could be whispered to the trees that would alter the formation of its leaves? What ethic could influence the approaching of day? The creeping of the beckoning grave? Or the next breath? And the next? And the next?

His exasperation was his misery. Emotions rolled like thunder inside of him, crashing here and there, touching down and searing the terrain. There was nothing he could do to alter the outcome of his curse. He was powerless. He was a pawn, incapable of affecting the outcome of his destiny.

The mourning papers would hurt someone. Nothing good could come of such evil direction. Dead spiders' legs, crushed maggots and weed! Dollar bills that caused ancient blood to run like demon ink from his fingertips. Messages from a forsaken time and place. Smelled like death to Alias…and he was the source of the deadly fragrance.

He sat up in the bed, thoughtful in a moment of clarity, and contemplated his fate. There was no edict written in stone pertaining to his life. It seemed impossible to him that it was preordained, that it was his lot in life to take the life of another. There had to be a way to lift the Curse from his life. Impossible is nothing. There just had to be a way.

Alias looked over at the mourning paper on his nightstand. It was inscribed with the words *Doin Doin*.

In a fit of rage he reached for one of the dollar bills and began to tear it up. He twisted, pulled and ripped with all his strength. But when the edge of the bill tore, Alias felt rips tear through his flesh. His heart felt as if it were being slashed open, twisted and torn…just like the cursed bill. He cried out in pain and dropped the bill to the floor. He collapsed in a heap on the bed, his chest heaving as he waited for the pain to subside. He lay there, staring at the cursed dollar. Thinking.

He sprang from the bed and grabbed his cigarette lighter, and with little forethought, picked up the bill by one corner and held the other end up to the flame. He felt instant heat on his skin. The intensity of the fire took hold and began to burn right through his flesh and into his heart. Alias closed his eyes and held on against the pain. As the flame licked higher, the bill burned brighter and the high pressure of an otherworldly burn settled inside of his skull and began to roast his brain. Alias growled and fell to the floor. The burning dollar bill floated out of his fingertips and landed next to his trembling body. As he lay there, gasping for air as the heat began to fade from his body, he watched as the dollar pulsed with a life of its own and began to heal itself. The burned edges, the tear through its middle, each began to waver and reform. Soon, the dollar bill was whole again.

Devil shit! Alias' body was hot all over. *Devil shit!*

There has to be a way to fight this thing, he determined. And I will. Somewhere in the night the spirit of the wind howled with laughter, and Alias finally fell into a deep sleep.

CHAPTER 8
Fighting Fire

Alias looked over at the blood-spotted urn. Its stout body seemed to pulse with heat and pressure. Its contents were a Curse of barbed pain, the essence of a brutal evil that spelled out death. The harbinger of demise to some unsuspecting soul.

Sometime during the night, Alias had determined that it was his lot in life to put an end to the Curse that haunted his family, to the many lives that were forcibly taken as a result of a witch's incantation. This was his moment, his line drawn in the sand, his stand against forces that were as old as fate. He was facing a reality that was beyond his comprehension.

Only one surety sat in the forefront of his mind, an anchor that firmly rooted him to his convictions. Alias knew that his soul would not withstand the spiritual darkness of murder that the Curse had laid upon him. His value as a human being was a direct reflection of his benevolence, which mirrored his belief that to harm another, especially to take a life, was a deed that was inherently wrong. Such action was the direct opposite of the meaning of his existence.

So he decided to fight.

The Curse was an age-old malady that afflicted him so he figured that the answers lay with the ages; back in the beginning with his ancestors. He would have to go back again.

This Curse had no earthly origin; in fact its manifestation could be attributed to nothing more than chicken scratches in the dirt. Therefore

Alias knew that he had to rely upon his spiritual connection. He had to see what came before.

Thus, Alias found himself back in his yard with his brother—preparing the hellfire concoction that would soon invade his mind, body and spirit. His hand unconsciously went to his ear. The tuft of gnarled flesh that remained there served as a penance of disbelief that was fated on that day long ago. His missing ear was a stark reminder that his plight was real.

The blood-red urn was waiting. Alias saw evil in its color, its shape… it was much more than just an urn. It was a gateway, a portal that opened onto his past, showing Alias his genealogy in a demonic Technicolor; the devil's own Hellivision.

"You ready, man?" Alias turned to his little brother Tyrone who was watching him with concern in his eyes. He didn't understand why Alias was going through the ritual again, especially after the body-wrecking experience of the first encounter. Alias nodded his head at Tyrone, but Tyrone made no move toward him.

"Alias, why are you doing this shit again?" Alias shot his brother a disapproving look. Tyrone was getting to the age of trying out his new arsenal of cuss words.

"Ooops!" Tyrone was used to that look. "My bad! But why are you doing this one more again? Last time you couldn't hardly get out the bed! You was like one of them crackheads trying to get clean. It's making your body bad for you, man!"

"Tyrone," Alias said. "You my man. You know that, right?" Tyrone paused for a moment before nodding his head in agreement. Alias paused to look at his young brother. "You got everything for me, right?"

"That's it," Tyrone said. "That's all you gonna say? 'Tyrone, you got everything.' That's all you got to say? Look. What if this stuff is killing you? There gotta be some cancer in there or something. Now you know if peanut butter can give cancer, then this shit can!"

Alias stared at him again.

"My bad!" Tyrone said. "But for real though. Why you doing this again, Alias?"

"Because it's the only way." Alias heaved a heavy sigh. He had talked with his brother, tried to explain his plan in terms that would be relevant, with words that would matter in his realm of understanding. But Tyrone saw the world through a kid's eyes. He saw relevance in immediacy. "Did you listen to me last time," Alias said.

"Yeah, I did," Tyrone answered.

"No. Did you listen to what I said, Tyrone."

"Yes. I heard what you said."

"Because sometimes you don't hear me."

"Now here we go with the la-di-da again." Tyrone rolled his eyes and shrugged. "I heard everything that you said and it still don't make no sense." Tyrone walked over to the urn and pointed. "You got dead spiders' legs; crushed, nasty maggots and weed all mixed up in there…and you gonna smoke it. Again! Now you tell me again…what did I miss?"

Alias looked at him. "Boy, you are a trip."

"No," Tyrone shot back. "You the one trippin'."

"Aiight. Aiight," Alias said. "Tyrone. This ritual thing…this is some real shit…and its got to stop somewhere. This Curse is hurting people…bad! I just can't have that knowledge running around inside of me. I just can't."

"But this thing is hurting you now!"

"Yeah. I know. But the hurt has to stop somewhere."

Tyrone watched him.

"You feel me," Alias said.

Tyrone nodded. Alias could tell that his brother wasn't convinced but there wasn't any time to break things down further for him. "Well, then," Alias said. "Let's get this party started." Tyrone prepared the pipe and held the lighter's flame up to the bowl as Alias sucked in the smoke. Soon, Alias was on a trip. Floating. Floating.

♠♠♠

Greenville, Mississippi. The year—1927. And it was raining. Day after day the rain fell until the days turned into weeks, weeks into month after month until the basin of the Mississippi River flowed over. The Mississippi Delta stretches nearly two hundred miles from Memphis to Vicksburg and since the Mississippi River overflows annually, the floodwaters would leave some of the richest soil on earth. Ironically, since the river overflowed every year, the land could not be harvested and farming was generally pointless. White planters began clearing the Delta in the 1800s but soon slaves were given the job of clearing the land and planting crops. Farming in the Delta was a risky venture due to the floods but somehow the farmers there managed to eke out a living. But every five or six years, a heavy flood would leave several feet of water that would wipe out the entire crop and devastate the local economy. After one particularly damaging flood, the United States Government came to the rescue.

The Army Corps of Engineers lined the Mississippi River with eleven hundred miles of levees. Enormous, earthen dams that were set back a mile or more from the natural river banks were said to be able to contain roaring flood waters and prevent the flooding of the crops. The levee was the first and only of its kind. Two hundred feet wide at the base and sloping up to a crown that stood four stories high, the levee peaked at a flat top that was only eight feet wide.

In 1927 the rain fell. Days, weeks, months—the downpour continued until the river flooded to the top of the levee, washing away trees, houses, machinery...anything that got in its way, thereby adding mass to the developing force of the torrent. By the time the flood waters reached the Delta, the river raged with the force of a maelstrom that was ten miles wide. The people of Mississippi reacted in learned desperation.

They gathered Black men—thousands of them; most by gunpoint, and forced them to work on the levee, day and night, fighting the force of nature. Hour after hour of backbreaking labor, piling sandbags against the back of the levee, against a rain that wouldn't stop, Black men were worked like slaves. The threat of a bullet spurred them on beyond the limit of endurance. But they were fighting a losing battle; the water pushed against the levee with tremendous force and finally the wall of the dam gave way. A hundred-foot wall of water burst through a crevasse that was three-quarters of a mile wide, killing hundreds of Black men who were on the ground, still piling on the sandbags.

Civil Rights groups in the North protested with appeals to the government about the treatment of Blacks in the Delta but their entreaties were met with disbelief. They decided to send representatives to investigate the conditions that had been widely reported by the Black press of the region.

"You're sending someone directly into harm's way," the Branch Director said. "Chances are that there won't be a good ending to this assignment."

"I'm aware of that, sir," the Assistant Director replied. "Everyone knows that. But they also know that this is what they signed on for. The greatest differences made are usually made with the greatest risks."

"You're preaching to the choir, sir," came the reply. The Director rose from his chair and walked over to his office window. He often enjoyed the view this vantage point offered. The calming effect of a gentle breeze as it moved through the leaves of the trees that were visible over the rooftops of the garment district. The visual serenity of the swaying trees was an illusion at the moment, a vision shattered by the reality of the events taking place in Greenville, Mississippi. "So what is our next course of action." He turned back to face the AD.

"We're going to send agents to Greenville. They will gather as much evidence as possible and report back to us here. Our goal is to throw mountains of evidence at Hoover when we have our next meeting. I think that Hoover is the key. He has his own agenda."

"Time frame," the Director said.

"We can't possibly implement one, sir," the AD replied. "This is going to be a 'play as we go' operation."

The Director eased himself into his chair behind his desk and eyed his assistant. The Director trusted his man. The AD had proven his competence and reliability on many occasions but his assistant was also ambitious and overzealous at times. "How many men are we committing to the Delta?"

"We have five men assigned to enter the Delta at different points and at separate times. Their movements will be coordinated and clandestine." The AD paused to look at the Director. "But we have to move quickly and decisively on this matter, sir. Now is the time."

"That's five men that we can't afford," the Director said. "I don't like that." The AD said nothing.

"You get one man," the Director said. "That's it."

"Yes, Sir," the AD said. "If I only get one…then I have just the man."

"Who?" the Director said. The AD turned and walked over to the office door. He opened it and called to someone in the lobby.

"Sir." The AD stepped toward his desk. "This is Agent Robert Abraham."

Robert Abraham stepped into the room. He was a big man, solidly built with a hint of agility and quickness in his step. His skin was a darkened walnut hue that had been blessed by the constant kiss of Southern sun. His deep-set eyes were steady and unwavering yet he seemed at ease, adaptable to any situation. He wore his hair short— cropped and neatly trimmed.

"He's one of the best," the AD said. When the agent turned and nodded at the AD, the Director noticed for the first time that Robert Abraham had one ear.

When Alias awoke later that night he felt physically drained and his head throbbed. He hadn't found any answers and he now faced what he dreaded the most: He had to implement the first stage of The Curse.

CHAPTER 9
Daryn's Mark

Club Midnite was the only juke joint in town. Music resonated from the short, squat building with the sound of old-school soul music blaring from a jukebox. It was ideally located on a corner just up the street from the projects. Its atmosphere was seasoned with the sweat and rhythm of the ghetto that peppered raucous Saturday nights. This was a place of temporary freedom, a garden of respite from the rat race, a mixture of libation and liberation in which a tired soul could lose its essence for the night.

Midnite was a dark brown den with a darker brown interior. The first step through the door was a step to the bar. Its beer-soaked surface stretched a good portion of the distance from the entrance to the dance floor. Alias took a couple of steps inside and waited for his eyes to adjust to the darkness. He leaned against a miniature electronic bowling game and looked out at the few tables that were spaced around the floor. Each table had a few chairs shoved underneath them—some with a few solitary patrons nursing their lonely drinks. Just past the end of the bar was a dance floor with mirrored walls that reflected fractured flashes of the strobe lights flashing from the ball that hung from the ceiling. Glass partitions protruded from the wall, forming a booth that the disc jockey stood inside as he spun a few records. Alias walked down to the end of the bar and took a stool facing the door.

His soul was heavy and, oddly, he didn't feel the need to numb himself with alcohol. He wanted to keep his mind clear; he wanted to walk out the front door and keep going; he wanted to scream and shriek at the fates for the Curse that tainted him, tainted his being. He was lost…and he knew it. He wanted to fight but there was no one for him to battle, no method to the madness that assailed him, so therefore the war was nonexistent. The enemy was within.

"Alias! Whattup, boy?"

Alias looked up as Dave slid onto the stool next to him.

"If you see a 'boy,'" Alias replied, "whoop his ass or suck his dick." Dave looked over at Alias through his blond locks and held his hands up in mock surrender. "My bad, dude," he answered. "My bad. Dude! I didn't mean anything…it's just an expression, okay. Sheesh!"

"Well, you need to watch that shit 'cause expressions express a lot of shit. Both said and unsaid, ya' heard!"

Dave was cool with Alias but he was just so *white* sometimes! Every once in a while he would make a comment that just sandpapered Alias' nerves.

"But, dude…" Dave was smiling. "You haven't even had a drink yet. I'm buying if you know how to soak up some suds."

"Naw, that's all right, man. Just chill with your 'boy' comments. I ain't got time for all that."

"I didn't mean anything by it. Okay?" Dave extended his hand.

"Okay." Alias bumped knuckles with him.

The bartender was at the other end of the counter talking to a light-skinned woman who wore a tall, beehive hairdo. An ice chest was pushed up against the wall behind the counter and the bartender sat on it as she talked animatedly with the woman. Bottles of liquor lined the wall behind her; so many different brands of liquor that there were enough to reach from the doorway to the end of the bar where Alias sat. The cash register, one of those old ones—the kind that rang a bell with each sale and the numbers popped up—sat on the counter almost directly in front of him. Alias eyed it with apprehension. Dave motioned to the bartender who was still involved in an animated conversation and totally unaware that he was trying to get her attention. In frustration, Dave slammed his hand down on the bar and the woman with the beehive pointed the bartender in their direction. She turned and looked at Dave with an annoyed twist of her lips before she rose to her feet.

Three old men came bustling into the bar in a cloud of ruckus but, it was a burst of familiar mayhem.

"Boy, you know I'll make you outrun me!" Alias turned to look. It was a murder of crows...a flock of old drunks—Johnny, Hosscolla and Squirrel. They were three hardcore, lifelong companions of "drunk." "Drunk" was their buddy, their pal, the glue that held the three of them together. Usually they could be found boozing it up at their other spot, The Hole. Apparently they had already taken a few shots down there and the liquor had steered them to Midnite.

"You ain't shit, boy," Hosscolla hollered. He guffawed loudly before he reached over to the beehive-haired lady and squeezed her butt. She turned viciously on Hosscolla who stood there simply smiling at her. "Oh," she said, the angry look fading from her eyes only to be replaced with a look of bemusement. "You better cut that shit out, Hosscolla." He gave her a big smile and turned to join his two buddies at the bar. Squirrel straddled a barstool and called out to the bartender. "Gwen," he barked out. "Could you get up off'n your beautiful, round, lovely, Black ass and get me a drink. Yo' ass is just lovely...I swear. Just. Lovely." Gwen responded with a smirk and reached for a bottle of rum. "Here comes your usual, Squirrel."

Squirrel was a skinny, smallish man with short gray hair that clung to his head in small naps. His eyes had turned a permanent bloodshot red years ago, giving him a look far beyond his actual years. Years of drinking had ravaged his body and now he walked with a pathetic limp that gave him the look of fragility. He said that he kept a knife in his back pocket because if a fight ever came his way, he was gonna be the one to tell the story the next day. His weakness was evident, yet he was the one who was always running his mouth and causing static.

Johnny and Hosscolla, on the other hand, were big, dusty bruisers, shaped by hard life, hard living and hard drinking. They both worked at the steel foundry across the river and they both drank toward the bottom of the vodka bottle. They were known to get ornery from time to time so most people stayed out of their way once they were into one of their marathon drinking sessions. They ordered two shots of vodka…straight with a beer chaser.

Squirrel turned to Hosscolla. "Boy! They couldn't melt you and pour you on me!" He paused to look Hosscolla from head to toe. "But if they did, though, you be some heavy syrup. With yo' big-ass self."

Hosscolla slammed his drink down his gullet and then banged the empty glass on the counter. "I'll make you outrun me rat now!" He looked down toward the end of the bar. "Another, Gwen!" He turned toward Squirrel. "You sho' do talk a lotta shit for somebody with so little ass! Look at you! You look like eight ass whuppings wrapped up in puny, bitch ass." His voice rose to a girlish octave. "*Glitter!*"

"Sho' do," Johnny piped up. "Sho' nuff."

"Who you talking to," Squirrel turned his anger on Johnny. "You big, black polar bear." Hosscolla and Johnny laughed. "You so black that when you was born…that's when they came up with shit like, 'black' and 'dark' and 'tar-nigga.' Nigga!"

Johnny drained his drink and ordered another. "Now, nigga, you know there ain't no such word as no tar-nigga! Ya'll Black folks always making words up and shit! Fo' shizzle my nizzle." Johnny tried to imitate Martin Luther King. "Now Jessie, you know that's not a word!" He swiveled in his seat to fully face Squirrel. "Yeah. Let me tell you something…" Johnny began.

"You ain't tellin' me shit," Squirrel cut him off. "You a heathen."

"You is a heathen though, Johnny," Hosscolla jumped in quietly.

"Ya' mama," Johnny replied quickly before turning back on Squirrel. "A downright heathen," Squirrel threw in before Johnny could open his mouth.

"Squirrel," Johnny finally spoke. "I will fold you up. Put you in my back pocket. And feed you farts all day long. You know that?"

Another group of people burst through the door and all eyes glanced discreetly in their direction, each patron taking note of each person as they entered. It was the genesis of the nightlife, the start of something new for the nocturnal, for the chances of sin, the pleasure of the things taken into the dark. Alias reached into the pocket of his jeans and felt the weight of the cursed bill that would end up in a stranger's pocket before the night was through. He wondered about the dark incantation that was scribbled on the front of the dollar bill. What did it mean? And more importantly, how was it going to affect the person who possessed it? Alias glanced around the bar. It was beginning to get crowded as people began to stroll in. The DJ struggled through the door carrying crates full of records over toward the booth in the back. It was almost time.

"For real though," Dave said. Alias had almost forgotten that Dave was sitting there. "Dude. You gotta have a drink with me. You gotta." The bartender wiped the countertop in front of them with a rag before she spoke.

"What you boys want?"

"I'll have me a brewski," Dave said. "You?" Alias nodded. "Let me have a sodbuster, too, then," he ordered. When their beers arrived they toasted and took a swig. *Time to spend it*, Alias mused as a couple walked by him and took a seat in front of the jukebox. He squeezed the cursed bill in his pocket and he felt his heartbeat quicken with the struggle.

He was at a crossroad, that juncture where the rubber meets the pavement... It was now or never. He could keep the cursed bill in his pocket and tempt the fates; he could hug the abomination to his chest and face the consequences, even if it meant his death. Or he could pass it on to some stranger, some unsuspecting anybody and let the chips land where they may. Every life deserves freedom and happiness. Every life is precious. Alias struggled with his dilemma. He knew it was now or never. As the old saying goes, "Shit or get off the pot."

He put the bottle of beer to his lips and turned the bottom toward the ceiling, chugging until the last drop was gone. Dave watched him, bemused, as Alias signaled to the bartender for another. She placed the beer in front of him and as Alias watched her, she seemed to be moving in slow motion. He couldn't hear what she was saying but he knew what she said. He pulled the money from his pocket—the cursed dollar bill sat on top—and handed her four dollars. She turned to the cash register and rang up the transaction, putting the bill in the till before counting out the change and laying it on the bar in front of him. She had left the cash drawer open and Alias stared at it.

Someone called her from the other end of the bar and she pushed it shut with her hip. Alias bowed his head. It had begun.

There was a crowd milling around. Many more people were standing than when he had arrived an hour earlier. But Alias blocked out the low hum of activity as he tried to bring himself back into focus. His brain felt fuzzy, he was slightly out of sync on the periphery of his vision, but when he closed his eyes he felt his brain merge back into clarity. With great care, he raised his head and looked around the room. There were quite a few familiar faces up in the club. The slow buzz of the weekend was slowly building as the syncopation of unbridled anticipation arrived with the night.

Suddenly the door of the bar swung open and Alias saw Joozy standing there. Her hawklike glare scanned the entire room before she finally stepped inside. Joozy was a thick, plush body with a stop-frightful face that spoke of a hard life and hard times. Her hair was full and thick, falling down around her shoulders in gentle curls. Her skin was dark black and pockmarked with acne. She searched the bar with sharp, piercing eyes, and her lips were full and set in a tense snarl. A pronounced line of pimples ran down her cheek like small bumps of protruding flesh. Her eyes seemed to be set too close together on her face and her nose was of the classic African profile—wide and flat. She had wide, full lips that held much promise; until she smiled, revealing teeth that were spaced unevenly and gave her the look of being slightly deformed. Joozy looked at the world with a hard attitude…and reciprocated venom for venom.

But Joozy's body was tantalizing. Like King Tantalus, who found that every time he reached for fruit to eat or water to drink, it was just beyond his fingertips. So was the lustful inkling of enjoying the pleasures of Joozy's body. Her physicality was tight and sexual, a moving masterpiece of sensual promise. She was tight; her hips were curved with smooth, solid flesh and she always wrapped them tightly with deliciously stretched skirts. Sensuality swayed her round, fleshy mounds of ass when she walked and eyeballs swayed hypnotically as they followed the rhythm. An electric thrill seemed to ripple up through her body, pulsating her full breasts which strained, trying to escape the confines of her bra. Her perfectly formed cups of chocolate flesh were delicately firm, poking out, forming an inviting valley between the two peaks.

Many men had looked, quickly, beyond her ugly face once they had gotten a dose of the moving promise of Joozy's body. Yet looking past the hard, dark lines and severe eyes of Joozy had eventually cost those hardened men more than the promise was worth. Alias watched her as she spotted her prey and cast her spell upon one of those men sitting at the bar. Joozy sauntered over to a guy with short, sandy hair, which was tucked under a baseball cap turned backwards, and wiggled next to him at the bar. She bent slightly at the waist and looked over the counter at the bartender. The man leered up at her and saw the curve of her waist tapering into the firmness of her round, firm ass, and was instantly mesmerized. He turned back to his drink, raised it to his lips and dive-bombed it down his throat. He paused for a moment to give the liquor time to hit. When it did, he swayed a little with the impact. Joozy smiled. She liked her men like that.

A few more drinks and she would have him in the alley out back.

Someone bumped her and she stumbled gently into the man's arms. Joozy turned back to see who had nudged her. "Please excuse me," the man said. Joozy saw the man flinch slightly when he looked her in the face. She was numb to his reaction. He turned and hurried on. She turned back to the man who now held her, with one hand wrapped around her waist, the other hand trapped between her breast and the counter. His grin was a mile wide. She let herself be held.

"Sorry. Excuse me," she said. He pulled her closer for a second and smelled her perfume. "Don't be sorry." His voice was slightly slurred. "As a matter of fact…" He helped her to her feet. "Let me buy you a drink." Her voice was soft when she answered.

Alias turned back to his drink. He looked up at the cash register that held the cursed dollar bill and a song popped into his head. *He could pour his heart into a glass and serve it just like wine. She'd drink up and still have time for the mourning paper.* That was some shit there! The mourning papers. Shit.

He looked up as another man came into the bar and paused in front of Joozy. She turned and stared at him but he seemed not to notice. He was about average height but he wore nothing but solid muscle on his frame. He didn't have much of a neck but he did have two bulges of shoulders that swelled stoutly. His chest pushed his shirt outward thickly but his back tapered into a streamlined waist. He had big arms that flexed out of the sleeves of his shirt in tight, hard cords, and he stood there in front of Joozy, looking around for an empty stool. His eyes settled on Joozy and he nodded curtly to her before he continued down the bar toward Alias, settling on a barstool with a seat between them.

He ordered a drink and nursed it for a moment. "Anything going on in here tonight?"

"Depends on what you do," Alias replied.

"Just chillin' tonight, yo."

"This might be your spot then." Alias paused to fully appraise the big man. He wore his hair in a close cut with hints of a wave flowing through a short fade. He had a long, thin nose and a barely-there mustache that gave him a somewhat studious expression. His eyes were dark and intense, reflective of his demeanor that demanded serious consideration. He was a dark man, intimidating by size alone. Alias realized that he was judging the book by its cover, but experience was his only guide in sizing up people. He was usually pretty accurate in his assumptions. In a word, the man was menacing.

The flesh-wrenching scar that ran across his face only served to reinforce the imagined terror of his visage. It was a jagged tear that ran about two inches wide slashing from the middle of his forehead, along his hairline and then ripping a path down his right cheek. It ended just slightly above his lip in a curlicue of knotted flesh, as if someone had tried to cut his face off. The very sight of the long knife cut nearly made Alias cringe in pain as he imagined how much it must have hurt when the guy's face had been cut. He could only wonder how much it would have affected his life if he wore such a disfiguration on his face for the rest of his life.

The man leaned toward Alias and stuck out his hand.

"Yo, I'm Daryn," he introduced himself.

"Alias," came the reply as the two men shook hands.

"And I'm not sitting here, right," Dave said.

"Yeah," Alias said. "This here's Dave."

Dave's head nodded. "What's up?" Daryn's head nodded him back. "Wassup."
"No DJ or anything tonight, huh?"

"Little later probably. They let everybody get their drink on first. Imbibe a little first."

Daryn smiled knowingly and Alias was struck with the transformation. His smile was ingratiating and warm; his entire face lit up and Alias couldn't help but grin in return. Daryn looked like he hid a little of the rascal, and Alias began to reconsider his previous appraisal of the big man. Daryn swallowed the rest of his drink and ordered another. When the bartender put his drink in front of him Daryn produced a ten spot and paid her. She took it and walked over to the register. Daryn raised his drink up in a toast. Alias and Dave joined him. Still smiling he said, "To the few good ones left."

"Damn few," Alias and Dave replied together. Alias glanced over Daryn's shoulder and noticed that Joozy was staring in their direction. She had maneuvered her way in between the white guy's knees while his arms encircled her waist, hugging her to him. Joozy's intense stare was fixed on Daryn.

"Anything else," the bartender said as she laid Daryn's change on the counter in front of him. Alias glanced down in time to see Daryn pick up his money and stuff it in his pocket.

"Look here, ya'll," Daryn began. "Have you ever thought about what women like?"

Dave piped up. "Hell yeah! They like Black guys with big dicks!" Alias and Daryn looked at him. "For real," Dave said.

"Real dumb," Daryn said.

"You stupid for real, Dave," Alias pitched in.

Dave stopped with his beer halfway to his mouth. "Look, I have done some research and shit. You act like that is some easy shit for me to admit. It's not, believe me. Now how am I, a regular white guy, supposed to compete with that type shit? Huh?"

Daryn and Alias shared a laugh as Dave took a deep pull of his beer. "Shee-et!" He turned to them smiling.

"What about you?" Daryn turned to Alias. "Have *you* ever thought about what women want?"

Yeah," Alias replied. "Plenty of times." He stole another glance at Joozy.

She was gently stroking the white guy's hair, petting him while he held his money out to the bartender. She was playing with him but she still was watching Daryn, fixated on him as he drank.

"Well," Daryn continued. "What conclusions did you come up with?"

"'Not me' is what they like. They don't like me."

Daryn laughed. "I hear you on that one! I'm definitely feelin' that!" He paused to sip his drink. He looked from Alias to Dave. "Now take me," he said. "Look at me. Look at my face."

Alias averted his eyes. Dave took another drink and looked toward the door. The scar on Daryn's face demanded attention even though decency dictated that they not stare openly. Alias looked over to the bowling game in the corner of the room and saw Hambone and Boody playing and drinking while the lights flashed and bells dinged. He saw Kaye sitting at one of the tables near the jukebox wearing a vacant expression. Alias had a desperate crush on her but she always acted as if he didn't exist. He noticed Joozy and the guy getting up from the bar and preparing to leave. She cast one last backward glance at Daryn before she took the drunken man's hand and led him out the door.

"Come on," Daryn's voice reclaimed Alias' attention. "Look at my face. It's aiight, man. It's cool. Both of ya'll tripping."

Alias looked. Upon closer inspection, Alias decided that the scar wasn't as horrendous as he had first thought, but it still carried a connotation of pain.

"Now, see my scar," Daryn explained. Alias nodded. "Some women like it and other women get all kinds a squeamish. So I always wonder. Like… sometimes…like…" Daryn paused to sip his drink. "Like I'll be in a bar or something and I'll try to guess which type of girl would like to get freaky with a freak, ya' know!" Alias and Dave smiled, partly in relief that Daryn could talk so openly about an issue that seemed so personal. Daryn laughed.

"And you wouldn't believe how many times I've been, like, *freaky situation, situation freaky*," Daryn sang.

"Right on," Alias exclaimed and extended a clenched fist toward Daryn who tapped knuckles with him before downing the rest of his drink. He motioned to the bartender for another drink and looked questioningly at

Alias who nodded a negative. Dave simply waved a few dollars in the air. Daryn pulled the money from his pocket to pay the bartender and paused to stare at one of the bills. Alias looked at the money in his hand…and his heart sank. It was the cursed bill.

Daryn turned to him, smiling with excitement. His eyes were aglow as he waved the bill at Alias and then at Dave.

"Check this," he exclaimed. "Check it! This money got writing on it!"

Alias stared at the floor.

"Guess what it says? Guess?"

"Give this money to the white boy," Dave said.

"I swear you stupid." Daryn had to laugh. "It says 'Doin Doin.' Now what the hell is the chances of that, huh?"

Dave picked up his drink. "Chances of what?"

"Chances of this! It says 'Doin Doin.' Get it?"

"No, I don't."

"Doin! That's my nickname. Doin. When I was a kid my mother said that I was always doin' shit so everybody started callin' me that. Doin. Ain't that some shit! I'm keeping this." Daryn tucked the dollar back into his pocket and pulled out a twenty. "This bill might change my life."

Alias looked away from Daryn…and swore.

CHAPTER 10
Joozy Beatdown

Joozy and the man walked up Warren Street with their arms wrapped around each other's waist. Her dark eyes darted back and forth, scanning the street for the police, taking notice of any midnight strollers with prying eyes. The streets were quiet and desolate; the only sound was the echo of their solitary footsteps that resonated into the night. Her drunken date stumbled against her but she held him tight and upright as they made their way toward the alley. He had been drinking quite a bit, slamming them down, mainly in an attempt to get her to drink with him. He began mumbling to her. All of his inhibitions were nonexistent now that the alcohol had taken effect, and he bragged to her about his sexual prowess.

"Really, though," he rambled on. "Most things that I do…I do better drunk than sober. Like driving. I do drive better when I'm drunk. I do. And my job. I handle that much better. And, and, and this…" He reached up and squeezed her breast. When he leered at her, the smell of liquor permeated the air. "And I fuck like a black man does. I fuck long and hard…and I know…you will like my technique."

Joozy was agreeable. "That's 'cause you a real man. I know you can take care of this. But you see my body…" She stopped to pose for him. "That means that you better bring a lunch and a hardhat, buddy."

He became instantly erect. "Well! Where we going?"

"You mean, where you coming, right?"

"Fuck yeah," he replied.

Joozy herded him around the corner onto South Third Street toward the alley where she had her gear stashed. She wanted to be done quickly with him and get back to the bar. She couldn't get the big, muscular man from Midnite out of her mind. She couldn't describe the attraction. She hadn't ever felt such a strong vibe from anyone before and she knew that in her heart, these were feelings that she just couldn't ignore. She had felt his presence, a raw magnetism, an energy that had touched her, awakening a delicious tremble that started at her center and hovered there until her knees felt weak.

And then there was that scar on his face.

She understood him. He was just like her.

Joozy was a realist. She had learned early on about the value that society placed on physical appearance. When she looked in the mirror she saw the darkness of her reflection and knew that it was counted against her. The raised line of raw-looking pimples that ran down the side of her face was hideous, and her mouth was full of teeth that were spaced unevenly. She knew what it was like to have your greatest flaw on display for the world to see.

Joozy forced herself to concentrate on the task at hand. The alley was dark and deserted, and she glanced in both directions to make sure that no one would see her as she guided the drunken man into the darkness. She barely paid him any mind as he clumsily pawed at her. She half-listened as he blathered on about how beautiful she was and how he had always had a thing for dark, black women.

Joozy knew that men were attracted to her body. In fact, they were more than attracted, they were mesmerized by their lust, by the ache of their fingers just to touch her. Yet the men who gave her attention never really took her emotions into account. They didn't care what they said to her or what they would try to do to her. They didn't care that there was a woman underneath. So she used men. Used their machismo, their macho to "get" them before they got her. She was totally unprepared for the exhilarating thrill and power that she felt over the men she victimized.

But the man in the bar awoke a spark in her. Her feelings were indescribable and she knew, somehow, that he would be able to provide some detail, fill in the blanks of the emotion that escaped her comprehension. She had to meet him.

She steered her inebriated companion into the alleyway behind the Boys Club. Joozy knew this alley well and she had told the white guy that she would ride him if he could stand it, in the back of a house that was halfway toward Union Street. The house was an old, dilapidated building that belonged to Mack; one of the few people in town that she could say was a friend. They had become so close that he told everyone that Joozy was his cousin and he would sometimes serve as her cleanup man whenever she took a man back to the alley. The back porch of Mack's house was set back about twenty feet from the alley and was shrouded in shadows. A huge, green garbage Dumpster was pushed against the house and formed a nice little nook where Joozy kept a woolen, Navy blanket that she would spread out on the ground. She also kept a metal pipe hidden there, just in case.

She led the man down the alley and stopped when they pulled up next to Mack's house. He paused unsteadily and squinted into the darkness at the back of the house.

"Where we going," he slurred.

Joozy pointed. "Over there. Behind there." He pulled Joozy close to him and they stumbled into the yard, locked in a lovers' embrace. He stopped abruptly and turned to Joozy, breathing the labored breath of the sloppy drunk. How in the world did he think any woman would want to be with him in this state, Joozy wondered, was beyond her. *Men!* His hand found her ass and squeezed it while he pulled her close and tried to kiss her. Joozy arched her neck and turned away from him, and his kiss landed on the side of her jaw. The drunk staggered away from her unsteadily and looked down at the ground.

"What's with the hesitation?" he asked in a high-pitched voice. "In the bar you said...you said...you said..."

Joozy almost laughed out loud. Slowly she unbuttoned her shirt. When the drunk looked up he saw the mocha mounds of flesh as Joozy's shirt fell away. She was wearing a black lace bra that strained under the pressure of her full breasts. He smiled as a tremor of lust rumbled through his body.

"I know," he exclaimed. "I know! You want some money, huh?" He pulled out his wallet and began to dig frantically in his billfold. "Yeah. I know what you black bitches like. You like the money, huh? That moolah. Dinero. Right?" He flipped open his wallet. "How much?"

"All of it," Joozy said.

He was unsteady on his feet but he continued to count until her words finally seemed to register with his liquor-laden brain. He looked up from his wallet in disbelief.

"All?"

He saw a flash of metal an instant before the pipe slammed into the side of his head. His body bounced off the green Dumpster and dropped to the ground where he convulsed once and then was still.

Joozy went over to the prone figure and nudged him once with the pipe. She had swung at him with every ounce of power that she could muster, but she was taken aback by the force of the impact. His body had ricocheted into the Dumpster as if he had no more weight than a ragdoll. Before taking his wallet she checked his pulse. His breathing was ragged and his head was swollen and red where the pipe had made contact. As she pulled her shirt on, Joozy eyed the lump of his skull nervously but then she dismissed her concerns for her victim; he was as nothing to her as she was to him.

She took all of his cash and his credit cards but left him his driver's license and other vital papers that he had folded into the little small pockets. She rifled through his pockets for the cash that he had flashed in the bar and took that, too. In his back pocket she found a small diamond-studded wedding ring with a gold inlaid band. She held it up and studied it in the pale moonlight with a grimace on her face. *A dog is a dog*, she mused, and then she spit on him. She threw his wallet and his ring on top of his prone body and stepped out of the dark corner of the garbage Dumpster. She checked in both directions before she headed back to Club Midnite. No one would find the unconscious man; he couldn't be seen from either end of the alley and if he was still there in the morning, Mack would throw his ass into the parking lot up the street.

Joozy walked swiftly toward the club. Urgency guided her steps and she silenced the voice that warned her that she was taking a chance by varying from her routine. Usually after she clubbed her victim she would go directly home and call it a night but now she had a different mission and nothing would stop her. Straight down the alley to South Street over to Warren Street until she stood fidgeting in front of Club Midnite, staring at the entrance. Now that she was at the doorway, apprehension invaded her nerves and doubt riddled her resolve but she steeled herself and went inside. She had to meet the man with the scar; her soul needed its mate.

She spotted him still sitting at the end of the bar on the same stool as when she had left, involved in an animated conversation with the guy with the dreads. As she approached him, countless thoughts raced through her mind, battling with her panicking heart that beat madly. "What if" thoughts threatened to seize control of her but her determination silenced their ill will. He belonged to her and she belonged to him. They would be together.

It never occurred to her that he might love another, that he wouldn't be available, or that there would be another outcome to their meeting than what she had determined. She just knew that she would have him. She would.

CHAPTER 11
What You See

Alias sat at the bar with his head cradled in his hands, tears just in the corners of his eyes. He had to warn Doin. Tell him about the Mourning Paper; the cursed dollar bill that he had in his pocket. He had to pull his coat to the facts…but how? *Let's see*, Alias mused, *how can I put this. Hey, Doin! Guess what? My family suffers from a curse that makes us write messages on dollar bills. Messages that kill. Yeah! For real, man! For real! And guess what? You got one in your pocket right now. It's got your name on it. Doin Doin. No, I ain't been smoking no crack!*

Alias leaned back and regarded Doin for a moment. The scar on his face was drastic and it seemed that the big man had suffered enough in his lifetime, destined to carry around his physical deformity for the entire world to see. No way to hide the infirmity, no way to keep the pain in a secret place, away from prying eyes.

Pre-destination. That was the only explanation that made sense to Alias. Coincidence? Shit, no! Alias was convinced that existence was fated, that he was destined to a lifetime of misery, to a lifetime of knowing that he was the bearer of bad tidings, bad things. And there was nothing that he could do to prevent his role in the urban tragedy.

Alias picked up his nearly empty glass of liquor. There was just a skim of liquid coating the bottom.

"You all right, man?" Doin had been watching him warily. Dave sat on the other side of him. He had struck up a conversation with a woman that he claimed didn't like Black guys with big dicks. "She's right up my alley, dude!" He had whispered to them.

"Yeah. I'm cool. I'm all right," Alias answered.

"Ain't that some shit though?"

"What?"

"The dollar bill!" Doin exclaimed. "Doin! On the dollar! Doin!"

"Yeah," Alias deadpanned. "Some shit." He spotted Joozy stepping into the bar. Just the sight of her in her short, tight little skirt made a man's pulse quicken…in two places. Her body was calling! It just wasn't calling him. It was calling for Doin and as far as he knew, Doin hadn't even noticed her. Joozy was known for robbing unsuspecting strangers, men who would try to sample the pleasure of her flesh only to end up broke and ashamed. Alias was really surprised that her tactics hadn't gotten her into trouble by now, because sooner or later dirty deeds always would come back to the perpetrator in one form or another. He had to admit that she seemed to be very careful with her methods. Once she left with one of her marks, she would take them, fake them and disappear for a few weeks before she stepped back out into the light of day. But not this time.

Here she was back in the bar and headed toward them.

Doin interrupted his thoughts. "Like I was saying, I can usually tell you which woman that I can approach. Ain't many, I'll admit, but when I see 'em…I know."

Joozy sidled up to the seat that separated the two men, staring at Doin with intense longing in her eyes. She moved around to the side facing him and languidly settled onto the stool, every inch of her body, tight yet soft, promising and poised. Doin's jaw dropped as his eyes absorbed the erotic display.

"What a body you got, girl. Damn!" Doin leaned back to look past her at Alias and started singing. "*La di da, la di da, la di di da da, baba. Well!*" He reached for his drink before finally looking Joozy in the face. "But damn! You ugly, girl! Sheyat!"

Joozy didn't respond to the insult. Instead she turned away from him and looked out of the window at the far end of the bar, her eyes glazing over with tears. She had heard worse from the mouths of children, from her mother,

her cousins; she had heard it countless times but she found that this man's words cut her deeply. From the mouth of a stranger, this stranger, those same words carried the weight of hurt and anguish. His words hurt her hope.

"You know what…" Doin was apologetic. "I shouldn't say that shit. I apologize. I'm sorry about that. 'Cause I'm ugly, too. Look at my face. I guess I'm just used to it."

They sat together in silence for a moment, contemplating their common bond. Joozy looked into Doin's eyes, words eluding her, unable to voice the feelings racing through her heart. For the first time in recent memory, she wanted to feel a man, to know that there was someone to reciprocate emotion for emotion and, more importantly, she wanted to be felt, too.

"Why you looking at me like that?" Doin faced her and looked deeper into her stare. "You got good eyes. Gawd gave you dem eyes! Sho did!"

Joozy smiled at him.

"And I like 'em, too. See, what I mean is this." Doin grinned back at her. "Most people got regular eyes. They can't see past the outside. Past the bad spots and shit. Can you?"

"I knew it." Joozy put her hand over his. She searched his face as if committing his features to memory and then she took her finger and traced the path of the scar that slashed across his face. "Are you used to people looking at you like this? Do you see what you seeing now? When you look at me?"

Doin took her hand and brought it to his lips, kissing the fingertip that had gently touched his face. He felt like she had looked deep *inside* him. "I guess 'ugly' was the wrong word, huh? It don't fit you."

"You neither," she whispered.

Alias watched the entire drama unfold and groaned loudly. They both glanced at him, puzzled, before turning back to each other. Doin cradled his drink in his hands.

"You know, you look at a man like that, the possibilities change. They get endless."

"I don't know." Joozy's smile reached the corners of her eyes. "I ain't never looked at anyone like that before…besides, I bet you clean up nice. Easily."

"Yeah. Right." Doin had to smile in return. "You probably want me to love you like a white boy! You know? If I buy you diamonds and pearls and cherish your little, baby feets!"

"Can you do that, huh?" Joozy was feeling that vibe. "You know that's nice though."

"Naw. I got to do it nigga style…straight out the bottle, no chaser. I give you me. How 'bout you."

"I can do it nigga style." Joozy laughed softly.

"Can you?"

"Yes, I can."

"I know you can." Doin looked at her body. His eyes roved, taking in her finely shaped calves, up past her thick, firm hips to her breasts, which whispered sweet nothings to his lust. *Dayum!* "So, can I buy you a drink and find out your name, address, phone number, social and all the other interview stuff. Or can I go straight to the menu?"

"Yes." Joozy eyed him. "To the drink part, with your crazy-ass self." She shifted in her seat to face him and crossed her shapely legs, brushing her foot gently against Doin's calf.

Alias couldn't contain himself anymore. "Aww naww."

Doin looked at him, snorted and then placed his order. After the drinks arrived he commanded all of Joozy's attention for the next few hours. There was no doubt about the outcome of their mating ritual, but they danced the dance anyway. They built tension with each moment.

Alias caught parts of their intimate conversation in bits and pieces, but he was only half-listening. He was determined to drown his sorrows in a few well-placed drinks. There was nothing he could do but lose himself, like he had lost his soul when he had come into the bar with that cursed dollar bill, the Mourning Paper. He should have set it on fire in his backyard. He should have ignored the unnatural burning he had felt in his skull when he had contemplated destroying it. His heart had contracted violently in his chest and beaten savagely. The Curse was strong but he should have fought it. It was either him or Doin. He heaved a heavy breath and looked over at him.

"Hey," Doin said to Joozy.

"Besides..." Joozy ran her hand across Doin's muscled shoulder. "You still haven't even asked me my name."

"I already know it. What is it?"

"Joozy. And you are?"

Doin returned her smile and held up his finger, signaling for her to wait while he reached into his back pocket. He pulled out the dollar bill and held it up for Joozy to read.

Alias swore under his breath. He knew, right then, that the fates loved twisted humor. She liked that cruel shit. Fate was a bitch who wouldn't even let him get his drink on, let him get totally fucking drunk before she jabbed a hot knife in his heart. She pointed the finger of destiny with the certainty of darkness at Joozy, undeniably, even before the words rolled off her lips when she read from her karma.

"Doin. Doin."

CHAPTER 12
Obvious Places

"So," Joozy asked softly. "How do you think of love?"

They were sitting close now, comfortable with each other after having shared the past few hours getting familiar beyond the first-date superficial conversation. Alias had left over an hour ago and Doin had decided that the young man was a little mixed up in the head. He had been giving Doin the craziest looks…like he wanted to try to kick some ass or something! But since he couldn't do that he just looked plain stupid! However, for the most part, he was cool, too, so Doin was glad that they had gotten a chance to hang out and chill.

Joozy rubbed her hand across his thigh. "Come on," she urged him. "Tell me."

"I don't really think of love." Doin watched her. "I think of lust. Lust usually lasts longer."

"You can love and lust at the same time, you know." Joozy looked up at him. She leaned gently into his shoulder. Doin was big and strong. She liked the way his body felt underneath her as she reclined against him, purring with contentment.

"No, you can't." Doin frowned. "Well, maybe for a minute but not for too long. I've had women lust for me before." Joozy leaned back to give him an incredulous look. "For real, girl. For real. I can get my mack on too, shit!" Doin smiled at her. "I have. I had women who would just lust for me, women who would mistake tear-jerkin', back-scratchin' sex…they would mistake that for love. It would always turn out to be just sex. They didn't really like me. Not for real."

Joozy regarded him coolly. "And you think that you could do that to me? Make me mistake my *real true* feelings for *one* feeling?"

Doin leaned forward and held Joozy gently—his face close, their lips inches apart. "I wouldn't ever want to make you feel like that." He kissed her softly on the lips. "We could still do the tear-jerkin', back-scratchin' part though, right?" Joozy kissed him deeply, letting her tongue dance sweetly against his, but just for a taste. "What chu think?"

"Dayum, girl." Doin caught his breath.

"Yeah, I know." Joozy ran her fingers over his lips.

"Sexual chocolate!" Doin stamped his foot. "Sexual chocolate!"

"You be buggin' sometimes," Joozy spoke between giggles. She couldn't remember the last time that she had laughed so much. It felt good to her.

Doin turned fully to face her. "I like your passion. At least, I see your passion. I like you, too, and I think I see you. Tell me…what kinda guy you like?"

"You mean to tell me that you don't know," Joozy teased. "Ain't you the man?"

"I am," Doin replied. "I'm like, King Dingaling! But you still got to tell me what you like."

"I like a strong man," Joozy said lightly. "Stronger than strong."

"Well, a strong man needs a good woman." Doin watched her.

He wanted her. He yearned to feel her body tremble to his strokes, to see the special glow that her dark skin radiated, to witness the sheen resulting from the friction of sex oils and heat. Her body looked so firm, that female firm, that perfect balance between soft and hard, pliable but malleable. He found himself wishing that he could spend hours just brushing her skin with his lips. They could do some good old-fashioned fornicating, bucking until it was all over but the shouting…but then what would happen next? His walls always came tumbling down.

"Joozy, I bet that you would be more than enough for me." Doin brushed her hair with his fingers. "But something always happens. It's the damndest thing, you know! And I'm a little jaded now because of it. It looks like I only get so much of the good stuff, you know, I get doses of good shit…like meeting you…and then I get the big payback and everything gets fucked up."

Doin paused for a moment before he went on.

He pointed at the scar on his face. "I think it's this. I call it the 'hurt me' mark 'cause it really changed my life. It changed me. Altered every outcome."

Joozy looked at Doin tenderly. *If he only knew*, she mused. Joozy wanted to tell him about Lucien, a man who lived up on Columbia Street, maybe a mile and a half west of Club Midnite. He had been working at the steel foundry over in Coxsackie for over twenty years, working his way up to the position of foreman. On the job one day, Lucien was caught in a flash fire, the result being that over half of his body was burned. When he got out of the hospital, a good portion of his face looked like raw meat, scarred beyond repair. But even after all of that trauma, he was still able to walk the streets, looked upon as a tragic man living a life marred by a horrible accident. A man could do that. A man could get away with less than perfection, a scarred face, a burned face, no face if necessary and he would still be able to earn a peaceful place in society. Free from the barbs and insulting glances that assaulted Joozy's mental state on a daily basis. Joozy could decipher thoughts and imagine slights whenever someone cast their eyes upon her. *Damn! Glad I don't look like that! What a shame! She's damaged in the most obvious of places.* Indeed, her face was her presentation to the world and she had features that danced at angles and positions that were vastly different than others. A dark surface, unattractive in itself in some corners, with a wide nose planted here, two piercing eyes that shot daggers and full-sized lips that failed to cover her teeth; teeth that hadn't bothered springing from their base in a straight, orderly fashion. A guy she had robbed a while back had told her that her smile was her best feature, that it improved her face value…but that was after he was drinking from the deep end of the liquor bottle. He had gone to the Dumpster, too; and she smiled as she stood over his prone body.

Yes, she knew Doin's pain. She put her hand to his chin and gently turned him toward her. With the tip of her finger, she gently stroked his cheek. There was a fire building in his eyes and she felt the heat of her desire smolder in return. For once, she felt the joy of reciprocation. He was what she was searching for in her life, someone to touch, someone who saw her with eyes that focused on her heart. She reached down and took his hand.

"But I like you," she stated.

"Yeah. I know." He looked down at her hand which softly held his. "I like you, too."

"More than like," Joozy urged.

"More than like," Doin agreed. They sat and held hands for a few minutes before Doin asked her if she wanted to go for a late-night walk. Joozy suggested they take a walk down by Promenade Park because it was only a few blocks down the street. It was also in the opposite direction of the Dumpster where she had left the white boy.

Hudson is a charming town with its reddish-pink cobblestone sidewalks framed with streetlamps made of black, lantern-shaped housings that cast soft light onto the stone streets. Stores and shops stood on the corners of Warren and Second Streets with a few other businesses sandwiched along the block between old, wooden houses and red brick ones. In the nighttime quiet, the tiny sounds of the nocturnal seemed to be amplified by the silence and echoed through the leaves of the large trees that were interspersed along the walkway the two lovers strolled down arm in arm. There weren't many cities that could boast of huge elms and willows rising up into the sky from its main street and Hudson basked in its rustic antiquity.

They walked in comfortable silence down Warren Street, enjoying the night air, the warm, gentle breeze and the peacefulness. Joozy rested her head on his shoulder. Doin felt the warmth of her body in every place that she touched. The soft flesh of her hips moved against him and heightened his arousal. He slipped his arm around her waist. Lust pulsed urgently, pulled at him, but Doin pushed those hungry thoughts away and tossed them into the soft shadows of the night.

They crossed South First Street, a block away from the park. The buildings on each side of the street seemed to be a little older than further up Warren Street. An old, ragged marquee that read Gallo's hung above an empty glass storefront and directly across the street stood Sam's Supermarket which was also closed up.

Joozy felt content and secure with Doin's strong arm around her; she felt warmth in his embrace. The night felt unbelievably right, as if there were a sweet conspiracy between the moon and the stars as they pitched a perfect night upon them. She was sure that Doin was aware of their connection, a *connected-ness* so deep that she couldn't touch bottom. She imagined lying with him, of watching his chest rise and fall after they had spent each other. Joozy had to have him.

But that was for later. At the moment, the city belonged to them. Their solitary footsteps were the only evidence of life on the quiet streets—not even a car passed by them. The slow cadence that accompanied them provided the opportunity to move closer.

The entrance of the park came into view as they neared the end of Warren Street. A small playground with a swing set, a merry-go-round and a sand-box stood to one side of the renovated sidewalk which was fenced in by a decorative brick wall that stood about four feet high. Directly across from the playground stood a building that housed the volunteer fire department. There was a big, red fire truck parked behind the garage doors that could be seen through the huge, glass panes. The playground and the Firehouse faced each other across an expanse of a red and pink concrete sidewalk that opened up to a brick stairway leading into the park. Rhododendrons splashed color under the night lights throughout the colorful scenery of Promenade Park as Doin and Joozy mounted the steps and took in their surroundings.

A tall bronze statue greeted them. Lady liberty stood with a serrated crown atop her head and a huge, iron sword held heavily with both hands as she presented her strength to her visitors. Expanses of grassy fields stretched off in both directions with man-made walkways of fine gravel that crunched underfoot providing artificial boundaries. The perimeter of the park was lined with an ornate iron fence that barred pedestrians from the precipitous drop-off of the cliff formed by the cavernous mountainside that faced the Hudson River. There was also a natural deterrent of woody expanse, mostly trees and bushes that sat on the other side of the railroad tracks, snaking their way south through the Catskill Mountains. In the moonlight the waters of the river twinkled in dark kaleidoscope with hints of the city lights bouncing off the far shore from Coxsackie-Athens, the city that sat across the Hudson. Old metal benches that were painted green and white were positioned near the fence, facing outward toward the scenic shores that spread out majestically in the starlight. Doin and Joozy moved to the first empty bench they saw and Doin extended his arm, inviting Joozy back into his embrace. She snuggled against him until she found her comfort and then they sat in silence, each content with their thoughts of warm satisfaction.

Suddenly, Joozy sat upright.

"What up?" Doin jumped, too.

"Nuthin.'" She squinted out into the darkness. "I just thought I saw a bee."

"Why? You scared of bees?"

"Yeah, I hate bees." She looked at Doin and his scar caught her attention. She could understand how some people might react to him in the negative ways that he had told her about. In the moonlight it had the appearance of an angry weal, a disturbing slash that was a shade darker than the rest of his skin and carried the suggestion of menace. His eyes contained a hard stare, penetrating, with a smoldering heat of intensity just below the surface; until he looked at her. Then his look softened, his eyes searched her soul like beacons. He was finding the hidden treasures there and hoarding them in his arms...and against his chest.

She leaned toward Doin and they kissed, gently, exploring each other's lips and tongues, conveying unspoken wants with the intimacy of their touching. Doin broke away from the kiss and pulled her into him, giving her a full hug, losing himself in her softness. She kissed him again and the sweetness of the first kiss was lost in the heated lust of the confirming embrace, a frenzied searching of wanting and tasting in a swirl of dizzying heat.

"Ooohhhh, Joozy! Umma tell mama!"

Joozy spun around and saw Annette and Barbara Ann standing behind them.

Annette and Barbara Ann should have been twins, and the more Joozy thought about it, the more convinced she was that they did indeed share DNA. They were both plumpers, each weighing in at the two hundred-pound mark but they shared much more than that. They both had smart-ass mouths…and they both talked mad shit. Annette held a huge ice cream cone in her hand, with extra scoops in it, which caused Joozy to wonder; where do big, fat-ass people get *"biggie"* everything from? They get biggie fries, biggie soda, biggie cake…and this girl got a biggie ice cream cone! With biggie scoops in it! The way she was licking the ice cream was border-line fat-girl pornographic. A few drops had dribbled onto her overall blue jeans, which she wore with one strap undone and hanging off her body with a light blue shirt underneath. She licked it off with her tongue. Barbara Ann had a giant bag of potato chips that she was happily crunching, nearly a handful at a time while smiling at Joozy. She was dressed exactly like Annette except her shirt was pink.

Joozy said, "Ain't you two supposed to be at home? In the bed?"

Annette repeated, "Ooohhhh, Joozy! Umma tell mama!"

Joozy laid her head on Doin's shoulder and snuggled in closer. Annette and Barbara Ann, like most teenagers, didn't take the hint. They walked over and stood in front of Doin and Joozy, blocking the moonlight and the view with their considerable bulks.

"Who this?" Barbara Ann pointed a potato chip.

Yeah." Annette slurped her ice cream. "You didn't advise us that you had a man-friend."

"Who this," Barbara Ann was still pointing.

"Ya'll are two nosy girls," Joozy purred from her perch.

"We ain't girls!" They were in agreement about that. "We. Are. Women!"

"Two nosy women then."

"We can be nosy, if…we…want to! Now!"

"That's right! Now…who this?"

"'Cause you didn't advise us."

"Sho' didn't."

Joozy looked up at Doin for help but he was barely able to contain his laughter at the two bad-assed girls who were all up in Joozy's business. Besides, he really wanted to see how Joozy was going to handle them. When it became apparent that Joozy was waiting for his reply, he spoke up.

He turned to them. "I'm Doin."

When he spoke the two girls focused on his face for the first time and he saw them flinch when they saw the path of the scar on his face. He was sorry for that, sad, really, when he realized that his scar had dampened the girl's spirit. He gave them his best smile, hoping to put them back at ease.

Annette smiled back. "Your name is Doin?"

Barbara Ann piped in, "Like, what you doin?"

"Uh oh!" Doin replied. "Watch out now!"

"I'm Doin the do," Annette started. "Well, I'm Doin Doin," Barbara Ann teased. "Uh-uh. Joozy's doin Doin!"

Joozy sprang up! "Okay now! Get out!" They had overstepped. Joozy was serious.

"All right." Annette drew away. "You don't have to get all sadity with it."

"That's right, Miss Thang," Barbara Ann added. As the two girls walked away, they began singing, "Batman, took me to the movies. Batman, the movies was groovy. Batman, took me to the park. Batman, the park was dark..."

Joozy and Doin laughed at them as they danced their way out of the park but soon they melted back into each other. Joozy could hear his heartbeat through his chest.

"You know I want you." He felt her voice through his skin.

"We can have each other..." he began.

"Tonight," Joozy confirmed. Doin didn't respond. Instead he tilted her face to him and gently kissed her. "What's wrong?"

Doin looked out at the winding Hudson River, its currents swirling, sending up clashing waves and whitecaps. Rumor had it that the Hudson River was bottomless, that men in submarines had been unable to touch the bottom of the polluted waterway. At least that's what Joozy had told him. The river was a dirty mystery to its depths.

He turned back to Joozy who waited intently.

"'Cause I got secrets. And I wouldn't hurt you." Joozy took his hand and gave it a gentle squeeze before she leaned into him and encircled his waist.

"Aww, Doin," she said softly. "Who ain't got secrets? And who lets that stop them from being with someone?" She kissed Doin's neck. "I feel for you, Doin. Already! And I got secrets. I got my past, too. And I don't take my feelings lightly. But I look past all that because I know we can have feelings together." Softly, she added, "I know we can."

Doin held her for a moment. He tilted her face so that she looked directly in his eyes.

"Me, too," he answered. "But not tonight."

She looked at Doin with a question in her eyes and a little hurt.

Doin said, "Tell me something. How many drinks did you have tonight?"

"Not too many," she replied warily.

"But are you seeing me clearly? Are you seeing me? 'Cause in the morning, things get awfully clear."

"I see what I need to see," Joozy replied. "The morning won't change that."

Doin smiled. "Sex on the first date will kill a relationship, ya' know?"

Joozy tried to hide her disappointment.

"So maybe," Doin continued. "We can start tomorrow."

Joozy smiled at the possibility of other days.

They sealed the agreement with a passionate kiss in Promenade Park, a promise of a future in the most obvious of places.

CHAPTER 13
Virtual Slavery

When the levee broke and the water burst through, thousands of acres of farmland were flooded and their cotton crops were destroyed. The livelihood of the people of Greenville, Mississippi was threatened, and they reacted in the only way they knew how.

The Delta returned to virtual slavery.

The National Guard took rifles and began to round up any able-bodied Black men they could find and marched them to the levee. Soon, the Guardsmen were joined by redneck farmers with shotguns who were more than ready to lend a helping hand and, together, they were able to corral over thirteen-thousand Blacks and force them to work and live on top of the levee. A city of bottomless tents sprang up on an area that stretched eight miles long but was only eight feet wide—the total width of the levee at its crown.

Agent Robert Abraham had been asleep in a safehouse when he awoke to the sound of splintering wood as the front door was smashed in. He rolled quietly from the bed to the floor and scooted over to the window. When he looked outside, he saw that National Guardsmen were gathered in the front yard with guns drawn. They were wearing their rain gear and Robert could see their vehicles lining the curb in front of the house. He glanced back up at the bed. Christiana was sitting in the bed, hastily fastening her shirt before sliding her pants over her full hips. Christiana was a full bodied woman—his woman—and she was strong and fierce. Her tenacious grasp on life was what fueled the attraction between them. She was tall for a woman, standing nearly at Robert's height. The curves of her cheeks suggested a beauty descended from royalty. Her skin was flawless and her eyes were deep and dark, a subtle hint at the promise of her wanton passion. Her lips were soft yet firm *and Robert had often found himself lost in the depths of their embrace, only to be rewarded with sweet kisses.*

Those days were gone.

Christiana climbed down from the bed, now fully dressed, and scooted over to the window next to Robert. She peeked outside and saw the National Guardsmen, along with a few white men from Greenville in front of the house.

"They musta heard you was here." Her voice was a harsh whisper. "They coming for every nigga they can. Damn!"

"We are not niggas," Robert hissed. There had been many heated arguments between them about the use of that word. Robert was adamant in his refusal to apply that word to his people. He felt like it insulted his ancestors' legacy, while Christiana failed to see the damage that the word could inflict. "Hand me my shirt." Robert took the shirt from her and shrugged his large frame into it before taking a quick glance out the window again. They were hidden in a concealed room in the attic of a farmhouse owned by Christiana's family that stood just outside of Greenville. The entrance to the attic was hidden behind a heavy, oaken cabinet that her grandfather had made with his own hands. Her grandfather had carved the base of the cabinet from an oak tree so it had good weight. It hid the door to the attic quite well but Robert knew that the way would soon be found. Sooner or later the Guardsmen would find them with the help of the rednecks who were too familiar with hidden caches and old farmhouses…and there was no way out.

"How did they know I was here," Robert said.

"Somebody told them, more than likely." Christiana sat next to him. She laid her head on his shoulder before she continued. "But sometimes they just go from house to house, looking for niggas."

Robert shot her a look.

"All right, Robert," she said. "We are not 'niggas'! Okay? So that means some Negroes told on you. And they gonna be coming up in here soon, too! They coming, Robert. They coming and they taking all the Black men…and the boys sometimes." She paused to put her arm around him. "They come and they take them and make them work on that damn levee up there in Greenville. They want all of ya'll." Robert felt Christiana's lips gently kiss his neck. He pulled her closer. "They put them up there on the top of that levee and work 'em damn near to death. They had 'em piling sandbags against the backside of it before." She squeezed Robert tighter.

"*Rednecks and the National Guard. They was running night raids everywhere. Taking grown men from they families. Hundreds of them. I remember the night they took my brother.*" Robert felt the breath leave her body in a heavy sigh.

"*Ain't no niggers in here, Paw!*" A muffled voice carried from the floor below them. Heavy footsteps could be heard stomping through the house downstairs. "*Oh, they's niggers,*" came the reply. "*They's niggers!*"

Robert knew it was just a matter of time. They were getting closer.

"*The levee broke,*" Christiana's voice was barely a whisper. "*All those men drowned when the water came pouring through that hole. The water came through that hole so loud, they say that it was the loudest noise they ever heard. Like a giant clap of thunder, a loud bang. And when it was over…they was all dead. All them men. And my brother.*"

Loud voices carried up from the house.

"*Ain't no niggers up in here!*"

"*Look, I'm tellin' you. They's niggers in here. Is you gonna let one of them darkies outsmart you? Huh?*"

"*Hell naw!*"

"*Then thank man! Thank! We know them coons is in here. We gonna find 'em, too. Shee-yat! We gots to get some more spades to work up top. They was hidin', too…*"

"*Robert.*" Christiana sat up and looked him in the face. "*I heard that they got all of us niggas working on top of the levee now!*"

Robert had heard the same thing.

"*You know they gonna put you up there, too,*" she said. "*Big, strong men are what they come for. And who knows how many of ya'll gonna come down from off the top of there. This rain ain't ever gonna stop.*"

"*Things aren't always going to be falling down around us,*" Robert said. "*It's my job to believe that. These circumstances are a temporary adjustment. A step closer than I meant to be…but this is my job. This is the reason I joined the struggle.*"

Christiana was silent.

Robert touched her cheek and turned her face to him. Even in the midst of the rain and madness, her beauty touched him, the maleness in him, always whispering to the echoes of yearning inside. Her eyes held the depths of regality, deep enough to see his own true meaning, and her skin reminded him that she was as unique as her touch. A touch that he wanted to possess.

"*You understand, right,*" *Robert said.*

"*Yes.*" *Her voice was soft. And then she kissed him.*

"*I will be back, Christiana. I will. And I want to take you with me when I go back up North. We can be freedom riders together.*"

A high-pitched squeal emanated up the stairway. They recognized the sound of the heavy china cabinet being moved. They had been found. Robert took Christiana's hand. "I am coming back. I promise. For your softness. Your morning sighs." Robert smiled at her. "And especially your morning dew."

The door to the attic banged open and the frantic pounding of footfalls echoed up the stairway.

"*This is my destiny,*" *Robert said. "The end of niggerization."*

"*They up here!*" *A voice rang out. From the edge of the darkness the ratchet of rifles could be heard as the Guardsmen locked and loaded.*

"*You and me,*" *Christiana said.*

"*You and me,*" *Robert agreed. They sealed their promise with a kiss.*

"*You two niggers get on your feet!*" *The Guardsmen stood over them, with guns drawn as Robert Abraham rose to his full height, his body blocking out the remainder of the dim light that shone through the window behind him.*

"*Gotdam, boy!*" *A local redneck had come up the stairs behind the Guardsmen with a shotgun in his hands. "You'se a big ole nigger! We better go on and shoot this one rat now!" He hefted his shotgun and pointed it at Robert. "Let me shoot 'em! Let me shoot 'em!"*

"*No,*" *a Guardsman yelled out. "No!" The redneck reluctantly pointed his gun at the floor. "Get down there," he said. "Get down on your stomach, boy! Hurry up 'fore I shoot ya ass anyhows." Robert dropped to the attic floor, face down, with his hands spread out above his head. One of the Guardsmen stepped over Robert's prone figure and clubbed him in the back of the head. Robert's body jerked once and then went still.*

"*No!*" *Christiana screamed and knelt down to touch Robert's face. "Ya'll are some low-down dirty bastards!" She turned to face them with tears in her eyes. Another soldier stepped behind her. "Ya'll cain't face him like a man, can you?"*

"*Don't worry,*" *one of the Guardsmen said to her. "You'll be going with him, too." The soldier behind her brought the butt of his rifle up and rammed it into the back of Christiana's skull. She crumpled to the floor and slid into the darkness.*

CHAPTER 14
Love Episode

It had been an interesting week for Doin—a testament to the ebb and flow of the human spirit and its sway from seething anger to the pleasure of erotic joy. He hadn't had any luck finding a job and he was getting to the point where his means weren't meeting his ends. Yet Joozy filled his nights with her touches and the nuances of her smile. For the first time in recent memory, Doin decided to take his time and let intimacy take its course with a woman. He could wait for her.

She was saving him from his daily frustrations. Days that were filled with rejections, a series of repeated questions on standardized forms designed with the intent of keeping him unemployed. Two or three days of the week he got a chance to dress up in his suit and tie, make the trip to a personnel office to sit across a desk from an interviewer. Each session ended the same…with a smile, a handshake and a gentle nudge out the door. After each interview Doin would hold hope in his breast for an hour or two but as the meeting replayed itself in his mind, his optimism faded into a lump of dejection that settled into the pit of his stomach. His frustrations grew with each day of missed income, of missed paychecks and his belief in his abilities was shaken with each rejection. His faith in a system that rewarded skill and diligence was derailed with each closed door. In the heat of the midday sun, Doin's disenchantment turned caustic, scraping at him until his thoughts took on criminal shape.

There were all kinds of ways to make money; easy money to be made.

And it could flow into Doin's pocket with the greatest of ease, if he were so inclined, but he knew that there was no such thing as a retirement plan for criminals. No dental plans either. *But damn it!* Doin vented. *What becomes of a man who wants to work, but can't? A man who wants to help support the balance of a capitalist system? A man who earnestly desires to become a cog in the engine of free enterprise?*

He gets doors slammed in his face, Doin answered his own rhetoric. His days had turned into a madness that lasted into the nights. That is, the fuse of his insanity remained lit until Joozy walked through his front door. His evenings were then transformed into comfort zones filled with her. They were in the beginning stages of their relationship so they were still reveling in the newness of each other, still finding joy in the simple pleasures. They lingered inside his apartment, alone together; discovering warmth in curves and valleys, untapped heat in gentle touches as they delighted in each other, intrigued, until they would fall asleep with her head nestled on his shoulder. Sometimes they would just listen to intimate songs and dance from lust to passion to tender breathing. His nights were all that! And he knew that they were worth the living.

Yet lately Doin had found the pressing matters of the daytime begin to creep into his nightlife. He supposed that it was inevitable, the bad blurring the good, but he had hoped for it to happen later, rather than sooner.

He looked up at the clock that hung on the wall above the television set. Joozy would be coming over soon so he did a quick check of his apartment. It was clean. Doin kept the apartment tidy; especially now that he had a woman. His bathroom, which stood adjacent to the backdoor and had a washer and dryer just inside the doorway, was clean and smelled of pine from the cleaner that he regularly used. He couldn't stand a nasty bathroom. However there was a load of clothes that remained in the dryer because he had gotten too lazy to take them out and fold them. The front room was the biggest room in the house, so it took the longest to clean but he had vacuumed the carpet, put his books in order on the bookshelves and straightened the papers on his small, hardwood desk. A color television set sat on a metal stand that faced a big, blue sofa. His bedroom was sparse, with a bed and two small end tables that sat on each side of it; an old, some-what ragged dresser that had a couple of the knobs missing from the drawers; and a hamper that he hid in his closet. It wasn't much but it was all his, so he kept it neat and orderly.

Doin paused to take in his surroundings and smiled. He felt his life chang-ing, felt an omen of good fortune coming his way. Joozy. She had touched him with her spirit. *That woman is together!* Considering what she lived with—a face that she despised—it was a wonder that Joozy didn't harbor hatred in her heart, didn't make darkness a necessary counterbalance for the weight of life's callousness. She didn't even display feigned indifference. She was serene, loving and strong.

And she cared for Doin. A lot. He could tell from the intensity of her eyes when she looked at him, as they lay in bed, naked and hot. Even afterwards, her roving stare drank deeply whenever they talked and especially when he held her. He remembered when they had been sitting on his couch watching a movie and they had gotten into a discussion about one of the actors. She had become so animated about the muscular action hero on the screen that Doin had to interject.

"Hold up, woman." Doin ran his fingers through her hair. "I'm the man up in this here mo piece!"

"And not just any man," Joozy pointed out.

"That's right." Doin poked his chest out.

"You're my man." She looked into his eyes before she put her lips to his.

"Fucking 'A' right," Doin agreed.

Doin knew the signs. He had seen them before. It never ceased to amaze him the way that women could mistake orgasmic sex for complicated love. Whenever he encountered what he called the "O" types, whenever he spotted those road signs, he would dump the girl. Quickly and harshly.

Until her. Joozy was something else. She was a keeper.

The doorbell rang and Doin rushed over and yanked it open. Joozy stood in the doorway wearing a tight, low-cut black top that plunged down into the roundness formed by her breasts, drawing his eyes and teasing his senses. Sparkles glittered brightly on the dark fabric that was stretched gently over her firm torso. She wore a skirt that reached all the way down to her ankles with a big, copper-colored button clipped to her midriff. On her feet she wore a pair of black, high-heeled stiletto pumps that displayed her copper painted toenails.

Doin took in the sight, stunned, as she stepped inside, hips swaying naturally before she took his face in her hands and kissed him fervently. It was a long, searing kiss that brought their bodies grinding together. After a moment Doin tore himself away and looked into Joozy's eyes.

"Uh-oh," he said.

"What?" Joozy tried to hide her smile.

"You know. Uh-oh."

"Uh-oh, what?"

"Uh-oh, you horny. That's what, uh-oh."

"Maybe I am." She stepped from his embrace. She watched him with hunger in her eyes as she reached for the copper button at the front of her skirt. "And if I was horny? Would you help a sista get her groove on?"

"Would I?" Doin reached for her.

Joozy stepped back out of his reach. "Do you remember that little fantasy that you told me about? That hooker fantasy." Doin nodded slowly. "If I was hot and fully charged..." Joozy moved her hips slightly and Doin's lust raced. "There wouldn't be nuthin' under this skirt but a gathering." Joozy snapped the button on her skirt and the black material fell in a pool at her feet. Doin's eyes roamed from her black stiletto pumps, up along her thick, shapely legs which were encased in fishnet pantyhose, up to a mini skirt that was so short that it was a mere formality. Joozy stepped toward him and, miraculously, more flesh appeared. Doin started thinking about baseball.

"That's right, honey." Joozy's voice took on the quality of a streetwise hooker. Her body was calling him with the suggestion of carnal pleasure. "This here is a gathering of smooth, soft skin; thighs you can't get at home; and one hundred percent woman."

Joozy purred as she moved closer to Doin. "That is," she whispered, "if I was horny enough to be your fantasy."

Doin gently touched her cheek. He turned away from her and walked over to the bedroom doorway. He had told Joozy about the hooker fantasy one night when she had brought up the subject of unfulfilled desires that he had never expected to be fulfilled. They had spent hours talking deep into the night but he had never expected her to act on it. It was just a fantasy, after all.

He turned back to her and smiled.

"I got fifty dollars, lady. And I wanna go around the world…in a day."

She crossed the room and took my hand. She led me into the bedroom and I lay on the bed and waited for her. I felt her softness, her womanhood, her fleshy vagina squeeze down on me. It was her signal to me that she wanted me, that my maleness meant something to her, that our sex was not a test of communication. Her pulsation was really a question, a shot in the dark. In truth: it turned me on. Well, I had an answer for her. My response? I made my hips sing a song…well, it was more like a hum. A steady, pulsating, throbbing beat that went inside and vibrated, building in intensity instead of fading into the background. I was so into my own rhythm that I didn't even object when Joozy pulled out the ropes and tied my hands to the headboard. At first I was panicked because I love the feel of her, love touching her but now I had to communicate without the benefit of using my hands. But then Joozy started to put it on me!

I was at her mercy, at her whim…and my only weapon was my tool. And the onslaught was fierce! Joozy had a look in her eyes that I hadn't seen before. *I think I can! I think I can!* I know that this chant may sound a little weak but it has helped me out of many a jam when the stimulation became a tad too intense. This mantra had helped me hold the building climax back sometimes and, besides, I can't stand baseball.

See, usually I'm a man about my sex. I mean, I'm proactive about pleasure…both mine and hers. To me, one of the most gratifying aspects of sex is giving a woman an orgasm. I mean a real orgasm! Ain't nothing like it! Shit! But don't get it twisted though…a woman can fake an orgasm on you, too. I know that. But not if she's MY woman.

Joozy is so real. She's my intimate. She dares to get close to me. That's intimate. She dares to answer the calls of my fantasies. That's intimate. She dares to touch me with her sex, to communicate with that touch. Now that's In-ti-mate! She's straddling me now and I can feel her settle down on me, letting the width of my core find its place inside of her. And then I feel that soft squeeze again; but this time I feel the delicious pulse all along the entire length of my shaft. Shit! I hope that she don't move right now! Shit! She moved! I pull frantically at the ropes that bind me. If my hands were free I would reach down and cup Joozy's ass, mold her cheeks and hold her still because if she squeezes me again, I might find myself apologizing in a few minutes. I'll be like, "I slipped! Damn! I slipped!"

I think I can! I think I can!

Joozy had this wicked look on her face. I hadn't seen this glint in her eyes before. She reached down and put her fingers around my throat...not choking me but enjoying the feeling of having me in a submissive position. With her other hand she ran her fingers over her breasts, the tips getting deliciously caught on the hardened nipples. I know how sensitive those nipples are and the thought of having one of those buds in my mouth with my lips clamping down on them sent more blood racing to my hardness. I puckered up my lips and started making sucking noises, but Joozy was in her own world and didn't notice my dilemma. She started rocking her hips, firmly, while adjusting to the feel of me, to the angle of my responsive thrusts and I paused to watch her body move. Joozy's body is perfect. Her dark skin is the perfect hue for the thickness of her hips, the curve of her back, breasts, shoulders...and she is all perfectly natural. Yet her sexuality is so much more than that. It's deep and real. It's the moist, hot love on top of me.

"My baby hungry?" Joozy finally noticed the insane gyrations that were causing even crazier-sounding suckling noises to come out of my mouth. She looked down at me, bemused. "You are one crazy man." Joozy laughed... but she fed me though! She leaned forward and dipped her nipple into the warm cup formed by my lips. I opened my mouth wide and tried to swallow the whole breast. *Her titties are so lovely! And delicious!* What happened next...I still find hard to believe. Well, "believe" may be the wrong word.

A better word would be "explain." Yeah. That's better because I know it happened yet putting it into words will be difficult. Okay. What had happened, was. All right. See. What it was! Was. That...I'm bullshitting now, huh? For real though! I locked my lips on Joozy's nipple, right, sucking and licking and rolling my tongue around it and then biting it kinda softly but firmly, and I feel Joozy start to rock and grind on my shit, right! 'Cause Joozy got this motion...this sideways, twisting, pulling and snapping thing that happens deep inside of her when she is getting ready to put the smack down on a muthafucka! But that's another story and way too personal. Anyway, Joozy gets real hot if I can find a way to keep pressure and suction on her nipple while maintaining pressure on her clit with my man-meat, so I go for it. I hit my mark and I'm there. I'm doing the damn thing! Sucking on her nipple—every once in a while I'm stopping to swish my tongue across it, bouncing the nub on the tip like candy but mainly sucking it like a baby bottle full of sugar water. Now the hard part to explain: Joozy dips her sex down on me and I feel a spot open inside of her. I hadn't ever felt that sweet spot before but when she presses her breast deeper into my mouth, I gulp as much of her titty into my stretched mouth as I can manage and then it happened. It is like an electric jolt...a shock wave travels straight down Joozy's breasts, past the firmness of her stomach, past her hips and down into her sex. It buzzes and crackles its way into my hardness like it is an antenna. I freeze with the impact and Joozy's body contracts and molds itself to me. I swear! We are one, Joozy and me. Our flesh merges, twistes, molds, melds...whatever it is called, we do it. And then she cums. Hard! I yell out. I don't want to cum yet. Not yet! But Joozy is moving on top of me, holding the back of my head to make sure that my tongue doesn't lose contact with her sweet breast while she breathes heavily in my ear. Sexy noises! I'm deep inside her world now and I can feel her moving in there, feel the beat of her sex, feel her catching me up. I feel her thick creaminess raining down on me. I feel her pulling me into her. I feel her heart racing against my chest. She's gasping. So am I.

I think I can! I think I cannn!!! Haallppp meeee!

She gotta hurry up and cum. Shit! I can't keep this up forever. I can't! I know!

I've got an idea. I'll just concentrate on this nipple until she finishes up. Yeah! There she go. Yeah. There she go.

Joozy collapses against me, spent. If my hands weren't tied...I'd pat myself on the back. I made it past the first wave. I kiss Joozy on her cheek and then I softly suck on her neck. She needs a few minutes to recover. I give her one minute and then I look at her.

"You came, baby?"

"Hell yeah!" She rubs her cheek against mine. *Nice!*

"Think you can withstand another one?"

She cups my face in her hands and looks me in the eyes. We are intimate again.

I feel her softness, her womanhood, her fleshy vagina squeeze down on me.

CHAPTER 15
Not Even a Reason

J oozy stood naked in front of the mirror appraising her body. Her hips were full and round, her stomach, flat and firm. She looked into the mirror again and met her eyes' reflection. An inflection was in her eyes, a sparkle that had been missing from her life and she felt a joy that made her want to jump. She was happy. She finally felt loved. She felt falling. She felt breathless. And she felt these emotions reciprocated from Doin. They spent so much time together, did so many things, shared so many moments, that their feelings were destined to be deep and tender.

She knew, in her heart, that she couldn't lose him. His closeness meant too much to her. It didn't seem possible that they could come so far in so little time but they had come together as if by design. She drifted over to the bed and languidly sprawled out on it, sighing in contentment. She stared at the ceiling while her mind drifted back to the night that she lay in Doin's arms. Their bodies were still glowing from the heated passion that they had shared as they lay with their legs intertwined, waiting for their breathing to return to normal. When it did, Doin let his fingers trace the curve of her hip. "I thought about you today."

"You should." Joozy's lips barely touched his skin.

"No, I mean, I heard a song. A lyric rather. But it was tight. 'Eloquent' is the word for it. Poetic kinda."

"Eloquent?"

"Yeah."

"Poetic?"

"Yeah. Wrote a song about. Wanna hear it? Hear it go!"

"You stupid." Her warm laughter thrilled him. He liked the heat of her breath on his skin.

"I can't control my body's madness. 'Cause the heat of you makes me weak." Doin paused to lightly kiss Joozy on her chin and then her neck, and then he peppered her body with light pecks until he reached her breasts. He took a nipple into his mouth and gently nibbled it until he felt it swell, firmly swished it with his tongue until he felt her urging him on with her hand gripping his head and guiding him. He suddenly stopped and pulled himself up to kiss her on the cheek.

"That lyric sums it up pretty good, right?" he asked her.

"Right." Joozy nuzzled in closer to him and smiled. They kissed deeply, deeply, before falling asleep in embraced slumber. Her last thought before she dozed off was that she hoped it was always as good as the first time.

With a contented sigh, she roused herself from the memory, rose from the bed and began to get dressed, smiling as she checked herself in the mirror once again. For once, she had found someone who saw past her darkness… her face, a man who was taking the time to unlock her passions, her realness and her heart.

Joozy pulled a pair of jeans from her closet that slid snugly around her ripe waist and selected a dark blue shirt with black buttons up the front. Doin said he liked her in dark colors and she wanted to look nice for him when he came over to see her. It would be the first time that he ever came to her house; Doin had insisted on meeting her mother and she was a little on edge about the potential for a disastrous evening.

She wasn't nervous about the house. A ghetto home is a ghetto home and she knew that Doin was familiar with the uniformity of manufactured projects: basic, square, white rooms; paper-thin walls; and brown doors. Besides, her mother was a homemaker; their house was always kept spotless so that what little they had was well maintained.

Just the thought of her mother, Miss Natty Mae, jangled Joozy's nerves and she acknowledged the discomfort that existed between them. Her given name was Natalie May, and to most people she was still known by that name, but whenever she had to deal with Joozy she would turn into Miss Natty Mae.

"Well. Well. Well." Her mother stood in the doorway watching her primp in front of the mirror. "This boy must be something, huh? You are actually dressing down! You ain't got your ass hanging out all over your usual places."

Joozy was about to reply, then thought better of it. She definitely did not want to even try to go there. Her mother had something on her mind; she always has something on her mind, and she would get around to it in her own sweet, evil time so Joozy let her ramble on.

Natalie was a beautiful woman. Joozy's mother had somehow kept her beauty in a potion that was hidden in her rich chocolate skin, which was still smooth and flawless. Her eyes were dark and commanding; her lips, her nose, her cheeks, even her hair all served to enhance a face that was the exact opposite of Joozy's darkness. Her auburn-colored hair framed her face in a delicate bob and she wore very little makeup, only lipstick of dark shades that enhanced her already full, lush lips. Most of her features she had passed to two of her daughters, Lika and Tasha, but lightning had struck her firstborn, Joozy...and Natty Mae supplied the damaging thunder. Joozy remembered the time when she and Tasha had been playing hide-and-go-seek in the living room. She had found a nice secret spot in the kitchen next to the china cabinet behind her mother's tall plant while Tasha counted to fifty. She settled quietly in her corner, listening to Tasha stumble through the numbers. "Forty-nine, forty-six... fifty," she said. "Ready or not. Here I come!" Joozy tried to make herself invisible while she waited for her sister to try to find her. When she heard voices in the living room, she scooted back further into the corner before she realized that they were adult voices and they were coming her way. Her mother had company over and they were laughing and talking about people. Gossiping.

"Girl," a voice rang out. "You betta watch out for them dog-ass niggas out there. Even these nappy-head little boys is out here trying to be grown. I seen one of them trying to run up on Tasha the other day. You know how they do!"

"Tasha know," her mother's voice rang out. "She know."

"Your daughters is pretty, too. So you know you better watch 'em."

"Yeah, you better watch all of 'em."

"Well, I know that I sure don't have to watch out for no Joozy."

"Why you say that," came the shocked response. "You sure betta watch her, too. Shit!"

Her mother was astonished. "Now who do ya'll think is gonna be chasing after her black ass!"

The quiet was deafening.

"My two babies just came out so pretty. They both favor my mother. I got a picture of my mother that she gave me of when she was a girl and my babies look just like her. But Joozy! Shit, she got damn near all of her black, rotten-ass daddy in her."

Joozy sat harder in her hiding place, her breath caught in her chest. Her mother's words hurt her...but she had heard these sentiments before. Natty Mae hated her.

"You know what," her mother had continued. "I was scared to have any more kids after I had Joozy. Hell no! She was just as black! I thought that one of them nurses had switched babies on me! Ain't nobody in my family look like that! Shit! I wasn't gonna have no 'nother baby that looked like that. Shit, naw!"

Joozy had quietly left her hiding place, tipped out the back door and found another hiding place behind a thick tree trunk...and cried her eyes out. Her beautiful mother hated her.

"Does he use you?" It was her mother, Natty Mae, watching her. "Does he just dump his stuff inside of that body that you so proud of?" And there it was; the heart of the problem. Though her mother and sisters each were so pretty to look at, they each had short, chunky bodies that held no hint of femininity. Where Joozy's body had the curves of sensuality, her sisters were more masculine and solidly built. Natty Mae hated that.

"I bet that boy got you thinking that he cares about your ugly-ass self! Look at you up in here primping in the mirror like you got you a gentle-man caller or something."

Joozy sat on the bed and waited. Miss Natty Mae always had problems with her. It was a root that reached deep and far, digging and growing, spreading animosity between them, creating an insurmountable barrier that separated mother and daughter.

"He must be serious," Natty Mae intoned. "Is it?"

Joozy didn't answer but just nodded her head affirmative.

"Then I have to see him," Natty Mae barked. "Tell him that he need to come see me! That's right! I got to see what this man look like. I got to see what kind of man would fool you into feeling like he feeling something. You hear me?"

Joozy regarded her mother with a puzzled look. Miss Natty Mae never talked to her about any matters pertaining to love or life. At best, her mother displayed muted disinterest in Joozy's rumbling stumble through the peaks and valleys of emotional development. In fact she had never given a hoot or a holler about the shambles that the journey had become. How ironic that now when Joozy had stability and the comfort of a loving man, when her heart was smiling...now her mother was trying to voice concern.

"Mama!" Joozy received a timely respite from Miss Natty Mae by her little sister, Lika. Lika came bounding into the bedroom and dove on Joozy's bed, popped up and began bouncing up and down with a smile on her face. She was a pretty, spoiled brat, a fourteen-year-old girl with a five-year-old's whine in her voice that curled Joozy's nerves every time she heard it. Lika was growing up to be just like Tasha, one of the beautiful ones. The ones who go smoothly through the years of life on the velvet paths built upon the fortunate curves of her lips, the depths of her eyes or the aching beauty of well-formed cheekbones. Joozy's sister was an innocent monster, constructed in Natty Mae's lab after years and years of negative reinforcement.

"Mama," Lika squealed. "There's a scary-looking man at the door. He asking for Joozy."

Natty Mae cast a sidelong glance at Joozy before she answered. "Well, go let him in then and tell him we'll be right there in a minute."

Lika hurried out of the room. Natty Mae turned to Joozy. "You know, you always thought that you was grown...a little wise beyond your years, but you're not. You ain't grown and you ain't beyond your years. You see, I know what you've been doing out there in the streets. You think I don't know! You better ask somebody! Folks love telling every time they see you. That lets you know something, Joozy. It sure does."

Joozy looked at her mother with an unspoken question.

"The world don't owe you nothing, Joozy! That's what you need to realize. The world don't owe you nothing. Not a job. Not a man. Not even a reason."

CHAPTER 16
The Unfortunate Path

Doin stood in the doorway, bravely bearing the sharp inspection of Joozy's family. Joozy stood next to her mother, whose eyes were locked on him in a calculating stare. Her eyes widened when she spotted the scar on his face and Doin knew that he was the object of some serious subtractions. It didn't matter much to him though. He was hardened to human insensitivity about his physical appearance. The only person in the room Doin concerned himself with was Joozy, who stood there smiling and beckoning to him. He crossed the room and kissed her cheek in greeting. Joozy made the introductions.

"Mama, this is Doin," she began. "Doin, this is my mother."

Joozy's mother was a classic beauty, Doin noted. She was the kind of woman that could make a man intense with a smoldering stare; the kind of woman who could make a man's backbone stiffen with her tease; that is, if a beautiful face was the requirement. Doin knew the type and the methods. He took great pride in his ability to look into people and see past the hollow pretense of their words and decipher the thoughts hidden behind their true meanings. It was all in the eyes, so he looked into hers...and saw a little bitch in there. She gave Doin a fake, plastic smile and a tilt of her head.

"This is Lika." Joozy turned him in the direction of a little girl who was a younger version of her mother, minus the dumpy, masculine figure she had to look forward to when she reached adulthood. She stood there with her mouth agape, childish curiosity getting the better of her as she walked toward them with her finger pointed at Doin.

"How you, Lika?" Doin knew what was coming.

"How you do that?" Lika was not to be denied.

"Lika, that's rude," Joozy said and turned Doin in time to catch Tasha emerging from her bedroom. "And this is Tasha."

"How you, Tasha? I'm Doin."

"How you, Doin," she answered curtly.

Joozy took Doin by the elbow and guided him toward the living room couch, with her mother and sisters following close behind. Lika came around to Joozy's side and sat on the large armrest, hastily grabbed the remote control and turned to watch the television. Tasha sat on the loveseat facing Doin, her attention openly fixating on his face. Miss Natty Mae took the chair that sat at an angle to the room.

"Well," she began. "First off…what's your real name?"

"It's Doin," came the reply.

"Well," Natty Mae was curt. "What is the name your parents gave you?" Doin hesitated before answering. He felt Joozy's grip tighten on his elbow in warning and he glanced at her in acknowledgment. On one occasion, she had heard someone ask him the same question and Doin had cursed them out. Joozy hadn't really told him much about her mother—not that he would have taken her evaluation at face value anyway. Her view would have been a tad slanted and he trusted his judgment above all. He tried to interpret Joozy's gesture but decided to rely on his own gut instinct before he turned back to look Natty Mae in the eye…and saw the "bitch" in there. It was there, dancing a frisky tango, jumping to and fro in the back of her eyes while it waited, poised to spring. Doin saw it…and smiled.

"It's Daryn," he stated.

"Where you get that scar from?" Tasha, who was standing by Natty Mae's chair, yelled out. Her outburst hung in the air like an accusation, followed by an ugly silence. Doin glared at Tasha; the anger in his eyes cut through her with stunning animosity. Her eyes went big and round in shock, a jolt to her senses that quickly subsided to be replaced by the hardcore-type-of-nasty-hate that only a lifetime's worth of ghetto could imbed into an attitude. It was the same powerful, killing cat that preyed, with paws extended, in her mother's eyes. The bitch. The only difference was that this one talked.

"You look like a monster." Tasha's mouth twisted with bitter spit.

Joozy's grip tightened on Doin's arm. His body flexed with madness, swollen with the harsh lyrics that he wished to spit at both of them. Words that rhymed with "switch" and "trick" and "luck" and "stick." And a song about how he put her nose on his dick. Yeah, lyrics bitch! And she would know where to find 'em...but no! No. *This is Joozy's family,* he reasoned. He chilled.

"Why you looking at my daughter like that Darvyn...Doolyn, Doin, or whatever your name is!" Natty Mae was ready to let her bitch loose. "You better stop looking at my Tasha like *you* got problems!" She stopped to let that statement sink in, drawing Doin's hostility from her daughter to her. When she had Doin's full attention...she finally let her bitch loose.

"You know you ugly, so why try to fool yourself. You got a mirror just like everybody got eyes. Your mirror reflects it back to you same as Joozy's does. Same as her dark, ugly ass!"

Doin regarded Natty Mae like a shut-off valve. She was shut off! Her voice no longer mattered to him. She was a leech on the warmth of life. Just like his stepfather. Coldness and weakness.

"Joozy ain't ugly." Doin leaned forward to look Natty Mae in the eye. "She just had bad luck. She was on the unfortunate path...and that was her bad luck. You see, her genes got mixed up with your genes. One of those cosmic tricks of the devil. Dark upon dark, lady. Dark upon dark."

Natty Mae rose up ready to snap but Doin shouted her down. "Easy! Easy! Witchy woman," Doin raised his hands in self-defense. "You may be dark, but Joozy..." Doin paused to take her hand in his, carefully interlacing their fingers. "Joozy has light. She has a spirit that shines through. It comes through. She has a spirit that's like a pretty light...and that is some very attractive shit." He smiled at Joozy before turning to Natty Mae. "And, if you'll pardon me for a second...that shit sure is prettier than you are. By far!"

Nattie Mae was beside herself with anger. She would have tried to split herself in two so she could cuss his ass out twice. Her eyes showed more white than could've been imagined. A thin sheen of sweat broke out on her forehead and a sliver of snot shot out the side of her nose. She didn't let no nigga talk to her like that. "Well, fuck you, Davin...Doobin...Doolin or whatever your name are! You don't know shit! Can't do shit, can't give shit, don't touch shit! You better bless your ugly-ass self right out my front door! You ugly and you a stupid mothafucka!" Nattie Mae's chest heaved from releasing her abusive torrent; she hadn't cussed anybody out that good in quite a while.

A heated calm settled over Doin as he rose from the couch. This was fucking ignorant.

"Yeah, you're right, Mother." Doin rasped. "I can't touch shit. I can't give her shit neither. Mostly 'cause she don't need me. She needs more than me. In fact, her needs are past tense and I can't apply myself to the past. Ya' know! Bygones are bygones. And bygones is what you did to her."

"What the fuck is this stupid mothafucka talking about?" Natty Mae asked Tasha who stood next to her, attentive and solemn, taking in Doin's words.

Doin reached down to help Joozy to her feet and together they headed toward the door, as her mother looked on, strangely silent. Doin turned back to look at Natty Mae.

"I can't give her a mother. A mother who will help her see where true beauty lies. I can't give her a mother's love either. I can't give her that. And you know what? You can't either. Can you?"

It was so quiet that they heard the tumblers in the doorknob ratchet into place when Doin pulled the door open. He spoke over his shoulder to Natty Mae as they left. "Your silence is sound, lady. The deafening roar of the guilty. And you are guilty. Guilty as sin."

Doin and Joozy stepped, arm and arm, through the doorway and out into the street. The night was deathly silent on the walk back. No words were spoken when they took a detour over to Promenade Park, the magical place of their first date. They sat on the same bench that they had shared on that special day. Joozy leaned into Doin's embrace and listened to the calming beat of his heart. She was hot with hate for her mother...and she knew that she could never go back there. She hugged Doin tighter, moved in closer, listening to the steady beat of his heart. It was the pacifying rumble of his chest and the warmth of his embrace that enabled her to hold back her pretty, trembling tears.

CHAPTER 17
Naked-Ass Coffee

Doin woke to the soft purr of Joozy's breath caressing his ear as she slept in his arms. They hadn't really found time to discuss the previous night's bout with her mother, and Doin could understand her need for mental space. Dysfunctionality requires a wide berth sometimes, needs room for emotional coasting in order to keep insanity from mooring at the spiritual port of the soul. The reality of steering those waters requires strength and elasticity, rage and laughter, joy and pain and an all-important on-and-off switch.

Joozy stirred next to him. She briefly flirted with wakefulness, reached to Doin and gripped him tighter before taking a short breath and settling back into the steady rhythm of sleep. He paused to let the feeling of her presence sink in, and he realized that her touch held more meaning than he cared to admit. This mystified him; mysteries that were soon to be uncovered joys. He marveled in her as she became a woman—his woman—because she was uncovering nicely. He kissed her gently on her forehead and then eased his body from her embrace, careful not to wake her as he tipped out into the living room. He sat on the couch and looked at his dollar-store alarm clock on top of the television. It was eight-thirty in the morning. *If life were truly fair*, Doin mused, *I would be getting dressed to be at work by nine*. Things being as they were, he might as well have stayed in bed. Doin needed a job…and he needed one yesterday, not today. He had applied at numerous places, to numerous types of business and he had even registered with numerous temporary agencies—all to no avail. So far he hadn't gotten a single call-back. He had the procedures down pat—from the first phone contact to the final interview—and yet he still came away rejected.

Doin got up from the couch and went into the kitchen where he started a fresh pot of coffee brewing and then took a few eggs out of the refrigerator. He fried his last two sausage patties and was scrambling the eggs when he heard Joozy stir. After the previous night's episode with her mother, Doin figured that she could use a nice relaxing morning in bed, breakfast included. When he slid the eggs onto the plate with the sausage, he remembered that he had some wheat bread for toast. He was reaching in the cabinet when he noticed Joozy standing in the bedroom doorway wearing one of his New York Yankees baseball shirts. He stopped dead in his tracks, just looking at her. There was a big, blue "N" on her left breast and the "Y" on the right one.

"I love New York," Doin rasped.

"I love breakfast." She pursed her lips. "Whatchu cook?"

Doin stared at her. "I bet you won't never get fat, huh? You can eat whatever you want, right?"

"Oxygen." Joozy waved her hand at him. "You need some oxygen."

"Well. You just sit it down and get ready." Doin started rapping, "*I got the macaroni soggy, the peas all mushed and the chicken taste like wood.*" Doin put the plates on a tray, turned to Joozy and took his rap to the next level. "*To the bang bang boogie and up jumped the boogie...*"

Joozy finished for him. "*To the rhythm of the boo-getty beat.*" She laughed as she crossed the room and took the tray from Doin. She slowly assessed his nearly naked body, and looked him up and down before she smiled. "You look good when you damn near naked-ass naked." She kissed his lips. "*Baby bubba,*" Doin sang. Joozy kissed him again but this time she went deep, her tongue dancing gently with his as he slowed to meet her pace.

"Stop this." Doin was breathless. "Take the tray and the food to the bed and I'll see if I can bring you some naked-ass coffee. You want some naked-ass sugar with that?"

Joozy took the tray and began walking toward the bedroom. Her hips swayed with purpose, teasing. She paused to look over her shoulder, catching

Doin with his eyes full of wonder at the sight. She knew he liked to watch her. And she liked the way she could entice him.

"The question is," she quipped. "Do you?"

"All right now!" Doin exclaimed. He poured two cups of coffee, added sugar, rushed into the bedroom and settled in the bed with Joozy. He handed her a cup. "You better stop teasing Daddy Longstroke like that."

Joozy almost choked on her coffee. "Daddy Longstroke? Now, you know you have more imagination than that." She put her hand down his underwear and grabbed his manhood. "You want to call him Daddy Longstroke? That's too worn out. Give me something else."

"How about Little Petey?" Doin asked. She looked at him like he was stupid.

"All right." Doin gave in. "Damn! Let's see." He reached over and gently stroked her nipple through the shirt. He was smiling when he next spoke. "How about Yum Yum?"

"Yeah." Joozy tried it on for size. "Yum Yum. Okay. You can do that. And baby? I wasn't teasing."

Joozy turned back to her meal. She enjoyed it when they were able to talk bullstuff with each other. Other men didn't have that talent, that ability to discern the fact that sometimes she just liked to talk and that talking didn't always mean that they had to climb right on top of her and start bucking. Doin could sense her mood and touch her when she needed it.

"You know what, Doin? You make me laugh, like, a happy laugh. It feels good to laugh with you. Feels real good." She reached over and touched Doin's shoulder. Doin pushed his fork into the pile of scrambled eggs and held them up for Joozy to eat. She took a bite.

"Well, Joozy. You make me smile all the time, so I guess it's an even trade. A smile for a laugh. Cool?"

Joozy nodded her head in agreement and then they ate.

"Doin," Joozy began.

"Yeah," Doin lay back on the pillow.

"I need to ask you something and I don't know how you are going to handle the question."

"Of course you don't," Doin replied. "*'Cause you ain't asted me the question yet, Miss Daisy!*"

Joozy nudged him. "Stop playin'. I'm serious. I really don't know how you gonna react to me."

"Go ahead. Ask me."

"Okay." She took a deep breath. "What's stoppin' you from loving me?"

Doin came up short. "Where...uh...what! Duh."

"Yeah. DUH!!!" Joozy could barely contain her laughter as she watched Doin wriggling like a fish on a hook. "I was just playing, Doin. That wasn't my question. Please...exhale! Breathe, baby! Breathe. Do I need to get you a paper bag?"

"No," Doin gasped. "No! I'm okay. I think I can make it." He reached out and took Joozy's hand, watching her intently before he spoke. "What question?"

"Listen. I don't like my mother."

"There's no question," Doin pitched in.

"No. Listen." Joozy was solemn. "I want to move in with you."

Doin was quiet. It was time to be straight-up with her. "Joozy, listen. I have to tell you something first. Listen. Joozy. I ain't working right now. I just got laid off. You know..." His voice trailed off.

"But I can't live with her, Doin," Joozy said. "I just can't."

"But Joozy...I ain't working."

"But you will. And so will I."

Doin was solemn. "So you wanna get real about it, huh?"

"I think that we could do it together anyway," Joozy reasoned. "We could."

"Yeah, Joozy," Doin agreed. "As long as I got...you got. We'll get it."

Joozy reached over and moved the tray of food to the side.

"*Come and give me some of that Yum Yum,*" she sang.

I want her to tie me up again. But not really. See, my hands are an integral part of my sex. They gets to feel shit! They get to measure her measure. I mean the beautiful, lush swell of her hips; that perfect roundness that makes me so glad that I am a man. Umma tell my son that shit one day: "The measure of a man is when he measures a woman's fullness with his own two hands." And I mean every inch of her—from the hooter to the tooter! Like The Artist said, "Touch it...and explode!"

So I want her to tie me up again. But not really. I want her to tease my manhood, make it rage and holla. I want to feel the torture as I wait anxiously at the next station, as I try to find her "G" spot and push it along. Push it along. Push it along. Yeah, push it along! I want lips. Eyes. Breasts. Ass. Friction and passion. I want all of that shit. That's why I want her to tie me up again. But not really. I know that this shit is hard to understand...but so is the depths of the satisfaction that she gets out of me. To understand my dilemma, you must understand my angst. You see, I run shit! Tha's right! 'Cause I got the thickness. I'm a tree with my own tree root! Ya know what I'm saying? And I lay it down! Now I know I sound like one of "them." Women...they know plenty of "them." "Them" brag about what they can do, how they can do it, and they even have statistics to back up their claims about how long they can do it. Not me though. I ain't one of "them." What I do is this: I get one woman in a one-on-one equation, let her know that her treasure is endless, that infinity is its pleasure...and then I fill her. I touch both sides and the bottom, and then I hold her when she tells me that it hurts...real...good! I figured out a long time ago that there is a thin line between love and pain. I ain't trying to cross over that line...I just want to hold the writing stick that draws it. Like I said...I run shit!

Yet I want her to tie me up again. I mean, this woman has got me lighting candles, playing slow jams and waiting by the phone, simply because I'm addicted to the dark passion of her skin, the way it glows when its in my hands. I can't fully explain it. It's like...it's like...it's like she has this special way of moving that moves me. Mesmerizing in its actuality. I guess she got me open, huh? Well, not really.

Tonight we do candles and mirrors. At least, that's my plan. Ain't no telling what she wants to do though. I think that maybe I opened up the freak in her. But tonight, she gonna do some Man-Sex. Tha's right! Some

Man-Sex! Some of my shit! Some straight-up, to the hole, downright huck-a-bucking! We ain't even gonna have no foreplay. Just straight up in there, and then…No. Waittaminnit. I better re-think that one. A little moisture is a good thing. A little wetness goes a long way. Okay. Maybe I'll pour some water on her ass, but for real…we having some Man-Sex! Shit!

I remember the first time I wanted to do the Man-Sex thing with her. She came over and knocked on my door. I knew it was her because when she knocked, my shit got hard. You think she might got me open?

I paused with my hand on the doorknob. She wouldn't tell me what she was going to wear over to my house because she knows that I love a woman who can dress sexy. Oh yeah! She ain't gots to be naked all the damn time. In fact, the very first time that I got conflicted was when she sexed me down with all of our clothes on. We had been out partying all night. She had wore this little, black mini-skirt with a red slit down the side that hugged the fleshy part of her thighs. She was also wearing one of them Wonderbras because I wondered how that bra was holding those two full cups of delicious without spilling over. I think that every man in the club wanted to be me that night. Joozy was moving that body with so much tease that when we got back to my place, I had planned on putting some ice in my mouth and tasting her. I figured that she was hot enough for at least two ice cubes. When I closed the door behind her, I was the one who needed the ice! She mashed me against the wall and jammed her tongue into my mouth. She spoke to me in tongue language and, hell, I'm bilingual, so I talked back. I sucked her bottom lip into my mouth and pulled her tighter to me.

"Say what you want," I finally told her. "'Cause I'm here to please you." She didn't answer. She lifted her leg up to my hip and I grabbed it, you know, trying to help. She leaned away from me, creating enough space for her to reach between our bodies. I felt the unique sensation of freedom as my chocolate piece sprang free. I looked down and watched as her fingers worked quickly between her legs. She had on black panties with a snap on the crotch! When I heard the button go "pop," my dick sprang to life; my chocolate piece turned to steel.

"You might think I'm crazy," she whispered in my ear as she guided me inside of her. I responded with hot kisses on her neck, her shoulders, her lips…anywhere that I could make contact with skin as we started our hot ride. And we rode any way that she wanted. As I close my eyes, I start thinking things…and I'm conflicted.

I want her to tie me up again. But not really.

I guess my anxiety stems from the fact that I want to be in control. I want to run shit! But at the same time, I want to surrender control to this woman, to Joozy, this antidote to my loneliness, this balm to the ache of my desires. Really.

CHAPTER 18
Bitches Room

I just knew that my madness would kill me the day I stood over Joselle's body. The heat of my anger and the errant satiation of a lust lost colored my insanity a burnt red by the darkness of her blood. My chest heaved from pain and exertion as my mind slipped away into the morass of my being. I cried. And D.Wayne died.

And then Ruh found me and made me brand-new. His light pierced my darkness, a pinpoint of whiteness that grew until its dimensions shone like a lantern. Ruh be praised.

He guided me…as he does every day now…he guided me with his gentle hands when I disposed of Joselle's body, as my soul began sifting through the debris left behind by my incestuous mother. Ruh even took away the vestiges of the nasty disease, the syphilis that Joselle had given to me. I didn't go to no doctor. I didn't need no stinkin' doctor or the devil's stinkin' medicine! Ruh made me new. He made me whole again.

It ain't my fault that Joselle is dead! She was already numb to every emotion that bound mother to son. She was just walking flesh with no heartbeat when she tried to tear my life from me! She turned me into a creation; and I became her damnation. The end is near! When Joselle took my sexuals that day, she was merely acting as the instrument of the degradation of society. Ruh told me that. The end is near! But my Ruh is beneficent. He has given me the answer. Ruh Water.

Ruh Water will save the world.

The trip from that time and place to this time and place is littered with the sacrifices that Ruh requires. Unbelievers will speak of the greatness of Ruh one day but presently they are limited to pagan comprehension. They can only speak of the lives that are given, not of the greater good that I serve. Each woman that I took was more than happy to be deemed worthy enough to give her gift; to bestow the life that she carried in her belly to the Temple of Ruh.

I first discovered the Temple when it called to me from the alleyway. It was a doorway that glowed like a celestial entranceway. The pale, blond wood radiated in the night against the solid lightlessness of the red, brick building. I found out later that the landlord had replaced the original door, which had been torn from its hinges by a couple of bums looking for a warm building to squat in, with an unfinished one that he had never gotten around to painting. The door stood out like a beacon...calling me. Ruh be praised!

When I first came down the stairs to the basement, the altar was the first thing that greeted me. It stood in the middle of the room by the back wall. The dark, mahogany finish cast murky reflections in the dank confines of the basement and as my eyes adjusted to the dim light, I noticed that the floor in that part of the basement was raised from the surrounding bottom surface of the room, lending it the status due to the exhalted. All that remained was for me to gather Ruh's worshippers. I set up six highchairs and arranged them in a semicircle facing the altar and began to collect the witnesses that Ruh required. This is where the magic would happen, where I would rescue the world from its dry hell. I would fight the fire with Ruh Water made from my god's elixir.

My place of worship is perfect. Ruh's altar sits fully majestic in the midst of greatness. He commanded me to make my sacrifices—six in all—and I have made a place ready for each one. Ruh's altar sits tall, majestic in the midst of greatness. It wasn't easy though. I had to measure each dimension perfectly, forming an exact semi-circle so that each highchair caught the perfect reflection of my deity's shine. It was important that each stillborn life was positioned to disperse its energy, its life-water toward the foundation of all creation. Removing the tray from each chair facilitates this transferral.

There are four dead fetuses sitting in the chairs now, their eyes closed, their water depleted and freely given to the most-high Ruh.

I had to hang a curtain up to the doorway of the other room, the Bitches Room, to keep that space from desecrating the serenity of Ruh. The Bitches Room is nasty; a necessary evil that I try to keep as far away from my mind as my mission will allow. I keep the mothers there. My own baby-mama-drama situation. What I had to do was take a sledgehammer and pound my way through the concrete floor in there and then I dug a hole as deep as I could. Once that was finished I had to go all the way down to the King Choppers at the mall and steal a grocery cart so that I could lug a couple of bags of kitty litter up in here. I lined the Bitches hole with two bags of that and after I extracted the baby from the woman, I would throw the lifeless body in the hole. Then I would spread the kitty litter over the top of the body to kill the smell. Works like a charm. I am one of the few men in life who has neutralized the wiles of women. I can't even smell the Bitches Room now.

Each and every one of those women has a special place in my memory; each one had a distinctive scream, yet their lives were fated to be fodder for the greater good and I took joy in the repetition. The last one to go into the Bitches Room had even bucked up a few times when I cut the fetus from her plump belly—but it was just the devil's reflex of her flesh giving up the ghost. I remember when I slid the baby out of her, careful to catch the afterbirth, the Ruh Water, in the tub that I had placed underneath her body. I wiped the little baby boy clean with one of the special towels that I kept in the room for my ritual, before taking him over to the fourth high-chair and positioning him so that he faced the altar.

Then I kneel down to give my prayers to Ruh. I feel the heavy wetness of my tears as they stream down my cheeks. Tears for my mother. Tears for my pain. Tears for Ruh as he lifts me up again.

"Is we almost there, Ruh?"

Sometimes I can see Ruh's face on the dark surface of the altar. He doesn't come to me with any man-like traits; his essence is the color of life, the feel of breath, and the gentleness of water. I see his face. I know his peace when the coolness of Ruh washes the pain and dark away from me. He lets me know that I am right.

"Please, Ruh, tell me why. Why did my mother take my sexuals? Huh? Look at her!"

I can hear myself screaming. My head is a red nightmare, flashing like rabies. Like insanity and childhood pain. I can feel myself pointing at the dead woman in the Bitches Room. My head throbs from the memories of being me, from the memories of Joselle. Of Joselle naked and on top of me. Her syphilis flowing from her sex and into me. Flo Jigga, digging into my neck. Red blood is the color of my rainbow. But Ruh has made me new. I am strong now.

"Two more, Ruh?"

His image dissipates in acquiescence and I know that I have to find my next queen. My life has meaning now. And the feeling is intoxicating. Damn near exhilarating. Ruh has been so kind to me lately. He's given me excitement. Juice. Like a never-ending clock. Tick. Tock. Tick. Tock. Night. Day. Day. Night.

"But I got two more to do though, huh, Ruh? And then you gonna give me water. Gonna give the world Ruh Water."

CHAPTER 19
Liquid Nature

Agent Robert Abraham had been living and working atop the levee for over thirty days and the rain had not stopped for even one day. The Mississippi River was still at flood stage and had remained that way since he had awakened in the makeshift jail that had been erected near the tent town at the bottom of the levee.

Christiana was down there.

The National Guardsmen had brought her to his jail cell during his first few hours there. He assumed that their objective had been twofold: to quash any notion that he might have of escaping and to let Robert know that they had her, too.

Christiana had been forced to work on the bottom, cooking and cleaning for the workers, but despite himself, Robert couldn't help but be relieved to know that she was safe.

The jailers let them have some time alone.

"Robert, what are we gonna do?" She spoke to him through the prison bars, her handcuffs jangling as she reached for him. Robert moved and took her hands in his before he spoke.

"Are you all right, Christiana?" He bent down and kissed her forehead. "Did those white boys touch you?"

"Yeah, they did," Christiana said. "With the butt of their rifle! Next thing I know, I'm here."

"Damn," Robert said. "They're even taking the women now! The situation must be getting really drastic." He looked Christiana in the eyes before he spoke again.

"Listen. You are strength. Pull from that. Lean on that. So no matter what they throw at you, no matter what they do…you and I are going to survive this." He pulled her as close to him as the bars would allow. "I've just found you. For me, be safe, baby."

"Okay." Christiana's voice was shaky.

"Okay?" Robert watched her intently. "Okay?"

"Yes." Christiana sounded a little more convinced.

"I'll come for you," Robert said. "No matter where you are. Remember that."

He hadn't seen her again.

Robert had been chained and marched with about thirty other Black men out of the tent town to a waiting boat and packed aboard like cattle. The ship took them to a loading dock called the Teardrop. It had been attached to the levee so that the human cargo could be off loaded and put to work. The surface at the top of the dam was roughly eight feet wide but the structure stretched lengthwise for hundreds of miles. Tents squatted in a staggered line atop the levee amongst the steadily falling rain. Not a day had passed without the steady downpour that steadily crept higher and higher against the dam wall, creeping up on them, threatening with the pure force of liquid nature. They faced the power every day and slaved away, regardless, stacking sandbags in cracks, tending to the weak spots that bulged under the torrent of water and grunting under the strain of keeping the boat safely moored against the levee.

Robert stood and surveyed the carnage around him. Nothing in his training could ever have prepared him for this. He was one amongst hundreds, living, eating and sleeping in a tent city. It was slavery. Pure and simple. And there was no escape. No liberation from the rain or the white men who put him there. It was a perfect prison perched high above the cold, wet freedom that sprawled out below them. It was a contrast that Robert couldn't put into words; he straddled the ultimate fence— on one side, a watery grave awaited him, while on the other side white men held guns. Thoughts of escape sometimes flitted through his mind but the steady, endless rain quickly beat down even those flights of fancy. Day after day it fell, beating down on them until the pounding rain began to feel like God's Chinese water torture. The rain poured until it became a part of their existence. They ate in the water. Slept in the water. The water became their toilet, and, predictably, disease became a serious problem.

Black men plodded through the tent city—wet, sick and beaten, their lives relegated to eight feet in width. Their existence became slush. Ankle-deep water pulled at their feet, adding weight to each step. Pounding rain soaked their food as they squatted to eat, or drizzling water beat on them whenever they relieved themselves.

Despair and madness intermingled; the harshness of their existence tested the mettle of their character and elicited the truth of their souls.

Sometimes in the darkness of the night, the dim light of the pale moon shone on the hearts of each man.

An open space had been cleared between the line of tents, creating an area where the men would sometimes gather after a long day of laboring in the rain to talk and commiserate. Robert would often sit with the group of men and discuss the grave situation of their imprisonment. Adversity could make mountains of men. It could also make molehills.

"There's freedom on the ground," Robert said one night. It had been a particularly strenuous day and tensions were high. One of the men from Linville, a man named Elijah who had been suffering from dysentery, had fallen off the side of the levee and drowned. He had been delusional, a symptom brought on by a fever that worsened in the unsanitary conditions that they were forced to endure. The living conditions were barbaric and the spread of disease was inevitable. Elijah had been bed-ridden, asleep in his tent on the soaked blankets, when he suddenly awoke, burst through the outer flaps of the tent and ran off the edge of the dam into the roiling water. Once the water claimed him there was no rescue.

"There's freedom on the ground," Robert repeated. "And it's imperative we find a way to get there." A murmur of agreement rambled amongst the group of men as they sat huddled in a wide circle.

"How we gonna get down from here?" A sonorous growl rumbled through the night in a tone that demanded an answer. Mandeep was a wide man and his look was hard. His face was set in intensity, his eyes spaced wide apart, divided evenly by a flat, flared nose. His mouth was set in a determined grimace and when he talked a few dark spaces appeared where there were once teeth. Robert remembered the day that Mandeep had been brought on the boat to the top of the levee. Four National Guardsmen and a redneck that Robert recognized as one of the men who had captured him, all with rifles at the ready, had beaten Mandeep badly. They had thrown him, face down with his hands tied behind his back to the concrete

platform that had been erected a half-mile down the levee. The platform had been built on a section of the levee that was called the Teardrop, due to its shape, that stood at the crest of an irregular, elevated strip of land. Due to the steep rise of land and the circular shape of the dam, the water pooled at that juncture and stayed steady enough for the boats to dock at certain times. The workers would often gather along the levee and watch as the boats docked, often loaded with National Guardsmen, country boys and the many Black men who had been captured that day.

Mandeep rolled over onto his back and looked at his jailers. Blood leaked from a gash on his forehead. Two rednecks jumped from the boat and yanked Mandeep to his feet. "You gonna learn, nigger," was yelled through gritted teeth. "You ain't no smarter'n nobody. Not no white man! Hear!"

Mandeep's voice was deep. Pained but somehow calm and sure. "Violence only begets violence until it corrupts your soul."

"Stop talkin' like that!" A loud guffaw rang out behind the redneck and Mandeep doubled over when he was caught by a blow to his midsection, followed by clubbing blows that put him on his knees. "It begets this!" The white man shook his fist in front of Mandeep's face. Mandeep looked from the extended fist to the redneck's eyes. Neither man moved. Finally the white man left Mandeep and got back on the boat.

"I wish you could tell me." Mandeep turned back to Robert. "Tell me what's the difference between down there and up here? Down there don't do nuthin' but get you up here."

"You giving up already, Mandeep?" Robert watched Mandeep warily. "I'm looking at my freedom…and that is always attainable. It takes struggle! Like it or not, we are Black men and we have to fight to remind people sometimes that we are just as human as they are."

"You preaching to the choir," Mandeep answered. "Freedom is not beyond my understanding. I can comprehend. But the fight down there is the same battle that we fighting up here. We just fighting on higher ground."

"You're serious," Robert said.

"I speak what I mean," Mandeep said. "This is my understanding of our situation up here."

"If so…" Robert looked at him. "Your reasoning, your understanding is narrow, sir! Down on the ground, I'm fighting against an institution called racism, against

peoples' beliefs, doctrines, laws…entities that are concrete. Up here! Up here, we are fighting nature. Rain, wind and now, disease. This is a war no one wins."

"An unbeatable opponent?" Mandeep looked around at the men gathered in the rain. "I think that we have more of a chance against the opponent up here, than the one that you want to fight down there. White men are more wicked than nature." A murmuring ascent rolled through the rainsoaked men. Mandeep's voice rose. "So we fight. They brought me here! So we fight. This! This is our proving ground. This is where we have to show them that we can overcome forces that they can't!"

"And in the meantime?" Robert was on his feet now. "To prove that we're better, men have to die of diseases that have long been curable? To live, eat, breathe, sleep, shit and die in water? No! This is a time for righteous anger and well-aimed bullets!"

"Violence is not the answer for us," Mandeep said. "There is not enough guns, and more importantly, not enough us."

A voice cried out from the crowd. "And how we gonna get us some guns anyway?"

"There are many guns to be had." Robert watched them. "On one of those boats." All heads turned to the two boats that were moored at the Teardrop.

CHAPTER 20
Dark Infantry

"I gotta find me a ripe one today. And I know that I will, because I got technique. Like my boy Mike said, 'My style—impeccable. My method—ferocious.' Shit! Ain't nobody out here. And it's getting late up in this piece...plus I'm getting tired of waiting out here."

Patience is the order of the day, dawg. *Patience!* I gotta stick to my usual mode of operation, my usual routine. It hasn't failed me yet, Ruh be praised, and I refuse to sweat any other technique.

"Two more and I'll get my water."

The method to my madness; it goes in steps. Step one, two, and three. And then I just, *step in the name of love. Step in the name of lo-o-ove!* That's my shit right there! *Step! Step! Side to side! Bring it back...* Let me chill though. I'm chillin' and shit.

Step One entails spotting a ripe one. She needs to be pretty much swole; maybe seven or eight months heavy into the process. But no less than seven months. I gets lots of water then.

Step Two is when I follow her. It usually takes me about two or three days to get to know her routine, what I like to call her "life points," because a lot of pregnant women will stay in the house for days on end. And I mean they don't come out for nothing! I personally don't know how they do it because most of them don't have a man around either to do shit for them. Yet they stay right in the house like they hibernating and shit. Watching women the way that I do, I've found out that most of them have a hole in their routines;

a weak spot that can be exploited, a vulnerable spot that can be used to snatch them from their "life points." I just take my time, wait for that moment, that glimpse into her downtime, and then I snatch me some ass. She becomes mine…her water becomes my water.

Which sequays, sekways, seqays—which leads me right into Step Three: That's when I use my gun. When I first started on my quest I was using a knife, but Ruh knew better. He told me to get a gun, so I went and got a .38 just like he told me. My own Flo Jigga. A woman will freeze right quick when she sees my piece, when she sees that I mean business. She'll do whatever I want her to do when she feels Flo Jigga in her back. What's funny is that I bet that if they were still alive they would probably kill themselves, each and every one of them, if they knew that I never put any bullets in my gun. No way would I take a chance like that again.

I remember the time I almost bit my own bullet! I remember that night well. It was the second woman that I had chosen to give her Ruh Water. She was really heavy pregnant, with the baby inside her, riding up high in her stomach. We were almost to the basement when she took me by surprise with one of those karate spin kicks right to the side of my head! And she was wearing a big pair of clodhoppers, too! Who would have thought her big, swollen ass could get her foot up that high! The gun flew out of my hand and clattered against the wall of the brick building in the alley. A flash of darkness passed before my eyes but my vision cleared in time for me to see her bending over to pick up my gun. I kicked her in the stomach and she fell to her knees, gasping in pain. I punched her in the back of the head a few times and dragged her to the basement. After that, I never loaded my gun again.

I have found that an unloaded gun works just as well as a loaded one so my Step Three is when I take her down to the basement, to the Altar of Ruh where she gives me the baby and the water. Shit! It ain't complicated! And it ain't no coincidence either! My Ruh is the answer to it all. He lightens my darkness.

My faith in Ruh is unshakeable. But lately, there have been shadows that are testing me. Phantoms have started haunting me, at night, in my dreams, torturing my sleep with sweat and fear. I ain't scared though. Ain't never scared. The noises, the cacophony, the clamor in the deep of the night are just maddening at times! The worst sounds imaginable are the ones that come from the darkness. The rhythm of the unknown, the cadence of chattering teeth hounds me from the edge of the abyss with some real scary shit!

I feel it sometimes on the back of my neck; the breath of the haunting that chases me but I have yet to actually turn back and look it in the face. I run from it…but I'm on a treadmill! The clacking of the teeth start gaining on me; echoes of it reverberate through my ribcage to my heart, and I know better than to turn and look back. But I can't help myself; fear can make a mind warp and do the strangest things and that is when I feel the tendrils of the darkness reach out and grab my soul.

Joselle is standing there! Naked! Nightmares do come true! The flesh on her face is ripped open, split wide and bloodless from where I beat her with the baseball bat. One of her eyes is twisted, mangled and hanging inside the socket. The other eye is watching me with a ghastly joy that terrifies me. My legs begin to pump faster; but I'm still on a treadmill to nowhere and for the first time since I was a kid, I hear my mother laugh. It is a sound I could have gone without hearing until hell froze over and I would've been satisfied. She didn't have any teeth left so her voice crawled out of her mouth with the wet resonance of snakes rolling over each other. I tried to scream but I squealed instead. In the midst of this madness it registers in my mind that Joselle is butt naked, that even in this deadly nightmare her body is still full with the ripeness of perfection. Blood suddenly burst from her nipples, flowing down her stomach to trace a horrid pathway between her legs. I feel the gorge rushing up my windpipe and spew out of my throat as I try to propel myself forward. Joselle simply points at me.

The din of clicking, clattering teeth grows louder and louder, intensifying, pulsing like a migraine, blossoming into a crescendo. The bright outline of a cartoon smile with the biggest, sharpest-looking teeth I have ever seen materializes at Joselle's side. Then another, and another, until she is surrounded by dozens of gleaming white teeth. Then the mouths start to open and close in a death cadence. Clacketty-clacketty, click! Clacketty-clacketty, click!

Joselle's mashed-up face breaks out into a ghastly grin and, as if on cue, the apparitions begin to materialize as they emerge from the darkness. An army of infants begins to advance on me. An insane thought stamps itself on my brain—it's an infantry! A fit of laughter seizes me and I fall to my knees convulsing and shrieking helplessly. Now I am at ground level and the babies continue to advance, marching toward me. Their teeth are so big and so sharp; but I can't seem to control my body's madness, I'm paralyzed. Darkness is reflected from each sharpened point but as they march into my field of vision I see that each infant is carrying a baseball bat. It only makes me collapse to the ground in hysterical laughter. The irony!

But the babies march on with purpose and as they get closer and closer to my prone body, I can feel the first infant's teeth as it clamps down on my face…and then I wake up screaming. I grow mad.

That shit is the devil's work…fucking with me. But I ain't scared. Ain't never scared. Ruh hasn't answered me yet but I know that he will. Who am I to question? In the meantime, I still have work to do. I still have water to make. Gotta find me a ripe one today.

CHAPTER 21
Ruh Water

I hate coming down to the welfare office. It stinks. The air is cloying, musty, stirred and jarred by body heat and proximity. I hate listening to muthafuckas bitching and moaning about government money that they think belongs to them. This shit is crazy! Pure madness! But I can quiet my hostility; I can gently force it down my gullet, suppress it with a smile and dance through the labyrinth of rage. After all, if you want to shop for shit, you have to go to the store…and the Social Services Office is my personal shopping ground.

I found a nice little spot so that I could watch everyone as they swing through the double doors on their way to find seats in the main room. The hallway where I'm sitting is cramped and stifling but the location is ideal; I can see whoever comes in while I remain nearly out of sight. Only problem that I have is that there seems to be an overflow of people up in here today. I already pushed my chair back up against the wall and the hallway is getting crowded with even more people. Three little kids, a boy and two girls, are squatted on the floor against the opposite wall playing a make-believe game of "gotcha." Their laughter and peals of joy are a stark contrast to the weariness on the faces of the adults. The noise is definitely getting on my nerves.

Time for a Ruh break. Time to take a moment and meditate with Ruh. I am going to settle back into my seat and let my mind float above this miasma of sweat-soaked poverty. Just for a minute. I can do that. Relax my mind and let it roam freely, up above, in the rafters where the dark demons of menace take shape. I can get there. Easily. I like all things dark; it's where I get my best ideas.

The children playing on the floor suddenly break out in squeals of laughter, poking fingers in each other's stomachs and giggling hysterically, just as I was getting ready to take off and soar.

Shut the hell up, you little brats! Somebody should have put a belt to your asses a while back, shit! Teach your little asses how to act in public.

I can just ignore them. I can calm down. Let me bring this thing down a bit. Let's chill. Just take it easy. Just slow.

I don't belong up in here with these people and I can't allow myself to get pissed off and start cussing and shit up in here. The one thing that I can do well is blend in with a crowd, sort of make myself a non-visible person. That is what I need to do now. Deep breath, baby. Breathe. Now I'm going to relax and take myself back up high, away from the poor people, away from the drab existence that they substitute for life.

"Next!"

My eyes pop open and the social worker is standing right in front of me. Now why did she have to scream like that? *Fat, white bitch!* She's fat and bulky, filling up the whole damn doorway, and now she got the nerve to smile with one of those shit-eating grins. She looks like one of those white women who thinks that she's sparkling with superiority, above it all while she moves amongst the downtrodden. She probably tells a mean ghost story—when she gets back home among her friends—about the spooks who sit by the doors. It's in her eyes. I see it there, in the corners where her stupid-ass smile don't reach, the bare spot of her pretensions. She doesn't know the realms of the high spirit of Ruh. She's a stranger to the picture of his genius and perfection…she only knows the mirage of pretense. Fat-ass girl! A few seats down from me an old black man jumped up and followed her into the office.

Later for her, I'm going back into myself. One by one, I'll just shut them out. Every extraneous distraction—I'm going to fade to black. The children. The stifling closeness. The hum of the furnace. They dissolve. Soon there is just D.Wayne floating in D.Wayne's world. Outwardly, I know that I am the picture of tranquility, the turmoil of my soul hidden from mere mortals, buried beneath a veneer of complete normalcy. Nothing about me hints at the depths of my impending greatness, of the legacy that I am destined to fill or the sacred path that I walk upon. True, I'm trapped inside of my skinny frame, but I won't be the first small man to command great respect. In fact, that underestimation of my value will make my triumph that much greater. By all accounts, I'm just plain normal. From my cocoa-colored skin to the short fade that I sport, there is just nothing about me that stands out…and that's no easy feat. I cultivate my non-entity status. My face has range; from serious to sensitive—whichever the situation warrants—and then I can switch up and present an openness that welcomes acquaintances with its friendly demeanor. I practice my appearance, my smile…perfecting my mortal self, in order to protect my messiah.

The darkness behind my closed eyelids flashes colors until I see light glowing in the distance, out on the horizon of my mind…waiting for me. I love it here. There's inspiration in this mind-play, joy in this mental journey to my spiritual playground. I love it here. This is where I first learned of my mortal legacy—The Wayne Foundation.

The Wayne Foundation is the exploration of obscurity…shining in its ebon flow, built, brick by brick, upon the ebullient work of my forebears. A spiritual flare of genetic wonder. That's how I see it. The Foundation is indicative of a lust lost, only to be regained by the few, the proud and the chosen.

The founding member of the Wayne Foundation was Jigsaw Wayne Jenkins. He was an artist, a sculptor of the human anatomy and the beauty of its missing pieces. Jigsaw Wayne saw the aesthetic in the square-peg-in-the-round-hole theory. He believed that flesh was pliable and malleable, able to conform to any shape or size. His carvings of astral emanations and lunar equivalencies were cut into the bodies of seventeen hapless victims, each one dying as Jigsaw watched and waited for his answers.

Jigsaw's machinations merely laid the foundation for those to come.

Wayne Chillcut was next in line to vie for the presidency. I think that Chillcut was lacking in many respects even though he had taken over thirty-five souls from the face of the earth. Reportedly, Chillcut had paced himself, capturing one woman per year, tying them to a steel table in his barn and torturing them by injecting them with syringes full of household cleansers like ammonia, bleach and drain cleaners. Then he would wait for god to speak through his victims because their souls were clean. Chillcut was a madman looking for a theme song that only he could hear.

Others followed…Wayne "Twang" Seale who favored guitar strings and piano wire as his instruments of death. Then there was Charles Wayne Kissler with his kiss of death accompanied by five, exactly five, killing thrusts of his razor-sharp knife. After him was Country Wayne Philbert who cut up his women and fed them to his pigs.

The Wayne Foundation had many members who came before me but they had all fallen short of the glory of genius. They had all been caught, jailed or executed for the hundreds of deaths accumulated at their hands. I'm different from them and not only because I have Ruh on my side. Some of them reeked of stupidity, some were just plain unimaginative, while others were simply obsessed. But none of them could look into the astral plane and receive the divine guidance that I am blessed with. Yeah, I'm different.

I'm Black.

White boys are always fucking shit up. They are privileged and they always let that get in the way, dulling the sharpness needed to operate at peak capacity, which results in mistakes and inevitable capture. It's difficult trying to maintain earthly focus when you're sitting on top of the world and the stars are always within arm's reach.

I'm a Black man. Anything they could do, I can do better…and I will be king.

I can feel a sigh inside my mind-play, the cool breeze of my secret life and my secret dreams. This is a part of me that even Ruh can't touch. This is the part of my essence that is surrounded by ethereal light, the pulse of my spirit that beats with a message all its own.

"Peace, I will." I speak to the echoes as the light fades and my senses return to the real world's invasion of my private place. I always enjoy my little trips into my secret place; it's my own version of a mental pat on the back.

"Oh yeah, oh yeah!" I have to sing, rocking in the chair to the chanting of my soul beat as the noise and clatter of the waiting room invades my mental space. The crowded hallway; the musty, dead air; the laughing children, all slowly come back into focus. My heart is humming inside my chest, no longer beating but riding the rhythm of my song. My fate is burned into my being, ingenious and spiritual and waiting to be fulfilled. And with joy in my heart and awe in my eyes, I look to the front door of the welfare office as the door slowly opens. And Joozy, my Queen, walked in.

CHAPTER 22
Falasha

J oozy heaved a heavy sigh and squared her shoulders against the anxiety that pushed up against her as she prepared herself to run the gauntlet called Social Services. She pushed through the doors of the big, gray building and consulted the directory in the hallway. The employment office was on the third floor. Joozy took the elevator up and stepped off into a large office with rows of chairs that sat facing a bank of counters with service reps sitting behind them. It had been a few weeks since Joozy had moved in with Doin and now she had finally decided upon a course of action. Doin had insisted that she take a few days to sit down and think, really give it some thought, about what she wanted to do with her life. He had told her that half of the battle in life was enjoying whatever job she chose and that once the objective was clear, she could set about achieving it. Joozy had spent her days trying to figure out which path to take and finally decided that she would start where the jobs were.

She stood at the entranceway and surveyed the waiting room. The rows of chairs were occupied by quite a few people. Some sat with blank expressions, others read newspapers, while some looked up expectantly at the video display screens that hung above each booth. Joozy went to the front of the room and snatched a number from the dispenser. She glanced at it, B701, and walked toward the back of the room and took a seat.

Heads turned as she made her way to the seat. When they saw that she wasn't the solution to all of their problems they turned back to the gossiping hum that accompanied the idle morning. From the corner of her eye she noticed a woman sitting two chairs over from her. She had the most beautiful skin that Joozy had ever seen. It was light brown with a little cocoa rubbed lightly into its surface, which was marble smooth and flawless. The dark brown blouse that she wore complemented the soft tone of her dark eyes. Joozy fought the urge to run her fingers across her own roughened cheeks. Skin problems had plagued her all of her life and, looking at the lady who sat beside her, Joozy wished that she could have lived at least one day without a blemish on her face.

Ugly memories assailed her but she pushed them away with the promise of hope that her life now held. She had spent the night with Doin, talking and planning the direction that their lives would take. They had silently agreed to build a life together and it had taken Joozy all night to come to grips with the joy that she felt. *Just once*, she prayed. *Just this once.* A smile crept across her face.

She had gotten up early in the morning to be the first in the office. But now the crowds were beginning to form lines from the doorway to the metal detectors at the entranceway to the room. Gray, ugly clouds darkened the early morning skies outside and the dreary atmosphere was clinging to the unruly disposition of the destitute. It wouldn't take much to turn the average person into an ass any time before eight in the morning; sort of like Cinderella at midnight with her slipper falling off.

A line was forming, snaking its way through the "S"-shaped rope walkway that led up to the smart-aleck, old white lady who sat behind a long, thick table. A Black man stepped up to her with his papers in his hand. He was dressed in a pair of baggy jeans and a dark-blue sweatshirt that clung to his skinny frame. His baby-blue sneakers looked out-of-the-box brand-new, and he moved with ease as he looked down at the lady.

She looked at him and smiled. "How may I help you?"

"Yeah." His voice was shrill. "You can give me my shit!"

Her smile disappeared. "Excuse me?!"

"My shit!" He spoke calmly, no threat implied.

"Oh! Your shit. I see. What about your shit?"

"They trying to say that I quit my job, so they sent me down here." He laid his papers down on her desk. "I want my shit."

The old lady took a moment to read his paperwork, handed it back to him and gave him a number. "Your 'shit' is back there. Take a number. Next."

He took his number but he didn't budge. Her gray head bobbed back up when the man didn't move on and after a tense moment elapsed, he spoke. "Thank you for your service." He turned and walked past the first few rows of chairs and took the seat near Joozy.

"Hey," he spoke to Joozy. She shifted and leaned slightly away from him.

"Hi," she answered.

"These people down here ain't shit." His voice was flat, empty. "There's more than just one reason for being down here. But they will try to dismiss you like you are something that they stepped in on their way here. Next! Next my black ass!"

Joozy turned her head and smiled. The lady with the beautiful skin, who had heard the guy rambling, returned her smile. There was the hint of understanding in that smile and Joozy felt compelled to return the warmth that it radiated. She looked down at the floor and then looked straight ahead. The guy next to her was still talking.

"She's an old white ass, too, ain't she? She needs to know the power of Ruh. Power of God." He shifted in his seat and put his full attention on Joozy. His eyes traced the outline of her face, inch by inch, taking note of each feature before rising up and looking into her eyes. Joozy returned his brazen stare with a glare of her own, daring him to go there. He leaned back in his chair and smiled at her. Joozy turned away from him and looked forward again.

A teenage girl stood in line. She had two kids in tow; a little boy walked next to her, clinging to the carriage where her newborn baby lay. She spoke to the lady seated at the table, shook her head once and took a number. She settled in the row of chairs slightly behind where Joozy sat. Joozy could hear her fussing at the little boy to sit still and behave.

"Hi. How you?" the guy spoke to the young girl.

"Good morning," came the reply.

"Good morning!" The little boy piped up.

"Good morning, little man!" The guy turned to Joozy again. "Excuse me, miss. I hope you don't get offended. I mean nothing but the utmost respect, but I notice that you have some dark-ass skin!" Joozy raised her eyebrows in response. "You Black! And I think that is the most beautifullest thing given from Ruh. My God above." He reached his finger toward Joozy's skin. "May I?" he asked. Joozy instantly went on the defensive, eyes hard as she regarded the stranger who wanted to touch her face. She looked in his eyes and saw that he was sincere, as if it would be an honor. Slowly, she relented. Without a word he ran his finger along her jaw line and then gently across her cheek. "Man! I love skin!"

A sudden blush crept inside of Joozy and a smile spread across her face. It was obvious that the guy had been earnest in his open admiration and she was not accustomed to such public displays. His touch had smoldered; but Doin's was fire. She felt her smile deepen with the lustful memory.

"That was a 'man' smile. Your man, huh?" The brown woman with the flawless skin smiled over at Joozy. "He was right about one thing," she said. "Your Black skin is beautiful. You have to know that."

Joozy shook her head and responded. "But yours is so smooth and soft-looking."

"Yours is beautiful, too." She looked at Joozy for a second. "We can't separate ourselves like that. We are sisters, right?" A commotion broke out at the front desk. A man stood over the gray-haired lady and glared at her. He stood with his legs planted slightly apart, rooted to the spot. His eyes sparkled with anger behind lips that were set in a determined tightness.

"We can't help you with that, sir," the old lady barked at him.

His demeanor never changed. He wore a woolen sweater with a giant "U" embossed on the chest, and his chinos were pressed and neat. He held the posture of an assured man as he slowly leaned forward and rested his hands on the table. His hair was short and wavy with a small part that was a few inches long. He seemed to be a man at home in the center of confrontation.

"This is Social Services, right." He watched her.

"Yes." Her voice was firm. "But we..."

"Well, serve society then! Do your job! Now...you asked me, 'May I help you?'...you did ask me that! You said, 'May I help you?' and I said, 'yes'...so help me! Come on with the reparations!"

"I can't help you with that!"

"Oh, and don't act like you don't have it," he continued. "Because you do."

"We don't do reparations here." The old lady was instantly wary.

"You don't 'do' them anywhere! That's the problem! You do jack doo-doo is what you do. You are strictly 'butt' on this issue! And I don't understand you. Does being Black mean so little to ya'll...and by 'ya'll' I mean white people, the government, crackers and any other cog of the machine that functions purely to deny me what should be mine...is our contribution colored by the color of our skin."

The entire room had gotten quiet while the man at the table spoke and now his words were echoing throughout the waiting room. Monotony was temporarily displaced. "I mean, you gave the Japanese people reparations for putting them in concentration camps! But slavery! I guess slavery was for free." He paused to regard the old white lady watching him from behind her desk. "Where your boss at? I betcha he a cracker, too! Come on with the reparations."

The old lady stood from her seat and motioned to the spooks that sat by the door.

"Is there a problem?" They suddenly appeared on both sides of the man.

"Yes, security guards, there is," the man replied calmly. "I'm here to apply for reparations. Your co-worker here seems to have a problem with that. She seems to think that I am asking for the money directly out of her pocket, and she's copping quite an attitude. But this government institution is the gateway to my money. Come on with the reparations."

The guards looked to the old lady for clarification, which led to an explanation, which led to further disagreement.

The woman next to Joozy spoke up. "The world would be a much better place if they gave us reparations for racial and social injustice."

"Reparations?" Joozy kept her eye on the man and the security guards at the front desk.

"Yes," she replied. "Payments for the work that our ancestors did during slavery. Straight cash value."

"You know that shit is right," the guy who sat near Joozy exclaimed. She had managed to forget that he was sitting there. "Twenty acres and a mule, shit! They owe, Pookie. They owe." He looked directly at Joozy. "By the way…my name is D.Wayne. What's yours?"

"Joozy."

"Hi, Joozy."

"Hi," she replied, followed by an expectant silence. Joozy looked over at the woman sitting next to her. She smiled.

The man at the front desk was involved in an animated discussion with the old lady.

"So how much would reparations be for?" Joozy asked her. "How much money?"

"I don't know," she replied. "But I'll settle for two dollars an hour."

"Two dollars?"

"Yessir. Take two dollars for forty hours a week times four weeks a month times about two hundred years! We would just have some money! And we're not counting overtime!"

"That would be a grip." Joozy shook her head, imagining the stacks of money. "But then they'll start charging us five hundred dollars a day for air!"

"They tryin' to cut off my air." D.Wayne shook his head.

"I'll probably blow all of that money though," Joozy reasoned.

"Me! I would put it all away and do like them Jews do," D.Wayne said. "I'll jew it away and save it and shit, Praise Ruh. You know how they do."

Joozy and the woman exchanged a glance.

"Now that is what you call stereotyping people," the woman spoke clearly. "Black folks…we supposed to know better than that but here we are, still doing the same thing. Judging people." She spoke directly to D.Wayne. "All Jewish people are not alike."

"How you know?" D.Wayne smirked.

"Because I know," she replied.

"No. No. How you know?"

"Simple," she replied. "Because I'm Jewish."

"You Jewish," Joozy exclaimed loudly. The sound of heads whipping toward them boomed like cannons in her ears and Joozy looked at the woman apologetically and uttered, "Oops." The woman watched Joozy squirm in her seat for a second before she smiled and then she laughed out loud. She reached over and covered Joozy's hand with her own, reassuring.

"Yes," she answered. "I am Jewish."

"How are you Jewish?" A young, dark-skinned man who sat in the row of seats directly behind D.Wayne looked up from the magazine that he was reading. "I mean…I didn't even know if that was possible. Is it?"

"Ain't no Black folks is Jews," commanded an older man who turned in his seat to voice his opinion on the matter. Whorls of gray swirled through his short, nappy hair. His nose was wide and dented at the peak in the shape of a monkey knuckle as he watched the woman with a challenging stare.

"Aw no, now that's not true." The young man sat up in his chair. "Sammy Davis said he was a Jew!" He turned back to the woman. "How is that possible?"

"Ain't no Black folks is Jews!"

"I. Am. Jewish." The woman was firm.

"How you a real Jew?" The older man plunged on, daringly. "The real Jews was, like in the Holocaust and shit."

"Aw no, I can't agree with that," the young man intervened. "A Christian is a Christian. A Jew is a Jew."

"Now how in the world can you say something like that? They's all kinda Jews now! There's the Orthodox and the Unorthodox, there's the…" The man stopped when he heard the signal that accompanied the next number being called and he glanced down at the stub in his hand. "That's me," he said and hurried over to the counter.

"So what kind of Jew are you?" The young man inquired. "I hope that's the right way to ask."

"Yeah." D.Wayne sat up and studied Joozy's face.

"I'm an Ethiopan Jew," the woman answered. "I'm a direct descent of an

African tribe. My ancestors were nearly wiped out for not converting to Christianity. After the slaughter there were only about 30,000 of my tribe left alive. We are still Jews."

"For reals," Joozy replied.

"For real," came the reply.

"So what happened to your tribe?" Joozy questioned. "Do you have a tribal name? What's the name of your tribe?"

The woman answered Joozy with a tolerant smile. "I was named after my tribe. Falasha."

CHAPTER 23
Nigga Ways

Joozy and Falasha walked briskly to the park in quiet desperation. The gravity of Joozy's problem was outweighed by the impending moment of truth that was dreadfully approaching.

Falasha and Joozy had grown close; their friendship was instantaneous and without question. She quickly became the best friend that Joozy had ever known, the girlfriend that she could talk to about anything at all. Despite her predicament of the moment, Joozy couldn't help but wonder at the improbability of their friendship.

At first glance, they appeared to be complete opposites. Falasha's skin was a burnished light brown; her face contained a classic yet modern beauty that was unique. She wore her hair gently down past her shoulders, curly and full, and her eyes were a dark shade of gray that was deep and hypnotic. Her lips weren't full and lush like Joozy's but there was never a shortage of hungry men who ached to taste them. She exuded a raw sensuality that flowed from her like hot water.

Joozy, on the other hand, was on the opposite end of the spectrum. Her face was dark black and laced with hard, rough edges. Pimples dotted her skin forming little, purple starbursts. Her eyes were hawkish, predatory and harsh, and her hair was short and rough. At times she still wondered what Doin found so appealing about her.

She and Falasha were as different as night and day, yet they had grown as close as night and day. Falasha's friendship was precious to her and Joozy was grateful that their bond was growing stronger with each passing day. So when Joozy needed moral support there was only one person that she could call; and Falasha had been right there for her.

Doin had a job interview scheduled, so he would be out of the house for most of the day. For once Joozy was glad that she had the run of the place, some time to herself so that she could creep on the downlow, and find some definitive answers, be they bad or good. She loved Doin and she hated keeping secrets from him but honesty wasn't always the best policy—especially this time.

As soon as he walked out the door, Joozy called Falasha and told her to hurry up because the matter was urgent.

Joozy had the pregnancy test set up in her bathroom by the time Falasha rang her doorbell. When she opened the door Falasha must have seen the worry etched into her face. "Oh, girl!" Falasha embraced her. "Come on, now! You know that you need to do this. Come on, now."

Joozy managed to smile through her tears. Falasha knew that she was scared and her comforting words found their mark. Falasha was straight and strong. She had a way of emasculating problems, stripping them bare and exposing them to the light, making them seem less imposing. Joozy returned her embrace and closed the door behind her. She led Falasha over to the couch and they sat facing each other. "Did you take it yet?" Falasha looked at her.

"I'm scared." Joozy looked at the floor. "Yes, I understand that." Falasha's voice was soothing as she took her hand. "What do you think might happen?"

Joozy knew what Falasha meant. If the results were positive, life would take a serious off-ramp for her. And she had no idea how Doin would react to the news. Lately, he had been coming home full of frustration at his inability to obtain employment and though he hardly complained, Joozy knew that his pride was taking a beating.

"I don't know, Lasha," Joozy answered on the brink of tears again. "I don't know what he's going to say. I just gotta let nature run that show." Joozy stood up and began pacing the room. "I mean, we didn't ever talk about having no baby. We haven't even been together that long. But I fell in love with him so fast though, Lasha! And he feels me, too! I know he does? But a baby! He ain't ready for that. Hell! I ain't even ready for that my damn self!"

Joozy suddenly stopped and turned to Falasha with eyes as round as saucers. "What if he thinks that I'm trying to trap him with a baby?"

Falasha regarded her calmly. "I thought you said that he loves you?"

"He does! He's a good man. That much I know."

"That means that he knows you," Falasha continued.

"Yeah?"

"So he should know that you would never do this on purpose, right?"

"Well, Falasha," Joozy thought for a minute before she spoke. "I see you still got some of that naïve shit running around in your brain, huh?"

Falasha looked at her, waiting.

"It's obvious. You don't know about nigga ways, do you?"

Joozy's voice turned hard as she recalled her life lessons learned at the hands of hard, cruel men in the days when she had been ready for love and open to pain. "Nigga ways!" Joozy repeated at Falasha's questioning look. "It's like this, Lasha. Say that you and a nigga were locked up in a room for eight straight months? Eight months! And a week after ya'll get out of that room you told him that you were three months' pregnant. Do you know what a nigga would say?"

Joozy rumbled on before Falasha could answer. She stood and assumed a dramatic stance. "Who baby is that." Joozy dropped her voice down low as she completed her verbal ghetto pose. "Ain't my baby! Where the blood test at? Where the blood test at?" Joozy had her act down perfectly and they both had to laugh at the sublime truthfulness. She flopped back onto the couch. "Niggas," she groaned.

Falasha finally spoke up. "So do you put Doin in that category? Because I see the way that he looks at you and I can't categorize that. Now, I know that I'm on the outside looking in, but you two seem to have something special going on here." Falasha fixed Joozy with her stare. "Can't you trust that?"

Joozy was quiet, contemplative. Falasha was right. She had nothing but tender spots as far as Doin was concerned and he touched them each and every day. She glowed with the warmth of loving him so much. And part of that love was the trust, security and sincerity that they found in each other's hearts. She had to trust that.

"Ai-ight." She stood. "Time to take this pregnancy test."

Falasha squeezed her hand reassuringly.

"Be back in a minute." Joozy headed to the bathroom. She emerged a short while later and quietly announced in a tremulous voice, "We gotta wait for fifteen minutes."

Her forced bravado had vanished and Falasha patted the seat next to her. Joozy plopped down and they clung to each other for a moment.

Time dragged by as if someone had tied a two-ton weight to each second. The waiting rubbed Joozy's nerves raw and she began to talk incessantly. Jabbering nonsense in her anxiety. "What if I ain't ready?" Joozy jumped up from the couch. She prowled around the living room, her hands holding her stomach, cradling it expectantly. "I know Doin ain't ready. We both ain't ready for no baby!" She paused to look at Falasha. "I guess we should have been thinking about this. We were in bed a lot. We made love a lot. You know how it goes when the newness is still there. Our feelings and touches and everything is still so new. But that don't make for a good daddy. Lasha! What am I gonna do?"

Falasha grabbed Joozy by the hand and pulled her down to the couch next to her. "Joozy, you're nervous," she said. "You're babbling."

"I know. I know. And I don't feel too hot neither."

"Joozy, you're going to have to slow your roll, okay! Slow down a little. You're sweating."

"Is it too early to have that morning sickness thing?"

"Joozy?"

"My heartbeat is too fast."

"Joozy!"

"I got butterflies. Lots and lots of butterflies."

"Joozy," Faslasha said. "Stand up. Walk around."

"No," Joozy answered. "I'm all right."

"Scared?"

"Hell yeah! What time is it?"

Falasha said nothing, but she kept her eye on the clock. She sat with Joozy as she agonized the time away. Twenty minutes later she nudged Joozy knowingly. Time was up. Time to quit the stalling. Joozy rose slowly and walked into the bathroom to meet her fate.

"Blue" meant "not pregnant." "Pink" meant that she had issues.

The sound of the toilet flushing preceded silence before Joozy emerged from the bathroom with a vacant look on her face. She turned to Falasha and uttered one word.

"Pink."

With that she walked straight out the front door. Falasha got up and quietly followed her. They were still walking. Joozy's expression bore the harshness of fear; a look that invited no conversation but Falasha was too worried about her friend to let her stew in such a dangerous void.

"Joozy?"

Joozy kept on walking. Marching seemed the more appropriate description of her stride.

"Joozy? What's on your mind? What are you going to do?"

When she didn't answer, Falasha grabbed her by the arm and spun her around.

"Joozy!" she demanded.

"What! I don't know!" Joozy snapped. "I might lose him. He might run. He might not want any children. See, Lasha. Doin had a bad childhood, so he might put that picture in this movie. But I know one thing! He is gonna take part of the responsibility for this baby 'cause I ain't giving it up. He ain't getting away with that deadbeat-daddy shit neither! You can bet your last money on that!"

"But you're already assuming the worst."

"No, I'm just keeping it real, Lasha," Joozy said solemnly. "Just... for real. See, this is more than a baby. This is eighteen years of commitment. From snot nose to 'who knows,' ya' know! Eighteen years of me and the baby. That'll scare the average bear, Lasha."

"So, that's your approach to this." Falasha sounded doubtful.

"Hardline and hardcore," Joozy rasped. She had gotten defensive, she had put up her dukes, and she was knocking out any buster in the vicinity. Her best offense became her defense.

Falasha tried to penetrate Joozy's newfound armor as they sat on the park bench overlooking the river but Joozy turned inward. Falasha was distressed by the anger on Joozy's face and she couldn't decipher her friend's mood or gauge the depths of her inner conflict. This was an issue that Joozy would have to handle solo. Falasha determined that her only option was to be a friend. Be a friend and be there for her.

"You know," Joozy said more to herself than Falasha. "One time. There was this girl who lived up by me. She got pregnant and her boyfriend went and got his 'nigga ways.' He ain't pay no child support, he ain't buy no Pampers, no baby food or nothin' else. You know her silly ass would not take him to court for nothin'! He walkin' around here now with his no-good ass! No worries!" Joozy's voice rose as she continued. "Not me though! I ain't havin' it!"

Falasha stayed with her until Joozy said that she needed some time alone to think things through. They parted ways at the corner of Warren Street and Central Avenue and Joozy headed up the street with no destination in mind. She needed time to think. For her baby.

Not once had she noticed the man who discreetly followed them; the man who had been trailing Joozy for the past two days. He lagged behind them on the other side of the street, careful to always stay out of their line of vision, stalking and rationalizing his madness…while praying to Ruh.

CHAPTER 24
Hymm's Stop

The bus stop at the corner of Iliff Avenue consisted of a cold, metal bench accompanied by a red and blue sign that listed the numbers of the buses that serviced the area. Doin waited patiently for his bus; he had a job interview with a janitorial service uptown. His job search was proving hopelessly futile and he felt desperation setting in. He was now to the point where he would take any position that was offered. There were three other people at the bus stop standing around waiting for the #2 Jay Street to arrive and Doin's glance settled on the old lady standing off to the side next to the sign. She wore a white skullcap and was mumbling curses as she rocked back and forth. Her face seemed oblong, her forehead bulged slightly, and her eyes were off kilter because her lips protruded at odd angles. A young woman who looked to be about Doin's age stood at a cautious distance while trying to keep a watchful eye and ignore her at the same time. Long, flowing hair framed her face and her makeup was flawless. Her eyes were pretty and expressive. They complemented the cocoa tone of her skin that played nicely against the tan outfit. It was over a full figure—evident, even though her clothes were loose-fitting. Doin took a moment to admire her figure, comparing her curves to Joozy's frame and realized that beauty comes in all shapes and sizes.

"Good evening." A slightly built man came bustling over to the bus stop, pausing to smile at the girl with the tan outfit.

"Hi," she said. He regarded her, expectantly, but the treatment he got was silence so he gave up the ghost and took a seat on the bench next to Doin. "You know what time the next bus supposed to be here," he said.

Doin paused a moment before answering. The man wore a gray suit jacket that was unbuttoned, revealing a black shirt with a mandarin collar, the buttons hidden by design. He spoke with the self-assurance of a man who has been "right" all of his life; a fact that was undone by the freshly pressed blue jeans he wore and the razor-sharp crease ironed into them. Doin had seen the type before; a Rico-Suave, smooth-talking nerd.

"Doesn't matter much, does it?" Doin said. "Either way you still have to sit right here and wait. Won't you?"

"Hah!" The old lady barked. She was still rocking back and forth all by herself. "Sho nuff will! Got to wait just like eva-body else. Young folks today..." Her voice trailed off as she returned to her private ramblings.

"Hey, I was just asking a question," the man said. "Just asking, was all."

"Well, let me ask you a question then," Doin said. "What is up with this combination that you wearing? Huh? For real."

"My combination?"

"Yeah! Now the jacket and the shirt... I'm with you on that. Those two are working. But the jeans, yo! I mean you are trying to impress somebody, right? So you have to explain the jeans to me. Inquiring minds want to know."

The pretty woman with the tan outfit looked over and smirked.

"It's just my style, my friend," the man said. "Just my style."

"E-e-e-e, y-e-e-ahhh!" The old lady was rocking furiously now. "Duh yeah!" They both glanced at her but they quickly averted their gazes, lapsing into silence as they waited. After a few moments of suddenly awkward quiet, the girl standing on the other side of them began to glance at her watch, alternately looking expectantly up the street for the bus.

"Damn!" Doin said.

"This bus is late, right?" Doin turned to look at the man seated next to him. "I'll be on C.P. time in a few minutes. I'll be feeding right into one of those stereotypes. Damn, I hate that."

"Yeah. But if you think about it, you're feeding into one of those stereotypes just sitting here waiting to 'get on the bus' anyway, so what does it matter?" After what seemed like a long moment, he broke out in a smile and extended his hand.

"Excuse me, my man," he said. "My name is Hymm."

"Him?" Doin said.

"H-Y-M-M," he spelled out.

"Nice to meet you, Hymm." Doin shook his hand. "I'm Doin."

"That's Doin?"

"Right. Doin."

The unmistakable clacking of high heels rang out into the air. Female rhythm. A definite female crunch, a sexy noise that both men recognized caused them to turn, waiting in quiet expectation, hoping that the watching would be worth the waiting. Doin imagined that he heard hips swooshing as the woman approached. A thinly veiled smirk of disgust spread across the young woman's face at the bus stop, then she looked repeatedly at her watch before she turned away from the approaching figure. When the woman came into view Doin and Hymm snapped to attention. She was a hooker. A "get your money out and throw it at her" hooker. And as she came strolling past the two men, wearing an outfit that left only dirty thoughts to the imagination, they didn't bother to hide their appreciation of the blatant flesh show. Her chest was firm, ripe and full; cups of perfection that rippled with carnality, without any unnecessary bouncing or flopping. She wore a top that was tight enough to conform to every inch of her tits, nipples extended, yet her stomach was tapered and flat, speaking directly to each man's libido and stunning their lust into a mute state. Doin managed to slap the bench in protest while Hymm could only stomp his feet in applause. She glanced at them with a bland expression, as if their response was neither vile nor insulting, just a blasé outburst, and she dismissed them as she went on her way. Yet even as she walked down the street, they were given the full view of the roundness that swayed to and fro, full and firm. She wore the shortest miniskirt that had ever come out of a paint can; it was painted onto her hips and thighs, and there wasn't enough room between fabric and flesh for anything thicker than a lustful thought. The fishnet pantyhose that she wore clung to her legs for dear life and only heightened the urge that both men could only express with thoughtless grunts.

Doin slapped the bench harder. "Damn! Damn! Damn!"

Hymm stomped his feet. "She poured them panties on! Poured 'em on!"

"You wouldn't know what to do with that," Doin told Hymm as they watched her walk away.

"Not the first couple of times, I wouldn't," Hymm said. They continued to watch the fleshy display until the hooker faded from view.

"But she might want my whole check though," Doin said.

"Might?" Hymm was smiling. "There's no question about that. And in this economy, she would break me *and* my nut! I have to live for more than that. Much more than a cheap thrill." The tan woman turned to look at them. "Or a pretty face." Hymm finished.

"But dayum!" Doin said. The loud screeching of the bus' brakes signaled that the #2 Jay Street had arrived. They quickly paid the fare and made their way to the back, taking the two bench seats that faced each other. There were only a few passengers onboard, scattered at safe distances from each other, each staring out of the windows watching the city go by as the bus pulled away from the curb and into traffic.

"So... my man," Hymm spoke to Doin. "Tell me something. What are you doing right now?"

"I'm headed up past the mall. I'm going to get me some work. Ain't that what you about to do?"

"Well, actually I'm involved in something that is much more than work. That's why I'm asking you... Not so much as what are you doing, as much as 'where is your head at' right about now. If you're not working, what are you doing about that?"

The two men eyed each other for a moment before Doin finally spoke.

"Well, um, I'm looking, that's what. Why? You got a job for me?"

"How has the 'just looking' gone for you so far? Got anything that looks good?"

"What do you mean?"

"Has 'just looking,' especially looking for whatever comes at you...has that gotten you to any type of financial satisfaction?"

"Yeah, it has. At times."

"That's just a fancy way of saying no." Hymm's tone was solemn. "You see, my man, financial satisfaction is a few steps above that payday-to-payday type of hustle. Financial satisfaction is when money is not the meaning of your existence; your existence begins to mean money. You heard!" There was a glint of quiet anxiety in Hymm's eye. Steely determination laced a stare that suddenly seemed to contain a deep, dark menace; as if he was a man of action who would run anyone over who got in his way. Yet his expression seemed open somehow, allowing for room in his manner; there was firmness, not a hard-line to his convictions. But the fact remained that he was here, sitting across the aisle from Doin...on the city transit.

"Yeah, that is indeed tight," Doin said. "That's tight. But can you accomplish that? Because you are talking this shit on the bus. With me."

"I'm on my way, bruh," Hymm said. "I'm on my way."

"What you saying then? That the bus is taking you there? 'Cause I got news for you!"

"Just a temporary break in the race is all." Hymm leaned back in the seat and looked out of the window. "I'm just getting back in the blocks right now."

The bus pulled up to a stoplight at the intersection of Chambers and Grant Streets. They were skirting the edges of the hood now as evidenced by the small, dirty houses that ran up each side of the street. There was a group of people standing in the dirt yard of a green and white house on the corner. They formed a circle around a man and a woman who were fighting, doing some serious knuckle busting and kicking up dust as they rolled around in the grass-less yard. The woman rolled on top of the man and a beer bottle appeared in her hand that she brought down viciously and cracked him on the top of his head. The light turned green and the bus continued up the street. Hymm turned back to Doin.

"What are some of your areas of interest, Doin?"

"Making money," Doin said. Hymm gave him a blank look. "Seriously, though," Doin said. "Mostly I do manual labor. Physical type work. Why you ask?"

"But if you had an option, a dream job, what would it be? What would be your field of expertise?"

"I don't know," Doin said.

"Just dream, Doin! Dream job!"

"I guess that I could get into some technical shit."

"Technical?"

"Yeah. Like computers. Programming or analysis or something like that."

"You feel that you would have strength in that area?" Hymm said.

"Yeah," Doin said, warming to the notion. "Yeah. Computers. I could use my brain for a living instead of killing my body all the time. And I would get paid out the gluteus maximal!"

Hymm smiled. "So you have an analytical mind?"

"Somewhat," Doin said. "Logical."

"Given that, answer this question," Hymm said. "If you combine all the factors of your life, the sum total of your existence, why are you limited?"

Doin was taken aback at the bluntness of the question but before he could recover, Hymm continued. "Now I don't need to tell you that analysis requires cold, hard and honest evaluation. Self-evaluation."

The bus rolled noisily to a stop. The doors screamed metallically in protest as they opened, and an old woman fought her way onto the bus, each step an obvious distress. Hymm and Doin watched her struggle until she made it to one of the seats in the front. The bus rolled on.

"Now me," Hymm said. "I'm a New York power hitter. I'm like Barry Bonds. I'm all over the park, spraying hits in every direction. Right field. Left field. Dead center over the fence. And I do it all straight out of the box."

Doin regarded Hymm with a bemused grin. "Now you know Barry Bonds ain't no New York nuthin."

"But analytically you know exactly what I mean, right?"

The bus pulled up to another stop and two young hoods boarded the bus. One wore a bandanna that covered most of his short-cropped hair, and the other had a head shaved so clean that light reflected from its smoothness. They both wore oversized jeans that sagged off their hips, jailhouse style, with matching throwback, Negro League baseball jerseys. They bustled past Hymm and Doin and went to the back of the bus, taking seats across from each other but facing forward.

Hymm seemed unconcerned with the two young men but Doin was wary. The world is a senseless place and Doin knew that youth could often be a wellspring for insanity. He wasn't that far removed from the crazy age himself, even though he considered himself a fully grown adult. Most of his foolishness had passed him by when his face had been ripped open on the storefront window that fateful, drunken night.

"I hit for power," Hymm continued. "And I don't bullshit. Now that's me. My own self-evaluation."

Out of the corner of his eye Doin noticed the kid with the bandanna on his head and wearing a Black Sox jersey. He nudged his partner, who wore a Monarchs jersey, and nodded his head in Hymm's direction. Hymm leaned toward Doin and held up his finger as if he had just captured an elusive thought.

"Doin," he said. "Let me ask you something. Do you believe that a person is the sum total of all their life's experience?"

"Nope," Doin said. "Can't agree with that."

"What don't you agree with?"

"The sum total of *all* of your life's experience! No. Sometimes the future can shape a person."

Hymm edged forward, intrigued. "So if I was a person who chased my dreams, that distant dream defines a part of me?"

"You simplified my answer and you got it wrong," Doin said. "Anyway… what does all of this have to do with a job?"

Hymm studied Doin intently before he spoke. "Doin. That scar on your face. How has that experience shaped you?"

Doin fought the angry response that leapt to mind. He had never given the question any thought and that struck him as funny. Usually, his scar was off the limits of conversation and most people would surmise that the subject was taboo. But Hymm had gone there anyway.

He couldn't possibly understand; no one could. Especially a nerd whose face was unblemished, clean. When Hymm looked in the mirror he could afford to self-evaluate. He could have good hair days and bad hair days, be unshaven and still be cool. Doin wondered what it was like to look down from the world of normalcy and have the nerve to question a deformed person about their deformity; sort of like asking the rape victim about the rape.

Doin's hand curled into a tightly clenched fist and he felt the heat begin to build under his skin. His anger was lifelong and deep...and fragile. Buried in a denial of muck and mire yet rekindled, reawakened with a stranger on a bus. He had erected a wall around the torn tissue, a barrier that sometimes threatened to encompass his soul in darkness, an emptiness that was serpentine and venomous.

Flames danced before his eyes; a madness that he fooled himself into thinking that he had dealt with years ago. At least he felt that he had shoved this demon into a mad box, locked it and cast it away; yet Hymm had brought it back to life with mere words.

The bus seemed to fill with a surreal silence that was pregnant with expectation. Doin clenched and unclenched his fist. His mind raced, desperate to find that place of control, the calm place. He glanced at the two youngsters sitting at the back of the bus. They had heard the entire exchange and now watched and waited, sensing the hostility in Doin, keenly aware of the tension that thickened the air. An old adage occurred to Doin. *Don't ever let anybody know where your goat is tied. Then they can always get your goat.*

Hymm finally broke the silence. "Yeah. I thought so."

Doin didn't trust himself to speak. He didn't sense that Hymm was being malicious; in fact, he felt that there was some deeper meaning to their conversation—a method to the madness but he was having difficulty divorcing himself from the anger that dug at him. He decided to count to twenty and take deep breaths in order to level himself off.

When he finally trusted his voice Doin broke the silence. "I'm not limited by myself. But my options are. I mean, I don't put myself in a box but it's rough out here. It's hard. So I do what I gotta do to get mine."

Sights of the city drifted lazily past them outside of the bus window. Anonymous buildings with anonymous addresses that were indicative of his anonymous existence. The realization came to him that his life was indeed fraught with limitations. He was bounded by the perpetuation of his body type; big, strong and black, bounded by the institutionalized notion of place; the ghetto hood, and bounded by the physical degradation of his face, both black and scarred. And as he looked across the aisle at Hymm, he began to wonder if those limitations were self-imposed.

"Hymm," Doin said. "And I want you to look at me like you are a man who has a job to offer. Now what do you suppose that I can do, huh? What kind of job would you hire me for? I'm what you would call the big, brawny type. Sheer muscle. So what would you want me to do? Labor!" Doin answered his own question. "That's what. Hard, physical work. You point at a rock…I pick it up and move it. You need a ditch dug…I dig it. Do you dig that?"

"I hear what you're saying, Doin." Hymm stroked his chin as if in thought. "You do, huh?"

"Yes, I do. But that's a ghetto mentality. That's the type of mindset that stunts your soul."

"Stunts my soul?"

"Damn right! Stunts your soul! I mean, look around you. There's hoods and there's hoodrats, thugs and thug life. There are brothers out here that maybe could have re-invented the wheel or found a cure for the common cold but their lives are doo-doo."

The two young men sitting at the back of the bus were watching the two men's animated conversation with unmasked interest; the mention of hoods and thugs seemed to have gotten their attention. Doin hoped that Hymm would take notice and be a little more careful with his words so as not to offend any thug mentality those two might have. If any trouble jumped off, Doin planned on being the last one to get hurt. He turned back to Hymm who was still talking, oblivious to the danger that lurked behind them.

"Everything that you want. Everything that you are comes from inside your peace of mind and strength of heart. Except when your soul gets stunted. That's when you live a life of misdirection. Going wherever the arrow points you. Whatever the man tells you to do—you do it. Wherever he tells you to go—you go. That's institutionalized slavery. The only thing missing is Uncle Tom and 'Yes, suh!' That type of shit stunts your soul."

"Well, I don't holla no 'Yes, suh,'" Doin said.

"You don't?" Hymm said. Doin thought back to the last job where he worked. He had worked long and hard for the money and his supervisor had been a capable, fair man who told him on many occasions that his performance was excellent. Yet here he was unemployed and on the bus.

"I guess the 'Yes, suh' was silent," Doin said.

"Man, you sho' nuff up in here bumpin' your gums and running off at the mouth!"

A deep, menacing voice blasted from the back of the bus. It was the guy wearing the Black Sox uniform. The Monarch looked on with a grin on his face.

"Like you don't holla, 'Yes, suh' just like everybody else." The Black Sox's voice was heavy with aggression while the Monarch lounged at a lazy angle in his seat. His eyes were dark and penetrating as he watched Hymm, waiting for a response like a caged cat, poised and eager ready to pounce on the slightest weakness. "As a matter of fact," he continued. "You said, 'Yes suh' when you gave the bus driver your money."

"You know that's right," the Monarch said.

Hymm paused a moment and looked from one young man to the other. "It's not that deep, fellas. It really ain't."

"But you are on the bus," Monarch said.

"Yes, suh," Doin said. "I's is on da bus. And when I fust seed da bus, I knowed their was a gawd!"

The two youngsters laughed. "He buggin'!"

"Straight up!"

Now it was Hymm's turn to smirk. "Gentlemen. Look at me. Look at my face. Look at my clothes. I'm like Ali. I'm so pretty!" Hymm had to raise his voice in order to be heard over the protestations. "But I say that with confidence. Because I got the look. It's all in the eyes of the beholder. If you look in my eyes you will see that I am beholding success. I see it right around the corner. Right now!"

"Man, what is this fool talkin' 'bout?"

"I'm sayin'!"

Hymm leaned forward, warming to his subject. "Man, I have dreams. Big ones. And you know what I've found to be the most surprising aspect of trying to achieve my goals? The harder I try—the more I bang my head against the wall. The more good things happen for me. That's when I realize that all things can be done."

"Ya talkin'," the Black Sox said. "Ya talkin'."

"And what are you doing," Hymm said. "Huh?" He looked Black Sox up and down. When he next spoke, his voice was feminine. "Now, let me see. You have a definite gang-man flavor, or should I say a gang-bang look working here. Yes, that look does say ghet-toe. It just speaks inner-city… well to my inner-city. Yes!"

"Oh Twan." The Monarch went along with Hymm's charade. "Don't hate, Twan! Do not hate me 'cause I'm beautiful."

Black Sox turned serious. "Look, dreams are necessary…stereotypes ain't though. Yeah, um from the ghetto…born and raised right down the street from the High Rise, but I don't say, 'Yes, suh' to the hood. I ain't stupid neither. And because I know that you got trouble with stereotypes…I graduate this year. And then I gets to get mine. And if you look in my eyes, you won't see no Uncle Tom-type shit in there either."

"We all got our own scam," the Monarch pitched in.

"So what are your plans then," Hymm said. "What are you two young men going to do when you get out of high school and into the real world? Because, gentlemen, the only thing worse than having no plan is having no plan at all."

The two youngsters were quiet.

"Hold up," Doin said. "Hold up a minute, Hymm. That's not fair. Eighteen-year-olds don't have plans. Not any solid ones anyway. Come on, now! What kind of plans did you have when you got out of high school?"

"Point taken," Hymm said. "But let me hip you guys to my game. I grew up in the High Rise Projects myself. I didn't like it. You ever heard that song…your mother's on welfare, your daddy's in jail, your sister got a sign sayin' 'pussy for sale'? You ever heard that song?"

"It don't go like that," the Monarch said.

"Yeah," Black Sox agreed. "Your rhythm is off, yo!"

"Well that's how it should go." Hymm said. "Because that describes the projects perfectly. Like I said, I didn't like it. The ghetto is so much more than the place that you live." Hymm paused and held up a finger to emphasize his point. "And so, having tasted poverty, I have no choice but to acquire fame and fortune."

"Where was that from," Doin said.

"I don't know," Hymm said. "But I could hip you, each of you, to the fame and fortune part. But you have to be down for the hard part. All work, no bullshit." Hymm took a moment to look at each of them in turn, looking them in the eye. "Interested?"

Doin nodded his head in agreement. The Monarch and Black Sox looked at each other and reached a silent agreement before nodding at Hymm. The bus squeaked to a stop and Hymm turned his head to look out the window.

"Gentlemen, this is where we get off."

CHAPTER 25
Footprints

D.Wayne sat on the bench across the street and watched the building. His bitterness colored his every emotion and poisoned his every thought. He had been following Joozy since the day he had met her at the offices downtown. There was destiny in their meeting; his spirit told him so. He was patient. Ruh would send the woman to him.

He was glad that other girl, Falasha, had taken her nosy ass home! She was always around! Never leaving him any time to be alone with Joozy, to bond in that special way that only solitude would allow. Falasha also seemed to bring her own elements of drama to Joozy's life, too, as the strange episode in the park had indicated. Something rotten was going on there but D.Wayne didn't want to take the risk of being seen so he could only observe from afar. Joozy had appeared quite upset, and Falasha seemed to offer comfort as Joozy paced and gesticulated in a frenzy. D.Wayne would bet even money that Falasha was at the root of the problem, whatever it was. She just seemed like the type of good-natured bitch that would keep her happy nose buried up in other people's shit, causing problems galore. At one point Joozy was sitting on the park bench with her face cradled in her hands and D.Wayne could see her shoulders trembling. She was shaking with tears.

D.Wayne watched the entire drama unfold from across the street. He went into a diner and sat at the counter, sipping on a soda, spying on them through the storefront window. He knew that the carbonation in the soft drink would come back to haunt him later in the form of excess gas and heart-burn but the mere thought of Joozy made him throw such minor worries to the wind. She was like a religious love for him. Every time that Ruh let him draw breath, he knew that he was meant to call on her, to never be lonely, because one day she would be his life. He would be Joozy's frame and she would be his perfect picture: love in a landscape, a Da Vinci and shit, a precious spill of water caught in perpetual perfection on canvas.

So the hardest thing in the world for D.Wayne was to love her and not have her. Yet the easiest thing that he could ever hope to do was to have her body to himself, to have that essence of Joozy bathe his spirit every day and every way. D.Wayne felt huge inside of himself, as if he had more to give than any one woman could take; and Joozy was more than one woman. She was a ghetto woman, black magic woman and the blissful promise of a bump and grind. D.Wayne was in the mood.

Joozy stood up from the bench. She seemed to have composed herself and she was giving the Falasha-bitch a hug before they went their separate ways. Joozy headed up Central Avenue, and D.Wayne hurried out the double-glass doors of the diner and went after her. She didn't seem to be in any particular hurry as he tailed her from the other side of the street, hanging back just far enough to keep her in sight. But he wondered where she was headed.

Block after block, Joozy kept walking, D.Wayne following her, and he began to wonder if maybe this wasn't his chance to talk to her. He knew from shadowing her for the past two days that her house was over on the other side of town now. She wasn't even headed in that direction. She had something on her mind; D.Wayne was sure of it, and maybe she needed a man to come to her emotional rescue. With the right timing, he was sure that he could be that man, that knight in shining armor come to save the day. *Sure,* D.Wayne reasoned. *Why not go for it. If not now, when? Okay, now I just need to seize the moment.* D.Wayne's heart raced with the realization that he was actually going to do it. He quickened his pace in order to catch up to her, trying to pull even with her on his side of the street without drawing too much attention to himself. When he saw Joozy stop at the intersection, waiting for the traffic light to change, he crossed the street and strolled up slowly behind her. As he approached the corner, the light turned and Joozy began to cross the street. She suddenly stopped in the middle of the walkway. D.Wayne stepped back onto the curb and waited. Joozy slowly resumed her stride and she made her way to the other side of the street. A woman and two girls were standing there, waiting for her. He heard the squeals of laughter from the two young girls as they rushed up to Joozy and hugged her. But the woman—he supposed that she was the mother—simply stood by watching with her arms folded across her chest. D.Wayne wondered if this was Joozy's family, even though the possibility seemed quite remote. All three of them seemed to be cut from the same cloth, light-skinned and dumpy with long hair that hung down past their shoulders, high cheekbones and smoldering eyes that were magnetic. Maybe they were her cousins or something.

D.Wayne waited amongst the crowd of other passersby at the corner and when the light changed, he crossed over, passing by Joozy who was in animated conversation with the two girls. He stopped at a storefront display of a sporting goods store on the corner a few yards away and pretended to window shop while he eavesdropped on Joozy's conversation. The first voice he heard was the mature voice of the older woman.

"So, how are you and that ugly muthafucka making out?"

D.Wayne liked her already.

"I hope ya'll ain't up there making no ugly-assed babies."

Maybe not.

"Ma," Joozy said. "I always wanted to ask you something but I guess I was too young to know what it was."

"Oh. So you all grown-up and shit now, huh?"

"Grown enough. I've learned a lot about myself in these past few weeks. Especially since I got up from underneath you. I know that I gotta be honest with myself.'

"So what are you honest about, Joozy?"

"I'm finally honest enough to know that you don't like me. And I ..."

"Now what do you mean that I don't like you? Just 'cause ..."

"Can I finish? I ain't even asked the question yet."

Her mother pressed her lips into a hard, thin line and waited.

"All I wanna know…and I think that I deserve this much…is, how did you get this way? How did you get to the point where you could blame me for being born? Because I sure didn't ask. How did you ever get to the spot where you didn't think that the things that you said and the way that you treated me, wouldn't ever touch me? Or hurt me? Please! Puh-lease answer me that!"

"Joozy," her mother said. "I don't know what you talking about. I don't even think that you know what you talking about. I treated all my kids the same…"

"Now Ma, that is what you call bullshit!"

"Oh, you done got grown enough to cuss me, huh!"

"I ain't cussing you…but that is bullshit. If you can't see that, then this conversation ain't going nowhere. Matter of fact…this conversation is over!"

Joozy spun on her heel and walked away. Her mother yelled after her. "Go on then. Take your ugly ass on."

Joozy turned back. "I ain't gonna cry this time, Ma. That's what I learned about myself. Not for you. Not ever again." She headed back up Central Avenue and she never looked back. D.Wayne followed her more determined than ever to have his queen. She made it two full blocks before she stopped and sagged against the side of a dark, marble building. She leaned her head back and looked up at the sky, oblivious to the lines of people that moved by her. D.Wayne decided to make his move.

"Joozy!" His voice was high and squeaky so he tried again but with a little more bass. "Joozy!" When she turned to face him he realized that he wasn't breathing, that he wasn't feeling, even while his heartbeat was thumping in protest. He paused to give her a chance to see his face, and his spirits lifted when he saw the dawning of recognition curl her lips.

"Hey," she said. At least she tried to smile but she couldn't quite pull it off.

"Hi," D.Wayne said. He felt like he was in the midst of a schoolboy crush. His tongue was tied in knots. In his rush to catch her, he had neglected to give any real thought to what he was going to say when he caught up to her. *To hell with it*, he mused. *I think I'll try the truth.*

"So how you?" he said.

"I'm okay. You?"

"I'm all right. I just saw you standing over here when I passed by and I remembered you from the other day. You and your beautiful skin… you were kind of hard to forget."

Joozy took a deep breath and looked down at the ground.

"Listen," D.Wayne said. "Are you sure you're all right? You look like you might be kind of out of it a little."

"No," Joozy said. "I'm fine. Just life problems. I deal. Ya' know." She paused to look at D.Wayne. "Hey. I appreciate you asking but I gotta go…"

D.Wayne held out his hand. "Listen. Before you go, I need to tell you something. Listen. I don't usually walk up on people like this, but remember? I met you a few days ago and…" Her eyes sparkled and D.Wayne momentarily lost his train of thought. "But listen. It's like this… I can't seem to get you out of my mind. I know that sounds crazy and shit, but I figure that I might not ever lay eyes on you again, so I just have to tell you straight. Because I know that we just met. I know that. But you are just what the doctor ordered for me. Like a queen."

He stopped himself when she looked at him with a sour smile playing at the corners of her mouth. Her lips, full, soft and firm. Ruh be praised.

She looked D.Wayne in the eyes before she answered. "You know what? My man thinks so, too." Without another word, she turned and walked away.

D.Wayne watched her, stunned. *Just like that! That's it! She just gonna! And she think that she gonnna! Mutha-fucking-son-of-a-gotdamn-motherfuck-ing-hell-to-damn-son-of-a-fucking-shit-bastard! Fuck that!*

I watch her. And when she turns the corner…I follow.

"I'm gonna get that bitch!" I see that now. After all the shit that I've done for her, she doesn't even know that she is meant for me. She can't see that she can chase the darkness from my life. Joozy is stronger than the dark infantry that haunts me. Stronger than Joselle even!

"'Her man!' Fuck her man! He's irrelevant." Less than irrelevant in the grand scheme of things. She belongs to me. Ain't no doubt. You hear me, Ruh? If I can't have her, then you can't have your Water.

Joozy is walking at a brisk pace now and I have to put some pep in my step just to keep my safe distance between us. She's a little too secure with herself. She hasn't even looked back once to see if I'm behind her. Underestimating a motherfucker. That's all right with me though. She'll learn.

Her stride is steady. She's humping her way down Central Avenue and now she's making the turn down Lark Street. She's headed toward my spot.

Lark Street is the demarcation line of the city, the unofficial starting line of the ghetto. It runs a long, snaking path through the hood, littered and unclean, a trail of constant neglect that is indicative of the economic status of the poor that are stuck there. In fact, one of the cross streets is Swan Street; which is just off the L-shaped alley where the Temple of Ruh is located. Swan Street is the part of the city known as The Sewer, the name given to the area back in its drug-dealing, wild, wild, west era. Back in the day it was common knowledge that you put your life at risk if you ventured down to The Sewer. Down there you were left with one of three options: fuck, fight or walk. And if you couldn't tell your story walking, even some of those options were eliminated. It seemed every weekend there was a shootout in The Sewer until the day two cops caught a couple of stray bullets. The city wasted no time shutting the drug dealers down after that and now Swan Street sits mostly deserted with only a few desperate drug peddlers still braving the storm.

Joozy is headed in that direction now and I would bet my last dollar that she is going to her apartment over by the Candle Young Projects. Candle Young Projects is composed of red bricks and welfare checks. At any time of the day, any day of the week, fatherless children can be seen running amongst the houses, wild and unchecked. Candle Young stands in the forefront of the High Rise Projects—the real hood. Twenty stories of shambles and filth. Most of the black folks who ended up living in public housing found themselves either in Candle Young or the High Rise as their final destination. Downing Street fronted the High Rise Projects, intersecting with the alley where I set up the Temple of Ruh.

The Temple was set up in an ideal location; that was how I knew that Ruh had sent it to me. The alley was constructed in an L shape, with the short leg of the L facing the High Rise Projects. This meant that most traffic moved past the short side of the alley. The Temple was set up just on the inside of the long leg of the L, sort of in a corner, which meant that for anyone to see me going in the door to the Temple, most likely they would have to spot me from the long end of the alley, which fronted on The Sewer. So whenever I took one of the women into the Temple, I was pretty sure that I wouldn't be seen. Most people stayed out of the alley anyway. Especially at night.

Joozy is going in that direction now.

Look at her. Ass swinging like she got it like that. Like she ain't got no footprints. Footprints that I can follow. Footprints that she left on me... ones that will never leave me. And she won't leave me either. Fuck that. What to do, Ruh? What to do?

She takes a left on Clinton Avenue where Swan Street zig-zags and resumes its snakelike wiggle toward the projects. Soon she'd be coming up on Welton Street, just a few blocks from the hood and I'd have a decision to make.

I want her. And I want her bad. Her beauty is meant for me. Only I understand it. And only she understands me. 'Her man'! Please! Where he at now, huh? Where he at, baby! He ain't nowhere and he sure ain't nowhere near here. I want her.

The blocks are flying by now. I gotta put some speed on my step now... get a little closer to her. Now she's crossing the street past Welton and the next block is Manning Place. I need to close the gap.

Just look at that body. Look at how she carries herself. Phat! What more could a man want? Okay, she's waiting for the light up at Manning Place and I've finally gotten close. Matter of fact, I'm way too close. Damn! She's turning around! I'm gonna have to dip and cross the street...smooth-like. I can only hope that she doesn't look directly at me because I sure ain't gonna turn around and look. Man! I hope she don't see me! That was too damn close.

All right, she's stepping back down Lark Street again but she's stopping at one of the storefront windows, doing some window-shopping. She's taking her time, too. Let me ease up on my side of the street. She's standing in front of a huge storefront. It's one of those stores with baby clothes: Baby Bib Soup. There's an assortment of infant mannequins in the window and Joozy is moving over toward the right corner of the display. She paused with her hand pressed to the glass.

A baby store! *Footprints, ya'll!*

Good thing I brought Flo Jigga with me.

CHAPTER 26
Behind the Pale Door

I caught Joozy by surprise when I stuck my gun—my Flo Jigga—in her back. We stood on the corner of Downing silhouetted by the afternoon shadows as night began to fall. Not a soul could tell that she was tasting my steelo. There were plenty of people milling around, as there always are in the hood. It's just that they never really see anything. Most of the people were settled on their porches, most of them getting high off one substance or another. But they were not about to pay too much attention to anything that wasn't in their immediate vicinity or affected their immediate high.

I had timed my move perfectly. Joozy and I stood on the corner of Downing that was directly in front of a softball field. Behind us was a huge parking lot with a few abandoned cars sitting between the lines. We were facing Candle Young, which sat across the street, bunched and crowded into a singular space as if that was all the room that the city had to offer. No one could see my gun hand.

My queen was stunned. I could feel her body stiffen, feel the paralysis that instinctively took control of her as the shock of a .38 digging into her spine began to dig into her mental. Even in the throes of my desperation I could see that Joozy was big and beautiful, more than worthy of being taken.

I jabbed her with the gun. "Don't look up and don't look at me. I first just want you to know that I mean all of this shit that I say." I felt her body shift toward me. "I know that you heard what I said, right?" I pushed the gun into her ribs much harder than I intended. I heard her grunt in response and I hoped, inside, that I wouldn't have to get too physical with her.

"What? What do you want with me?" Joozy's voice was loud. I saw a few heads whip around in our direction and I pushed right up on her, like we were lovers. Nut to butt. I leaned close to her ear and made my whisper as harsh as I could. "I guess you can't tell how desperate I am, can you. Your mind hasn't really jelled to the fact that I got a gun in your ribs in the broad daylight. That you is my ride-or-die bitch right now. So if you really want to get loud, you can just go right ahead. We'll see how many of these ghetto muthafuckas gonna care when you drop."

Right then, I couldn't help myself. I had to put my lips on her neck. I had to rub them back and forth and feel the tenderness of her skin. The dark beauty of my queen. I felt her body recoil from my touch and that just pissed me off. I jabbed the gun hard into her back. "Head back toward the alley."

"The alley?" Joozy said, her voice more steady.

I think that I am going to have to really keep ready for her. She's not begging. Not my baby. No. She seems to be getting herself together. Looking for a spot to make a move. My best bet is to try to keep her feeling threatened with a steady line of my bullshit. Keep her moving and not thinking.

"I can see myself shootin' yo ass!" I kept my voice as guttural as possible. "Now I ain't trying to do nuthin' to you but you gonna make me. I see that shit as clear as day."

"Why? What you want?" Joozy moved slowly toward the alley.

"I want a Queen."

Joozy stopped dead in her tracks. Without turning around to face me, she said, "A Queen? A Queen! It's you, ain't it? D.Wayne. You the one that got that like on me, right? Is that what this is all about? D.Wayne?"

"Fuck no! Get in the alley, bitch!" I see that I got to manhandle her ass. I punch her in the small of her back and watch her stumble into the alley. I didn't swing with all of my might. All of that extra motion would surely draw some unwanted attention. But I caught her unexpectedly, and the impetus propelled her forward into the alleyway. She caught her balance and turned her head to look at me.

"Yeah, I knew it was you," she said, looking me in the eye. I didn't care anymore. I didn't care who saw me and I definitely didn't care if Joozy thought that I didn't love her. I stepped into the alley and raised the gun, pointing it right at her head.

"You know you kinda pissing me off right now." As I walked toward her with the gun held out in front of me, Joozy started backing further into the darkness of the alleyway…just like I wanted. "First, you gonna tell me that you got a man when I know that you don't. Where that bastard at now, huh? When you need him. I'm here for you, Joozy, but you pissing me off for no reason at all." I had to laugh at the craziness of it all. "Joozy, you know you remind me of this woman I once knew. Her name was Joselle. Joozy. Joselle. Ya'll both have that same cracked beauty. And ya'll both act like bitches."

"Bitches!" Joozy stopped to glare at him. "You the muthafucka with the gun!"

"Shut up!" *Ruh! Please don't let me kill her!*

"Fuck you! You shut the fuck up. Pussy ass with a gun!"

"And my gun got bullets, too!" *Ruh! Please don't let me have to kill her.* "Bullets that go 'pop' and 'pow' and shit. So get to stepping down that way." I pointed toward the bend in the alley. "Before I have to kill your ass right where you standing. Shit!"

Joozy looked at me for a hard minute. I think that she was running it through her mind that maybe she could take me, even with the gun. This woman is *bad*. She not scared of jack-shit. Finally, she turned and began to walk down the alley toward the basement where I kept the Altar of Ruh. I could see the pale, blond doorway from where we stood, beckoning to me. Joozy has the most beautifullest ass that I have ever seen in my life. It just moves with so much life and promise.

"Why you doing all this shit anyway, huh? What you want? Pussy? And you feel like you got to take it? With a gun?"

"You know that you are my Queen." I push her toward the darkness. "But you got a dirty mouth. Get your ass down there." I move her toward the door that leads to the basement. We are deep in the alleyway, just at the point where we can't be seen from either end of the alley, hidden in the shadows from the passersby. "I know that you scared. That's why you talking so nasty, but I will shoot you, Joozy. Dead in the ass. I've come too far for you to doubt that." I step back from her and point down. "So lay down there. On the ground. Face down." Joozy stares at me, unmoving. This could be her final moment…and she knows it. I think that she's about to try to make a move, so I play a hunch. I point the gun at her stomach.

"This is the last 'bitch' that I'm gonna call you. Next time it's gonna be real. Now, bitch! Face down on the ground!" I know that I played her right when she drops to her knees and then assumes the position. I watch her closely as she lay there and, suddenly, I just can't resist the urge any longer. I just have to do it. Before I die and go to Ruh, I just have to know what it feels like. I reach down and firmly run my hand over the curve of Joozy's ass. Pure perfection. I would kiss it, and lick it and bathe it with my tongue if she would allow me but I realize that I still have time for dreams. To my surprise, Joozy doesn't utter a word in protest to my violation, which only serves to make my maleness come alive. I remove the keys from my pocket and unlock the door to the basement. I reach inside the doorway and grab my Louisville Slugger and set it behind the open door. The Altar of Ruh awaits.

"Now Joozy, I want you to get up real slow and face the wall." Quietly, she complies. It's getting really dark now and I know that I have to get Joozy inside as quickly as possible.

"D.Wayne. Why are you doing this to me? Shit! Why?"

I ignore her questions. I put Flo Jigga up to the base of her skull. "Good. I see that you are finally realizing the seriousness of this here situation and shit. Good for you to know that I ain't fucking around. Now. Inside." I guide her inside with my gun against the back of her head, prodding her toward the door. The first step into the Altar of Ruh is the landing at the top of the stairs that lead to the basement. The rickety handrail is barely holding on but the stairs are still sturdy…every single one of them. I checked to make sure. There is a light switch at the bottom of the stairs and there is one at the top of the stairs where I'm standing now. But I leave them off to help add to the disorientation that Joozy is bound to feel at this moment. She's at a total loss in the darkness of an unfamiliar place. I reach inside the doorway and grab my baseball bat. I take a quick step back and swing the bat at Joozy's shoulder blades. The sound of the impact reverberates through the silence of the black night and the force of the blow sends Joozy flying head first down the stairs. I didn't mean to hit her that hard and when her body comes to rest in an awkward position at the bottom of the stairs, I step inside the doorway and slam it shut, throw the baseball bat against the wall and rush down the stairs to tend to Joozy. She's unconscious and her breathing sounds funny. I didn't mean to hurt her. Didn't want to hurt her. As I kneel down to tend to my baby, as I gently pick her up and hold her in my arms, I would never know that my love for Joozy, my yearning to touch her would be the cause of my biggest mistake.

CHAPTER 27
Ghetto Drama

Hymm and Doin sauntered leisurely toward Downing Street in the direction of the projects. As they neared the inner city, the detritus of the city's abandonment and disrepair became glaringly evident as gutted buildings, frequent litter and hopeless eyes began to dominate the ghetto scenery. Candle Young loomed before them, monstrous in its poverty—an eight-legged monster that eats the downtrodden, yet stops just short of devouring them. The insidious nature of Candle Young is that it swallows its victims whole and sustains them in its belly, alive but unable to escape.

Each man felt no animosity at the state of hood life that greeted him like an ever-present monolithic ailment; neither associated the destitute children that played in the gushing fire hydrant with any particular antagonism drawn from compassion. Instead they both dealt with the ghetto scenery by administering emotional patches to spiritual wounds.

The High Rise Projects stood right next to Candle Young—distinctive not only because of its twenty-floor height but also because of the run-down condition of the surrounding neighborhood. Anything goes when grief is the order of the day and hope is surrendered to mayhem. Despair is heavy in the air, pervasive and cruel. Its insistent weight could be read upon the faces, deciphered in the demeanor and the defeated postures of the working denizens as they plodded about their daily grind.

The ghetto has its own unique, dynamic brand of disorder. A mixture of pain and numbness, determination and submission, eloquence and rawness that, when intermingled, produces its own color of desperation. No rules apply in the ghetto; a world of anonymous sensations waiting to be explored.

Hymm and Doin made their way in silence, each man alone with his thoughts. They were returning from a meeting in which Hymm had gone over his plans to start his own business. It was a fairly ambitious dream and Hymm had captured Doin with his enthusiasm and his realistic determination toward fulfillment of his goal. Jamal and Derek, the two youngsters from the bus, had taken to the idea of entrepreneurship with the gusto of youth even though Hymm had questioned their enthusiasm over the long haul; when the real work began and hard issues would require hard men to meet the challenge. Doin had listened to Hymm with a reserve born of caution but as the idea began to take root, he reluctantly admitted to himself that his hesitation was possibly due to fear. Whether it was fear of success or the fear of failure…he couldn't say, but he knew that it was an apprehension that was ingrained in him so deeply that it would be the most formidable foe he would ever face.

Hymm walked over and stood in an alleyway between two brick houses that were burnished a smoky, dirty brown by the polluted city air. Hymm paused to take something out of his pocket. "Hold up, Doin." He glanced quickly up and down the street.

"Whattup?" Doin joined him by the side of the building.

"I need to light this joint up." Hymm paused. "You smoke, don't you?"

"Is doodoo brown?"

"Sometimes."

"Exactly."

"Well, this is some Ted Bundy-type shit here."

"Ted Bundy?"

"Yeah. Some killer weed, man! Death-defying smoke." Doin regarded the man who earlier had spoken of climbing social mountains, of reaching the financial echelons of riches, of grasping the highest rung of the ladder. A man who now stood in an alley, getting high off a big, fat joint.

"You get high a lot?" Doin asked. Hymm flicked his lighter to life and touched the flame to the end of the cannabis.

"Not a whole lot." Hymm inhaled. "Why do you ask?"

"Because I guess it's a 'do as I say, not as I do' thing, right? That type of thing?"

Hymm exhaled. "Not really. It's more of a 'do what you need to do' circumstance. See, I can smoke me a joint, relax my mind and let my conscience be free, and then take my situation to the next level."

"Yeah, right!" Doin exclaimed as Hymm passed the joint. "You just trying to justify your shit. You can't preach purity while you're getting polluted."

"What are you saying, Doin? I can't be like Mike?"

Doin smiled.

"Seriously though," Hymm said. "On some level, ganja seems to open my brain up to a newer plateau. I mean, sometimes my mind seems to just open and I get a little more creative. My juices start flowing in all directions."

"No shit," Doin agreed. "That always happens when you get blunted but it's still an illegal substance, Hymm. It would still get in the way if you are trying to become a legit businessman."

"I guess so," Hymm replied. "But after the first joint! I really don't care."

"I feel that! But that is still some hypocritical shit though."

"Doin, take two and pass. Take two and pass." They were silent for a moment as they smoked and watched the ghetto scenery unfold in front of them. A porch light went on in the corner house across the street at Candle Young. A group of people filed out of the house with a card table, arguing about the rules of the game before they got started playing.

"Naw, man! It's Big Joker, Little Joker and then the two of spades. That's why they call the game Spades!"

"Fuck dat shit! It's Big Joker, Little Joker, two of diamonds, then two of spades. The diamond is a wild card!"

"Your ass is a wild card, aiight! Somebody hit the music."

The smooth sounds of a mixed tape flowed out of the window of the house. A Jay-Z joint mixed with the beats of A Tribe Called Quest. After a few more minutes of shit talking, four players took their seats and started to play. The flashes of lighters lit up the porch that they were sitting on. In the projects, blunts are as much a part of the game of Spades as trash talking. The graying fingers of dusk had long since darkened and the hum of activity was taking on a different timbre. Gone was the animated strain of youthful playfulness, replaced by the bass of adult rumblings and dirty whispers. Nighttime noises.

"Doin, listen," Hymm exhaled a plume of pungent smoke. "I'm not trying to be a shining beacon of morality. I don't think morality really pays these days anyway. As a matter of fact, I don't think that moral 'right and wrong' has any economic payoffs that could be measured in the pocket."

"You know what." Doin nodded in agreement. "I'm feelin' that! Because morals change with the wind." Hymm arched his eyebrows for clarification. "That's some good buds," Doin passed the joint back to Hymm before he continued. "Morals do change, though. Society dictates morality! I read that someplace...but that's on point. Because, morally, at one time...morally, it was just fine and shit to own slaves. Shit! Everybody had slaves, right? So it would have to be morally 'ceptible."

"Not just that," Hymm spoke solemnly. "Morality has no history. The only thing that matters is victory. Now me...I want quiet victory. I'll leave the pleasantries in my will." He paused to pass the joint back to Doin. "To the victor go the spoils."

"I know that's right," Doin replied before he hit the joint.

"Morality is subjective. Subjective to the victor's whim." Hymm's voice rose in answer to the doubtful look on Doin's face. "Take the Civil War, for example. If it wasn't for Black folks back then, I think that this country would have a totally different look to it. There would probably be two very different United States right now. I mean, think on it, Doin. In the North, you had city boys who worked in factories or went to school to be lawyers and accountants...these were the white boys that went down South trying to fight! Imagine them out in the woods! Trying to fight! Those city boys, out in the woods, were trying to fight some redneck crackers who learned how to hunt with rifles in peckerwood 101! Now who do you think was winning that war?" Hymm paused as Doin passed the joint back to him. He took a hit and held the smoke in his lungs before he continued his discourse. "Now the Black man had already went to Abe Lincoln and said that they would fight, but freedom for slaves would be the price. Lincoln didn't want that shit so he said, 'Like, like...no!' and the Black man was like, 'Aiight.

Cool.'" He paused to blow out a thin gray stream of smoke. "See, they knew about those Southern crackers. They knew those white boys were going to be hard to handle out in those woods, so they just sat back and waited for the inevitable." Hymm passed the joint. "Two years later, when the Northern boys were getting their asses chewed, Lincoln started thinking. He knew he was going to lose, so he called the Black man up. When he let the Brothers start fighting, we started tearing shit up, and soon the tide was turned and the North won the war."

"For reals," Doin exclaimed.

"Yup. Now. Morally, don't you think that the history of the United States should reflect upon our ancestors' contribution? Tell the world that Black folks were there? Trying to change the color of the face of this so-called morality? No. Instead history wants to tell me that Lincoln was altruistic in some way. That Black folk owe their freedom to him. I think that history owes us an apology and to recognize a moral authority that stands any test of time. Think about what the geography of this country would look like if Black folks refused to fight. Would a sense of morality let you ignore that?"

"Self-preservation." Doin spoke around a cloud of smoke.

"Point taken," Hymm replied. "Anyway...I want to be quiet about my business. Have you ever noticed that when people know that you have money...that's when they try to take your shit! They'll have you in court for stepping on their toes! I want to avoid that if I can. We have to be on the down low with most things that we do." The joint was gone now and Hymm tossed the small bud on the ground. "That was some good weed." Doin's eyes were red. Hymm turned to him. "Doin, I know that I'm asking a lot. I'm asking you to put a great amount of trust in my dream, but I need to know that you are serious about this shit. Committed."

"I hear you, man," Doin said. "I hear you. But I got to survive right now. I got a girl at home and we need some dough, yo! And I don't need it now but *right* now. You feel me?"

"Yeah, Doin. I 'feel you,' as you say it." Hymm began jive walking. "I feel you, yo! Um feelin' that!" He paused. "Well, actually...I am feeling absolutely buzzed right now. That was some killer weed!"

"Some Wayne Williams-type shit!" Doin pitched in.

"I said Ted Bundy!"

"But Wayne Williams was Black."

"Well. Well. Damn then! You can't just take my saying and just turn it around like that, Doin."

"But Wayne Williams was Black."

Doin was still uncertain what to make of Hymm. He was bookish with a touch of nerdiness about him. At the same time, he seemed to be firmly grounded in reality. And he had some killer smoke, too…a definite plus.

"You got a girl at home?" Hymm glanced at Doin.

"Yeah."

"Kids?"

"Nah."

"A serious relationship?"

"I think that we're getting there." Doin was thoughtful. "But we ain't going nowhere unless I find a steady income to support us. She's been cool so far about me not working, but I know that she's not liking it right now. Dollar, dollar bill, ya'll."

"Come on, Doin." Hymm motioned toward the alley that ran in an L toward Swan Street. "Let's cut through here…it's a shortcut. You know what?" Hymm said as they made their way into the deserted alleyway. "I can't wait to make some serious money, myself."

The alleyway was dark and quiet.

""Dollar, dollar bill, ya'll," Doin chanted.

There was sinister in the black nooks and crannies.

"Cash rules everything around me," Hymm joined in.

Movements carry in the dark.

"Dollar, dollar bill, ya'll."

They were halfway down the alley when two figures emerged from an abandoned building in front of them. One of them had a baseball bat slung casually over his shoulder. He wore a baseball cap with the bill tilted and turned to the back, thug style with a loose-fitting jersey that didn't hide his sturdy build. The man with him was a slightly pudgier version of the base-ball player but he had an Afro with half of it braided in cornrows. He stepped forward as if he were the designated spokesperson of this menacing tandem. "You ain't supposed to come down this alley at night, nigga."

Hymm took in the situation. "Listen, man. I know that your friend there has a baseball bat and all...but let's have an honest appraisal of this moment, okay? You two guys do look like some serious thugs...I mean the baseball cap and the bat! That's some excellent shit. And you?" Hymm pointed. "With the Afro! And half of it in cornrows...that shit is classic. Ya'll have passed Thug 101. Hurray for a muthafucka. But will you look at my man here." He motioned toward Doin who stood next to him like a mountain of muscle. "Now either one of you would have a serious problem even handling me...so which one of you is going to dream the impossible dream?"

"Bigger they are, harder the pussy falls," the baseball thug said.

Hymm regarded the men with bewilderment. "Ignorance is indeed bliss." He turned to Doin. "Let's skip this." And they turned back the way they had come. A large, muscular figure emerged from a doorway further up the alley in front of them. This man dwarfed his two partners; he was a hulk, even bigger in bulk than Doin. He wore a red bandanna on his bald head. A wife-beater tee shirt, which seemed to have its own set of muscles, was tucked into a pair of blue jeans.

"What do you think?" Hymm was tense.

"Can you handle yourself?" Doin spoke without averting his eyes from the hulk in the alleyway.

"Do you have any other options?"

"Not even."

"Doin, you know that I need you to be my right-hand man, right?"

"For reals?"

"Yes. So you better meet me on the other side of this mess. Okay?"

"Yup. Yup." Doin faced the huge figure in the alley. Hymm faced the other two men.

Suddenly the night was filled with blinding lights. A police car came squealing into the alley with its blinding lights searing the darkness. The big, hulking man with the bandanna quickly stepped back into the doorway and closed the door. Doin turned and began to sprint around the corner and down the adjoining alley. Hymm was already a few steps ahead of him when they were stopped dead in their tracks by another cop car coming from that direction, blocking them in with the other two men. The baseball thug and his partner with the half-Afro were blurred figures in the headlights of the car, frozen…for a second. Just as quickly, the baseball thug turned and ran straight toward Doin. Doin didn't have time to think about what happened next…he only reacted. The thug came at him, cocked the baseball bat and swung at Doin's head. Doin ducked under the arc of the swing and came up, springing off his feet, in a vicious shoulder tackle. He lifted the baseball thug off his feet and slammed him flat on his back as the bat went clattering to the ground. He felt the air whoosh out of the man's lungs, but the baseball thug managed to hold on to a front face lock with one arm around Doin's neck. Doin got his hands under him and pushed up off the ground, but the guy would not let go of his grip. Their combined weight brought both of them crashing down on top of the baseball thug. Suddenly, a fist slammed into the side of Doin's head. He turned and looked into the face of the guy with the half-Afro. He pulled his arm back to deliver another punch and Doin frantically dug his fingers into the baseball thug's face, trying to loosen the death grip that was clamped onto his neck. Before the punch arrived, Hymm came flying through the air and caught the half-Afro with a forearm across the neck, knocking him straight off his feet. Doin wrestled himself free from the neck lock and brought both of his hands down into the baseball thug's chest, clubbing him. The thug wasn't fighting back. Instead he was frantically shoving his hands into his pockets, digging hurriedly and throwing the contents onto the ground.

"Nobody fucking move," a disembodied voice blared from the darkness. "Nobody moves, nobody gets hurt." The policemen emerged from their cars with guns drawn. A paddy wagon came up behind the first car that had come into the alley, and a cop jumped out with a drug-sniffing canine on a leash. "Get on the ground, face first." This voice came from behind them and was much closer and much more urgent. "Hands behind your head, fingers interlocked."

Doin knew the drill. He knew that there was only guilt in his innocence.

He knew that once the police spoke in anger, that there would be a price to pay; somehow and some way, be it in blood, sweat or tears. It didn't matter what he thought that he didn't do—his crime was getting caught in the headlights of the law. He was barely cognizant of the canine passing over his prone body.

"Well, looky, looky what we have here!" The cop was standing over the thug. He had a baggie full of white pebbles. "Crack! You boys know that this is illegal shit, right? Poison kills. And it's mostly killing a whole lot of 'brothers.'"

Doin's heart leapt a fearsome beat when he saw the bag of drugs. "Officer! Me and my partner were just on our way home! We don't mess with no drugs. We don't even know who these guys are!"

"That's right officer," Hymm said. "Absolutely right, sir. We were just minding…"

"They were trying to jump us when ya'll came, officer. For reals! I swear…"

"We do not indulge in crack-cocaine, officer. That is a highly addictive…"

"Didn't you see him swing that bat on me? Shit!"

"Heard it all before," the cop said. His voice was cold, his demeanor, colder. "You can tell your story to the judge. Tell him how I found you lying on the ground, with crack all around you but it ain't yours." Doin looked down. There was crack spread all around him from when he was fighting with the baseball thug. "As a matter of fact," the cop continued. He opened the bag of crack and took out a handful of the remaining rocks. He stood over Hymm. "I think that we have each one of you for possession." With that, he dropped a few pebbles on all four of the prone figures and proceeded to indict each one of them, counting off the years. "One for you and two for you and three…"

Doin looked over at Hymm and they shared an unspoken thought.
Dreams die.

Doin nodded at Hymm. The thug's baseball bat lay on the ground, inches away from Hymm's outstretched hand. His fingers slowly curled around the handle. Hymm returned the signal.

They sprang to their feet in unison and sprinted directly at the police car blocking the far end of the alley. The night air rushed past them, like life's breath, cool and fleeting as they ran up, onto the hood of the squad car, leaping onto the roof before the first volley of shots rang out. They were both lifted up into the air with an awful tremor as the bullets found their mark. Doin could still hear the echoes of screams as his body was sent sprawling in the dirt of the alley.

CHAPTER 28
Teardrop

The rain began pouring heavily that night when Robert heard a voice outside of his tent. He pushed the flap open and saw Mandeep standing there.

"Yes." Robert looked at him.

"I got a message for you," Mandeep said. "From Christiana."

Robert crawled out of the tent. "You know her?"

"Yeah. You could say that."

"What does that mean?" Robert's voice was a deep growl.

"Relax, man. She's my first cousin." Robert watched him. "Anyway, she had me give you a word."

"What?"

"She told me to tell you that she pregnant with your child." Mandeep looked at him. "She say it's yours."

Robert was silent.

"She say it's yours," Mandeep repeated.

"Then it is." His mind raced. He thought of the love that he had for Christiana and the love they had shared. He wished that he could hold her and look in her face when she told him the news of the family that they would have together.

"She say that she missed her cycle this month…and she never miss her cycle."

Robert looked up at Mandeep. "She needs me. She can't have this baby by herself. She can't raise the baby by herself! Was she all right when you saw her?"

Mandeep smiled and clapped Robert on the arm. "That's all I wanted to hear!"

"I really need to get down from here," Robert said. Mandeep watched him in the pouring rain. The wind began to pick up, howling and rocking the flimsy tent.

"This water is coming in here hard," Mandeep said. "Wind's pushing up, too."

A loud, steady rumble emanated beneath their feet. A steady tremor rolled under them, tremulous and menacing as the volume of the noise grew. The hollow sound expanded and stretched away from them, traveling north toward the moored boats near the Teardrop. "What the hell is that?"

"'Not good' is what that is." Both men turned in the direction of the keening. They could see the tops of the boats bobbing in the water, rolling up and down on the waves. "Look at those boats. It's rocking something bad." The rumbling grew louder and was soon accompanied by an ear-splitting squeal that escalated until it climaxed with a loud snap. They watched in fascination, as a fissure was blasted open in the Teardrop between the two moored boats. The pressure of the water as it came pouring through the newly formed hole, began widening the opening in the dam. They felt the structure move beneath their feet. Hundreds of faces along the levee emerged from their sleep, awakened by the unnatural noise in time to see the tents that were on the collapsing section of the dam as they were washed over the side. The screams of the men inside could be heard echoing through the night air. Robert and Mandeep were shocked into action as they ran between the tents toward the break.

The crashing water was deafening. The two boats bobbed up and down in the Teardrop, tied together with the ropes that had torn from the moorings when the wall collapsed. The Guardsmen aboard both boats were scrambling across the decks, hurrying to get the engines started as the sucking water attempted to pull them toward the breech in the wall.

There was chaos on the eight-foot width on top of the levee. Hurried movements had to be made in measured steps as Robert and Mandeep bounded between unevenly spaced tents. As they neared the Teardrop, Robert saw that the water level was dropping. In fact, the water had dropped to the level that the starboard rail of the boat was nearly even with the top of the dam. Water was pouring through the widening hole in the levee, viciously eroding the opening in the man-made barrier and pouring out into the sodden Delta. A long section of the dam that stretched from the Teardrop to where Robert stood had been damaged by the initial force of the blast. Mandeep had made it to the edge of the fissure and was dragging an injured man back toward Robert. One of the boats was suddenly lifted by a wave of water and slammed into the side of the levee. The force of the impact knocked Mandeep off his feet. He tumbled over a partially collapsed tent and went down hard. When he rolled over, both of his legs went over the side of the dam. Mandeep reached out and grabbed onto one of the tent poles, clutching desperately as he tried to haul himself back up onto the flat top. The pole slipped from his grasp and, slowly, his body began to disappear from view. Robert ran down the levee. He reached out for Mandeep and caught him by the shoulders, grunting as he pulled upward with all his strength. Mandeep reached up and took hold of the edge of the levee, heaving up as Robert pulled him to safety. They sprawled out on their stomachs next to the injured man that Mandeep had dragged from the edge of the cracked levee. The back of the man's head was bashed in. He wasn't breathing. Mandeep looked at the man and then looked at Robert. He closed his eyes and bowed his head.

The boat slammed into the levee again.

Sections of the levee buckled and the two men were thrown sideways again. Robert hung from the side, frantically clawing, trying to latch onto something; anything solid that would support his weight. He could hear Mandeep's labored breathing next to him but couldn't spare a glance in that direction. His hand hit something solid and his fingers quickly latched onto it. Robert yanked at it with all of the force he could muster to determine if it could hold his weight. It held. He swung his other hand over and got a firm grip. That was when he realized that he had the dead man's ankle. He hauled himself up the dead leg and saw that the man had been impaled; his body was fixed to the surface, unmoving. He pulled himself up until he was safely back atop the levee. Mandeep screamed.

Robert struggled to his feet. He saw a movement from the corner of his eye. He whirled and saw the ship's mast moving toward the levee. As the boat surged toward him, Robert jumped to his feet, sprinted three steps across the width of the levee and jumped. He landed on the deck of the ship an instant before it crashed into the levee. His feet touched down on the afterdeck, and the force of the ship's impact with the dam sent him crashing into the bulkhead. He fell to his knees and saw with clear horror as the section of the levee he had been standing on, collapsed... and Mandeep was gone.

An anguished cry escaped Robert's lips as the ship bounced away from the wall. The two boats were still tied together, trapped on each side of the hole in the levee, *unable to move beyond the aperture. There were other men desperately leaping from the levee toward the boat. Many didn't make it. Suddenly, the ship's engines came to life and the weight of the boat shifted under their feet. A Guardsman staggered down the starboard side onto to the aft deck, glanced to his left where Robert was still on his knees, and began to crab crawl over to the capstan that stood about four feet out of the deck.*

"We can't move her!" he yelled. "Their engine won't start."

"So what can we do?" Another Guardsman emerged from the port side of the boat. He glanced at Robert dismissively. "Can we pull them past the hole there?"

"No," came the answer. "Their engines won't start. They won't make it."

"Well, we can't stay here," the Guardsman spoke with trained authority. His salt and pepper hair was plastered to his head and his thick, bushy eyebrows were knitted in thought. "Did you get them on the short wave?"

"No go. Can't raise them."

"Ain't nuthin' but niggers on that boat noway." A man emerged from the hatchway near Robert. He steadied himself against the bulkhead with one hand when the ship swayed. He had an axe in the other hand. "We never got no chance to unload 'em when we got here, and when the dam broke, most of the rest of 'em just jumped onto the boat. That's why the engine won't start." He paused to nod his head. "Too many niggers."

Robert knew his type. Peckerwood.

The boat lurched forward and the thick, corded rope that connected the two vessels went taut with the tension.

"I say we cut it." The man hefted the axe.

"No," the Guardsman said. "Not on my watch."

"Watch!" the axe-wielder said. "Yeah, you jes watch." He moved toward the rope with the axe held high. Agent Robert Abraham leapt.

His fist caught the redneck squarely in the jaw, sending him sprawling and he crashed against the bulkhead of the ship. He looked up at Robert in disbelief.

"What the hell is wrong with you, nigger?" He struggled to his feet and held the axe out in front of him. "You don't hit no white man, boy! You don't touch me, boy!" He looked at Robert, sizing him up. "You seen that shit, Cap'n," he said. "Down here that action ain't tolerated. Ain't allowed. Down here that's a bullet to this here nigger's head."

The two Guardsmen stood there, watching, their rifles now at the ready. The younger man sneered, deliberately raised his gun and pointed it at Robert.

"Belay your last, soldier," the older man said. The young man shot him a look before lowering his rifle.

"Give me the gun," the redneck responded. "Hell, I'll do it my damn self."

"Not on my watch!" The Guardsman pointed at him. "Now put the axe down. Now!"

"Sho' will," the redneck said. He charged at Robert and swung the axe. Robert jumped back out of the arc of the axe, the blade barely missing his midsection. The axe came at him again, this time, chest high. Robert ducked under the blade and felt it whiz over his head. He pushed off his right foot and threw his shoulder up and into the redneck's midsection. The two men hit the deck and Robert felt the air rush out of the man's body. Suddenly, the redneck pulled the handle of the axe forward and Robert howled with pain as the point of the pickaxe dug deep into his back. He seized the handle and yanked it back toward him, trying to dislodge the piece of steel from his flesh. But the redneck held tight. Robert pulled back again and the white man swung his fist, catching him in the face. His nose flattened and blood shot out both nostrils as Robert was knocked backwards to the deck. The redneck struggled to his feet.

"Get up, boy! Shee-yat! I love the sight of nigger blood! See how dark it is! Come on!"

The axe lay on the deck next to Robert. He picked it up and rose to his feet. Blood flowed freely from the wound in his back and Robert staggered, unsteady but determined. "This," Robert's breath came in heavy gasps as he brandished the weapon. "This is a testament to your weakness. You need this, don't you?" Robert wore an amused grin on his face. He glanced at the two Guardsmen who stood there watching him…and then he tossed the axe over the side into the roiling waters. "You see, everything about you is 'boy'…you need guns and mobs to confront your fears. And at the end of the day, I am your fear…boy!"

"What you say, nigger?"

"At the end of the day…I'm a man. And you ain't."

The white man roared and charged straight at Robert…but this time he was reckless. Robert sidestepped him, yanked him by the arm and using his momentum, swung him face first into the steel bulkhead. The white man went weak in the knees but before he could fall, Robert fired three vicious rights to his back. The man crumpled to the ground. Robert fell on top of him and applied a headlock.

The strength was ebbing from his body as Robert put pressure on his stranglehold. He was in a frenzy and barely registered the shouts of the Guardsman as he tightened his hold on the man's reddening neck. Desperate gasps escaped from the redneck's throat as his air passage was cut off and his breaths began to die. Robert felt the man's body go slack.

"Let him go!" yelled the Guardsman. "Now!" Robert squeezed harder. His vision was getting dim, darkening around the edges. He knew, with certainty, that he was destined to die but he also hoped that a hundred Black men would not be dying with him. His last thoughts were of Christiana and their baby. How he would have loved them. He heard the white man's neck break with an audible crack an instant before he felt the bullet tear through his chest. Then he was free. He wouldn't be anybody's nigger, anybody's boy anymore.

CHAPTER 30
Doin Doin

Doin gasped from the pain, felt it spurting up inside him with each breath as he writhed on the floor of the alley. He dragged himself upright against a building, a haze of agony coloring his vision, when he spotted Hymm, laid out in front of the police car, spread-eagled on his back. His breath sounded ragged and loud in the dark night. Blood gushed from the side of his mouth in a stream, and Doin could see the whites of his eyes when Hymm began to convulse. An odd cadence, a tapping sound could be heard coming from Hymm's body; the sound of wood hitting concrete. Doin realized that Hymm was still gripping the baseball bat, his muscles locked in a death grip while his body twitched. The bat was striking the ground in a death beat. Finally, Hymm's body gave one last shudder and Doin knew that he was dead.

"Shit!"

He tried to pull himself to his feet but his body wouldn't respond. He had bullet holes in him, blood leaking, but he refused to acknowledge the damage. His brain was dead to any mortal realizations; he simply had no capacity for concern and he didn't care how many there were. The sound of the police filtered into his brain, registering as no more than sounds as they neared; making their way around the police car with guns drawn.

"Clear on the left side! You got that side?"

"Can't see through over here. Wait one!"

Shit! They coming!

Again, Doin tried to struggle to his feet but the searing pain blazed to life anew, stinging him so badly that he could only flop back to the ground helplessly.

"I got him!" One of the cops was looking at Doin. He quickly glanced down at the bullet-ridden body of Hymm, stepped around the front end of the car and slowly began to inch his way toward Doin, his gun pointed. Doin saw the blue-clad figure through a slow-motion haze, not really seeing the gun or the uniform, but instead focusing on the cop's face. In minute detail, he saw the stark whiteness of his skin where the cop hat sat down on his forehead, the thin cop lips, the aquiline cop nose and the intense glare of the cop eyes.

Doin's brain suddenly kick-started. As the cop made a steady approach, his thought process began to jump furiously, desperately attempting to conjure up a means of escape. The cop stood directly in front of the car now. Watching.

"You're just about a done deal now, ain't you?" The cop never did hear Doin's answer because the next thing that he experienced was the violent collision of wood to his head. Hymm stood, silhouetted in the headlights of the police car with a defiant smile playing across his face. He had blood everywhere; his face, his neck, his entire chest was one bloody mass. Doin knew it was a miracle that there was any life left in his body.

"Mutha-fuckas!" Hymm said.

"Put that fucking bat down! Now! Step back and put your hands over your head!" Hymm was surrounded. But it really didn't make any difference. He wasn't going anywhere.

"Fuck ya'll." Hymm was swaying on his feet.

"Put the weapon on the ground! Put it down and put your hands up. No sudden moves!"

"We didn't do nuthin'! We. Didn't..." Hymm dropped the bat. He looked over at Doin...and a smile played across his face. "Um a New York power hitter!" Then Hymm made a quick move to his left like a gunslinger and reached into his pocket.

The police opened fire.

Hymm's body danced on his toes before the force of the bullets threw him backward. He lay in a heap, lifeless. Doin looked on in horror as a wallet fell from his hand.

"NO!!!"

Desperation fueled Doin as he leaped to his feet and sprinted along the wall down the alley. The pale, unfinished door was his only hope. If he could make it to the door he felt like he had a fighting chance. Shots rang out; splintering pieces of brick flew around him as he ran toward the shining door that beckoned to him; as if it guaranteed escape. The unmistakable sounds of triggers pulling on empty cylinders hit his ears. *Click. Click. Click.* A voice bellowed from somewhere behind him. "Reload!" He hit the door with his shoulder, putting every ounce of energy he could muster into it even as the resultant pain nearly caused him to pass out; but it swung open easily. The door was unlocked. He crashed into the banister, which sent him careening headlong into blackness before tumbling down a steep set of stairs. He landed flat on his back at the bottom of the stairs, screaming in agony. He saw a gaping wound in his shoulder. The fall down the stairs must have caused more damage to his wound because there was blood flowing heavily. His shoulder felt as if someone had stuck a blade in him and left it there.

Fuck the pain! Cops coming!

He rolled over and tried to grab onto something to haul himself up when he felt an electric jolt of pain when a kick landed solidly on his bloody shoulder. He went down in a heap. His legs began shaking with the intensity of this new onslaught of pain so he tried to roll over on the other shoulder. Another kick. This time, he screamed. He felt his body begin to slip away from him, a darkness descended like a curtain accompanied by a faintness and the final realization that this was it. Time to go.

He barely felt the harshness of the cold steel through the sweat that covered his body as D.Wayne stepped forward and pressed Flo Jigga to his forehead.

"Who the fuck is this?" D.Wayne prodded. He reached down and propped Doin up against the wall, looking at him. "Why are you here desecrating Ruh?"

"Doin!"

Joozy's voice penetrated the darkness that was settling over him in a heavy mist but Doin couldn't get his mind to register any sensory details that would penetrate the big sleep that was calling him.

"Doin!" Joozy called him again.

D.Wayne looked over at her. She was securely tied to an old headboard that he had found in the basement. Her legs were lashed together with a rope that, in turn, had been tied to a pole that descended from upstairs. He had tied her well and she was immobile.

"Doin, huh? Oh yeah…Doin! This is him, huh? Your man!" D.Wayne bent over and spit in his face. "Well, I'm doin, Doin!" He raised the gun and put it to Doin's head.

"Hold it, right there!"

"Freeze, mister!"

"Put the gun down! Drop it!"

Four sets of guns were pointed at D.Wayne from the top of the stairway. D.Wayne looked at them incredulously. "How did you get in here?" He turned to look at Joozy. "You see what he has done." He indicated Doin. "He brought all of this impurity down on Ruh. To his altar. To our altar! Ruh be praised."

He turned back to face the police.

"Don't do it, man! Put the gun down!"

"Nobody has to get hurt here! Put it down!"

D.Wayne swung his arm up and pointed Flo Jigga toward the cops. They opened fire in unison, fighting fire with fire, blasting D.Wayne's body back into the darkness of the basement.

Joozy screamed when she felt the first bullet tear into her stomach. Her body went slack when the second bullet hit her and she welcomed the darkness. Her last thought before passing out came as a tear… for her baby.

CHAPTER 31
Niggerization

Joozy tossed and bucked in the bed; lost in the violent throes of her nightmare. A tormented fire burned her belly, a pain so severe that it radiated up her body and into her brain. She lay in the bed, her frame ravaged by the shooting agony that flared through her stomach while she fought the demons that threatened to take her sanity. In the darkness she looked down at her body toward the source of her pain, her emptiness, and she gasped in horror. There was a gaping hole where her stomach should have been! She opened her mouth to scream but found no air. Instead she began to regurgitate pieces of her baby. First, a bloody hand; then a severed, tiny leg followed by ten, red frothy toes. She stared down at the mess… and finally, she managed to scream.

A cold, clammy wetness covered her forehead. The shock of the soothing dampness touched her senses, calming her, bringing her out of the dark dream. Joozy's screams subsided as the nightmare faded and consciousness began to filter in through her pained eyelids. She felt a welcoming chill glide over her cheeks accompanied by the realization that her dream was just that; an unreal nightmare. She opened her eyes. Falasha stood over her.

"Joozy," she said. "Wake up. Everything's going to be all right. You'll see."

What is she talking about? "No!" Joozy tensed. "No!"

"You're just having bad dreams, is all. Just dreams."

What is she talking about! Joozy stared at her as memories came rushing back. Air escaped her in huge gulps as she remembered; her chest rose and fell frantically and she looked around the room wildly. She cried out, her sobs akin to that of an injured animal, wrenching and painful. Falasha held her hand and soothed her, holding on through the initial stages of pain while waiting for the imminent hurt that was soon to follow. Joozy twisted and screamed, trying to shake the agony that came with the realization that she had lost something precious that couldn't be replaced. She felt a pounding throb in her stomach; an ache that penetrated her heart so deeply that she looked down and saw that the bandage wrapped around her stomach had become spotted with blood. A stab of pain caused her to cry out. She looked up at Falasha and saw the confirmation of sadness in her eyes. Tears sprang to Joozy's eyes. Torrents of tears that overflowed were soon followed by terrible sobs as stark realization hit her like a ton of bricks. Her heart, her face, her soul, was unable to contain the emptiness and loss of the baby that had been taken from her. Her baby.

"Joozy, I'm so sorry!" Falasha stood next to her bed, tears streaming down her face, sharing Joozy's pain, agonizing and wishing she could take some of it as her own. She knew that life could be tragic and that her friend had suffered more than most. Now there was even more wood to be put to the pyre that scorched her.

"My baby!" The words tore from Joozy with the anguish of death. Falasha leaned down and gently pulled Joozy to her, holding her as they cried together. It was all that she had to offer and Falasha was going to hold her hand out to her for as long as Joozy wanted to hold it. A nurse came into the room to check on Joozy. She told Falasha that Joozy had to get some rest, that her injuries needed more healing time. Falasha eased Joozy's head back down to the pillow and gently wiped her tears away. "I'm not going anywhere, you heard? I'll be right outside the door. I'll be here when you wake up, okay?" Joozy didn't answer. Her gaze was fixed on the ceiling, on a point of nowhere. She was drained. The nurse was right. What she needed now was some rest and some time to let her mind adjust to her new reality. And she hadn't even mentioned Doin.

The nurse looked at Joozy's chart, looked up at the monitors for a second, taking time to make notations on a clipboard before she began to prepare an injection. "This is going to help you rest for a while," she said as she rubbed alcohol on Joozy's arm. Joozy hadn't given any sign that she knew that the nurse was there. "You need lots of rest so that you can recover. And you will be all right." She administered the shot, turned and pushed the cart out of the room.

Joozy suddenly sat bolt upright in the bed and yelled, "No!" She reached for Falasha. "Doin! Where is he? Doin!" Falasha held her until the medicine put her back to sleep.

Doin knew that he was pretty fucked up as soon as his eyes popped open. His chest felt like it was sliced open with the raw nerve endings exposed to the elements and flapping in the breeze. His shoulder felt numb except for a small ribbon of flesh that held it connected to the rest of his body. His knee was racked with pain as if someone was trying to amputate it with a dull buzz saw. He moved his body, testing to see if any parts were missing and instantly regretted that move. Pain covered his body like a liquid blanket, agonizingly slow and so intense that it took his breath away. He wasn't even afforded the luxury of a scream.

"I would advise you to be still…be still and listen." Moving only his head, Doin looked in the direction of the voice. It was a big, Black cop in full uniform standing over by the window. Doin hated him on sight. The cop looked just like his stepfather.

Doin looked around the room. He was in a hospital. For an instant he was glad because he thought that he was going to wake up dead. The feel of the hospital sheets, the hospital quiet and the hospital smell were proof that he was alive; the cop in his room was proof that he might still be dead.

"You with me now?" the cop said.

Doin scowled at him.

"Good." The cop walked over to the side of the bed and looked down at him. "You might not know me but I'm an important man. So I'll clue you in. I am John J. Gaye, Chief of Police."

"Chief Gaye?" Doin's voice was heavy, doped. "Probably 'Head' Chief Gaye." He laughed but then he choked on the pain that it caused.

"Oh, you've got jokes," Chief Gaye said. "Well, here's one for you. Thug nigger in an alleyway with a bag full of rocks. What's that called? Nigger in a can! And I'm thinking maybe fifteen, twenty years before you even ask about parole. Funny, right?"

"I didn't have no..."

"Save it! I don't want to hear your bullshit."

"So," Doin talked slowly. "Why you here... You fucker?"

"You know what," Chief Gaye said. "You better pull your lips back in. Because I can only imagine what it would feel like if I washed your mouth out with soap."

"Why?"

"Now that's better." The Chief paused and walked across the room to look out the window. "Because of this shit!" He yanked the window open. A chorus of chants echoed from the sidewalk. "Fuck the Po-leece!" "Blue Clan murder!" "Twenty Six shots!" Doin couldn't see from his bed but it sounded like quite a crowd was outside. And if there was enough protest there might even be a few television crews filming the whole thing. At least now he knew why this cop was in his room. The Chief slammed the window shut. "See, Black folks! Black folks, we got us a problem. We have been oppressed for so long, victimized for so long, died innocent for so long that it has become a part of our racial makeup. I mean, we have been treated unjustly, we have died innocently and we have taken it beyond belief. So now, if a Black man gets accused of anything, we race to his defense. Doesn't matter if he did it or not. Doesn't matter if he's right or wrong. They come running back to us and we forgive them. We are just a forgiving people."

"You a cop," Doin said. "Who forgave you?" A bout of spasms seized his body and he coughed painfully.

"I swear to God, I will slap you right in your lips," the Chief warned. He looked hard at Doin. He was serious! "I mean, take you and your thug friends. Pockets full of crack, selling to your own people, thugging and just generally being a blight to society. A hemorrhoid with shooting power. But the minute one of you gets killed...the masses fall behind the thugs. Go figure."

"They...killed...Hymm!"

"So what! Should've killed you, too! If you want to know the truth about it. I don't know how they missed you with all of the bullets they fired. But now, you see, that's where our problem lies. Black folks around here are in an uproar. They're ready to call Cochran up here!" He looked out the window again before speaking. "Excessive force! It's only excessive until one of you hoodrats are breaking into their house, robbing them blind or drugging up their neighborhood." He turned and looked at Doin. "You're the new man of the moment. It seems as if your fate has now become symbolic of theirs."

"Maybe it is," Doin said. He took in air in huge gulps, trying to bring his pain under control.

"Say something else!" the Chief snarled. "One more smart comment and I will smack you right in those lips! Hard!" There wasn't much anger in his voice, just a steely quality, hard. "So now you are like, 'The Answer.' They've been out there for days. Raising all kinds of hell. Calling me out..." He stopped and looked around the room. It was a standard hospital room, stark and naked except for the two beds and hospital finery. A chair was pushed back against the wall by the adjacent bed. The Chief pulled it over and sat down. He looked up at Doin in the bed for a moment and then decided to stand. "You've been out for a couple of days, so let me bring you up-to-date on what's been going on. After you and Hymm tried to super fly over my police cars, you assaulted one of my police officers with a baseball bat."

"Bull – SHIT!"

The Chief held his hand up. "I'm just telling you the criminal court version. You can just save the drama for your mama. Because I don't want to hear it. Anyway, after you hit my officer in the head with a bat, they were forced to open fire. One of you, Hymm, was hit with nineteen bullets...dead on the spot. You, however, escaped and charged into a building. When the police entered the premises, you were nearly unconscious and a man was holding a gun to your head. The officers told him to drop it, he refused and opened fire. The police returned gunfire, killing the gun-toting madman and saving your life and that of a young woman that he had kidnapped and held hostage in the basement."

"So. What you want?" Doin said. He felt pain seeping out from under his bandages. "Open and shut." He took a deep breath. "Why you fucking with me?"

The Chief pulled the chair up, turned it around and sat cowboy style facing Doin. "Okay. Here is where it gets interesting. See, that guy in the basement who had the gun to your head...he was insane. He had dead babies and dead women down in that basement. He was getting ready to do another female when you crashed through the door. Now here is the real interesting part. When he put that gun to your head in the basement! He didn't have any bullets in the gun! So now everyone, the public, the people...they want to act like we were supposed to know that simple little fact. Hence the marching and the protesting. Amazing, right?"

"Yeah," Doin said. "Amazing. But what has this got to do with me?"

"Simple. You are the only one who can tie this all together. All you have to do is tell them the story that I just told you, except for the empty gun part, throw in some of that 'Can't we all just get along' mantra, and I will make sure that all the charges against you are dropped. You'll be a free man."

Doin looked at the Chief. He thought about Hymm. Thought about his death. Thought about how easy it was going to be for the police to put both of them in jail for crimes that they didn't commit. Thought about how many times it had happened before.

"Chief Gaye? Blow that shit right out...your ass!"

"What!"

"Your ass!"

"You're serious!"

"Your ass!"

"So, you want to be a hero, huh?" The Chief walked toward the door. "Fifteen years is a long time for a hero. They won't even remember your name."

"You will," Doin said. The Chief just smiled.

"Oh yeah," he turned and came back into the room. "Remember when I said that the madman had killed some women and babies in that basement? He had another woman down there, too. He was getting ready to cut her up, too. Her name was Joozy." He walked to the door, paused and looked back. "She lost her baby, too. Say! You know her, don't you? Joozy. You might want to think about her before you make any decisions. Room 223." He turned and walked out the door.

Doin hobbled down the hallway of the hospital to the elevator. He didn't notice the man with dreadlocks sitting outside in the hallway; he was too intent with purpose to pay attention to anything else. When he had found out what room Joozy was in, nothing—not even the pain that agonized him with every step he took—was going to stop him from getting to her. The elevator took forever. He had to slump against the wall to remain upright but the pain didn't matter; it could be ignored. When the elevator arrived he nearly fell inside but he managed to push the button for the second floor. When the door opened again, Doin stumbled out, ignoring the stares of the people in the hallway. He leaned against the wall for a moment, gathering himself. A door at the other end of the hallway opened, and the man with the dreads stepped out and watched Doin slump against the wall.

He called out, "Doin!" He rushed over. "I'm so sorry, man." Doin looked at him warily.

"Alias," the man said. "Remember? Club Midnite? Remember?"

"Alias?"

"Yeah. How you feeling, man?" Doin was breathing heavily. "Come on, man." Alias stepped over and offered his shoulder and helped Doin to his feet.

"What you doing here," Doin said. "Why you here?"

"Just wanted to see how you were. Make sure you all right? It's okay?"

Doin looked at him. "Yeah. We straight."

"Where you going?" Doin pushed himself away from the wall, mumbling a room number under his breath and unsteadily making his way down the hallway to a door. He hit the door with his good shoulder and pushed his way into the room where Falasha was standing near the bed. When she turned and saw him the first thing he noticed were her tear-filled eyes. She tried to smile, but the effort proved too much, and she could only put her hand to her mouth to cover the bitter twist of her lips. She walked over to him and gently embraced him. "Doin," she said. "Please! Help her." Her words seemed to shake him from his trance. He looked beyond her at Joozy lying in the hospital bed. She looked small and defeated. She looked ravaged. He needed her.

"How is she?"

"Doctors didn't say."

Doin walked over to the bed and looked down at Joozy. He touched her face.

Jumbled thoughts rushed across his mind. Heavy thoughts. So many that he didn't know what to say to her…where to begin. He took her hand. Tubes were sticking out of her. Yellow fluid dripped through the intravenous needle accompanied by the rise and fall of her chest which was so soft that her breathing sounded unnaturally quiet.

An anguished cry escaped Doin's lips. He brought her hand up and kissed her fingers. A single tear trailed a long line down his cheek. He looked down at the bandages around her ravaged belly. "I can't lose, Joozy. Why does this have to happen, huh? We ain't ask for much. Just each other. Why?"

Silence filled the room as Doin bowed his head and whispered a prayer; his essence, his being, begging his higher power for answers. "Oh God! I don't ask for much. But this is what I have. My girl. I mean…my life has been pretty shitty so far. You ain't showed me a whole lot." Doin paused to look up at the ceiling. "I guess you don't owe me shit, do you? We ain't never got personal, have we? I know we should have, but I couldn't see you. I couldn't *feel* you. And it was crazy that every day that I look in the mirror, I see my stepfather. I see the devil. Except this devil got a mark on his face. A life mark. But I'm sorry. I'm sorry. Just give her back to me."

Doin leaned down and kissed her lips.

"Joozy. Joozy. Come on, baby. Wake up."

She didn't stir. He turned and looked at Falasha.

"They gave her something a little while ago," she said. "She's asleep. We just have to wait for her to wake up." She saw the anguish on Doin's face. "And she will."

Doin turned back to Joozy. He couldn't imagine what he would do without her. He raised her hand to his lips and held it there for a moment. When he spoke his voice trembled. "Joozy. You gotta come back to me. I ain't never had nobody else. Never. Remember you used to tell me, forever. Forever! Forever, ever?" He choked out a laugh. "Remember that shit? Ain't no forever without you, Joozy. Just ain't."

Doin turned to look at Alias. "She used to always tell me stuff like that and I was too mannish to respond." He turned back to Joozy. "It's like I did something right for once. Me and you are like that. We are like that time you took me around the world in a day…but only like so much better. I love you more than I love me." He bent down and kissed her lips. "I do."

Joozy's eyes fluttered open.

"Hey, baby," Doin said. "It's me. Come on."

She tried to focus on his face.

"You all right, baby? Can you wake up?"

"Doin?"

"Yeah. I'm right here."

"Doin?"

"I'm here, Joozy. I'm here."

"You all right, Doin?"

"Yeah, I'm gonna make it. How you feeling?"

Tears sprang up in her eyes. Doin was taken aback. "What?" he said. "What's wrong, baby?" She was silent but the tears rolled down her face. "What is it, Joozy? What's the matter?" He paused to wipe her tears away. "Listen. We have come too far to hide from each other. And you're scaring me now. Tell me something, Joozy. What?"

"Doin," Joozy said. "I lost the baby."

Joozy took his hand and put it on her belly. Doin felt the big bandage that was wrapped around her entire midsection. "Oh baby." He held her gently, pressing his lips against her.

"I was gonna tell you when you got home. But then all this happened."

Doin looked at her. He thought about how much a baby would have meant to her…to them. He saw the pain in her eyes and knew that it was all about the love they had for each other. Love they would pass on to their child. And for the first time in his life, he knew this was something that he couldn't lose.

"Don't worry, baby," he said. "We can make another one. We got time."

She looked Doin in the eyes before she spoke. "No, I can't." They looked at each other in silence, sharing their loss and deciding that, together they had enough love to last for the rest of their lives. Doin knew that he couldn't live without her.

"Falasha," Doin said. "Could you do me a favor?"

"Whatever you need," she whispered.

"Could you go down to the front desk and tell Chief Gaye that I need to speak to him?"

Falasha left. Doin and Joozy held each other in the hospital room, letting tears wash away the remnants of their heartache. Alias felt the movement of the two dollar bills in his pocket.

CHAPTER 32
The Truth

Alias and Doin waited quietly in Joozy's hospital room. Minutes earlier the room had been crowded with city officials. It was emptied quickly after Doin had given his statement to the press. Chief Gaye had stood by listening solemnly as Doin read a prepared statement that exonerated the Police from any wrongdoing. Being that Doin was the only surviving witness to the shooting, the entire police force breathed a collective sigh of relief. Tensions were high in the city as the outraged citizens reacted to another police shooting that had taken the life of another young, black man. Hymm had been an upstanding member of the community and his violent death had a polarizing effect on Blacks. It spurred protests amid a public outcry that simmered with hostility in the face of the police misconduct. D.Wayne, however, was swept under the carpet of public opinion. His crimes were deemed best forgotten by both sides.

Joozy lay asleep in the hospital bed. Her ordeal had left her battered and beaten both emotionally and physically; Doin had refused to leave her side, even after the doctors had assured him that she would recover.

"You need to get back in bed yourself," one of the young doctors had told him.

"Shit that, doc," Doin replied. "Shit that."

"Come on." The doctor took him by the arm. "When she wakes up, she's going to need you...and she's going to need you conscious. For her." He led Doin to a chair by the bed and began to check his bandages. "You've been through a lot of damage yourself. I thought that I told you to stay in bed and get some rest." Doin looked at the doctor, puzzled. "Yes," the doctor answered his unspoken question. "You were completely out of it so you probably don't remember that I am your doctor. I'm the one that stitched you up, so it's my duty to make sure you recover, too." He paused to look at the bandage wrapped around Doin's shoulder. "I knew you were going to be the stubborn type the moment I laid eyes on you." He cast a quick glance at Joozy lying in the bed. "She's going to be okay. She's pretty strong. But you! We don't want you to reopen any wounds, so you need to get stationary, okay? You have to keep movement to a minimum. Keep in mind that you run the risk of internal bleeding, which can lead to all kinds of problems that we don't even want to discuss. So if you stay here, you still need to get some rest. This is the healing time. Give yourself some time to heal."

Doin nodded his head in acknowledgment.

"Good," the doctor said. "Right now, you have to take your medication."

"I'm good, doc." Doin looked at him. "I'm good."

"No you're not." The doctor spoke to Alias. "We need to get him back to his room." Alias walked toward him. "No. We don't." He looked the doctor in the eyes. "He ain't going to leave her. Know this."

"Well then." The doctor walked over to a tray that lay on a table near the bed. He picked up a syringe and stepped over to Doin. "This is to ease the pain that will be sneaking up on you in a few minutes." He pulled up on Doin's sleeve, exposing a vein. When he next spoke, he was looking at Alias. "It looks like I will be leaving him in your hands now." He deftly slid the needle into Doin's arm. As the drugs began to seep into his system, Doin shifted in response to the effects the medicine was having on his body.

"He's going to be out for a while," the doctor told Alias. "Just don't move him and don't let him move around too much. Remember what I said. Internally he can get screwed up pretty badly and he won't know it until his condition becomes critical." The doctor stared hard at Alias for a moment and then turned and walked out the door.

The dollar bills in Alias' pocket blazed to life. Their heat pulsed against his skin bringing home the realization that the pain and anguish pervading the hospital room was a direct result of his plight. Joozy lay in her bed with bandages plastered to her wounded stomach, tubes sticking out of her body, monitors clamped to her fingertips and tears in her eyes. *This is the Curse*, Alias mused as the dollar bills wiggled madly against his leg. *This is what it feels like to be damned. Life just dies on the vine.*

Doin slumped in the chair by the bed, twisted in pain. It seemed as if the medicine was finally taking him. Suddenly, he rose from his seat and, with eyes closed, reached behind him, picked the chair up and dragged it over to Joozy's bedside. He flopped back down and laid his head on the bed, finally succumbing to the pull of the drugs, falling into sleep with his hand touching Joozy's arm. Alias had watched Doin move around in pain, every movement causing an involuntary clench that rocked his body. He had shared Doin's agony. *Life just dies on the vine.*

He felt like retreating into the shadows of the darkened room. The shades had been drawn on the sole window, muting any natural light that may have filtered through. The lights had been dimmed so as not to disturb Joozy and now the silence that hung in the room seemed to darken the atmosphere; Alias shadowed with a Curse in his pocket. He felt the weight of the two remaining bills, felt their heat burning the high octane of hell-fire from his soul. "I gotta break this thing, man." His voice sounded hollow in the stillness of the room. "This Curse thing…look what it's doing! And just because of me." Alias buried his face in his hands. A desperate cry escaped from his lips and a desperate tear fell from the corner of his eye. "I can't get rid of this thing." He scowled. "I just can't get rid of it."

"The truth can."

Alias' head snapped up at the sound of the voice.

"The truth is your measure."

Robert Abraham stood before him. His image was sharp; the mirror of the visage that Alias had seen in his visions. His granite stare of determination pierced Alias with soul power, a sharp dagger and dark, fiery blades of purpose.

"How?" Alias stepped back. "How did you get here?" He cast a quick look at Doin who was slumped over, half-sprawled on Joozy's bed. "I ain't smoked nothing today! Why am I seeing you now? How?"

"You want answers, correct? Then I am your answer."

Alias moved cautiously toward Robert Abraham. "You are?"

"*Don't you see me in the smoke?*" Alias watched the apparition as his mind wrestled with sanity. He knew that he couldn't be crazy, that he couldn't be looking at—or talking to—Robert Abraham. His grandfather was dead; the victim of a racist's bullet. Alias reasoned that this vision was a lingering result of that devil smoke. He wondered at the possibility that he may have done much more damage to his brain than he could have imagined.

Robert Abraham seemed to sense Alias' disbelief. He turned his head to the side so that his misshapen ear could be seen.

Alias stepped forward. "Yeah," he said. "Yeah. That makes sense. You the answer." Robert Abraham looked down on him. Soul power eyes. "So what do I have to do?" Alias said. "The answer to this...is what?" Robert Abraham's image began to waver. He seemed to lose cohesion; his image flickered like a flame but then he coalesced and burned brightly.

"What...the...fuck...is that?" Doin was slouched in the chair, watching them. His head lolled to the side, his eyes squinting as he fought to stay conscious. He tried to raise his arm to point at Robert Abraham but the task proved to be too much and it flopped back down heavily on the bed. "Alias?" There was an unspoken question that Alias didn't want to answer, but he understood. When he looked over at Doin, he realized that the drug had him and he couldn't say much more.

"It's like a dream, Doin," Alias said. "You dreaming."

"So what...you doing?" Doin worked the words out. "In my dream then, mothafucka? Shit! Now, what the fuck is this?"

"Go to sleep, Doin. Rest."

"No! Who that is?" Doin tried to move again and Alias suddenly remembered the doctor's warning. "Be still," he told Doin. "Doctor said you got to be still. No moving." Doin sucked in some air and tried to sit up in the chair. "So tell me who...who...that," Doin said. Alias rushed over to him and gently nudged Doin back into the seat. "All right," he said. "Just be still and I'll tell you." He looked from Doin to Robert Abraham. "How come he can see you?"

Robert Abraham shrugged.

"Doin," Alias said. "I'm going to keep this simple because you tripping, okay." He paused to glance over his shoulder at the image of Robert Abraham. "Don't ask me how, but this is my grandfather. Robert Abraham. My grandfather who died a long time ago."

Robert Abraham regarded them with no expression on his face. If the news that he had a grandson shocked him, he gave no indication. Alias remembered the manner in which Robert Abraham had died, remembered how he had given his life to save hundreds of enslaved Black men, remembered how death had robbed him of the opportunity of witnessing the branches of his family tree grow. He stood and faced his grandfather.

"You remember that night when Mandeep told you that Christiana was pregnant?" Robert Abraham waited. "Well, Christiana had a baby boy… your son…who then had a baby boy of his own. Me. My father is gone now, too. He was haunted, chased by the demons of the Curse. He loved life as much as you did. He died trying to find the answer to this." Alias pulled his hair away to reveal his shredded ear.

"Damn!" Doin's voice rang out. "No ear!"

Robert Abraham and Alias stood facing each other. Robert Abraham's eyes were strong and Alias realized that his grandfather really had soul power. Strength born from the soul of necessity and compassion. A pair of hands materialized from the darkness, thick and strong yet somehow still intangible. Solid light yet ethereal. Scars crisscrossed the knuckles. Worn brown skin flashed ebony and touched Alias with the heated fingers of time. They reached out and Alias felt the coolness of wisdom settle on his shoulders.

"The truth," Robert Abraham began. *"You have to seek it. The truth. Living in the danger that we live in. The truth. Fighting against an injustice so bright! But it fails to lighten the bad of my Blackness. So I must tell you, in truth, that I really can't give you any answers. The answers are all questions. Our lives are all questions. And the essence of what we are compelled to deal with is one big question mark."* Alias felt the strength of Robert Abraham as the words washed over him. *"I think you need what we had in my lifetime. A Black man who will step to the forefront…and I mean unfiltered! A black prism that contains unexpected light. Question is…will the truth ever be enough?"*

"That's niggerization, right there," Alias answered.

"The inability to see Black light unfiltered," Robert Abraham said.

"Am I seeing this!" Doin yelled. His voice was thick and ragged. "For real! You like...talkin' to a ghost and shit."

"Doin! Rest!" Alias was harsher than he intended. His voice softened. "Doin, the doctor said for you to get some rest, man. Chill, all right!"

Alias turned back to face Robert Abraham.

His grandfather was gone.

Alias stood facing the darkness for a moment. He felt the heat of the remaining two dollar bills in his pocket as they burned and snapped. Slowly he headed for the door.

"You leaving?" Doin sat in the chair watching him through squinted eyes.

"Yeah," Alias replied. "It's time."

Time for another badness.

ABOUT THE AUTHOR

Nane Quartay was born in upstate New York and attended Augusta College in Augusta, Georgia. After a tour in the U.S. Navy, he traveled extensively before returning to New York to begin writing his first novel, *Feenin*. He now lives in the Washington, D.C. area. You may email the author at nquartay@yahoo.com.

Feenin

BY NANE QUARTAY

PROLOGUE

Tokus Stone stood looking out the window at nothing, wondering what would happen next…and he wanted to say good-bye. "Peace" to the violence that lay outside, on the desolate streets below. "Later" to the hunger that plucked at his insides, that gnawed at him until his soul went raw. "See ya" to the cold harshness of people, to their salty numbness that dripped like bitter syrup into their eyes and mouths. He felt them all…and he dealt with the barren landscape as hell. An entity that was very, very real. He brought the binoculars to his eyes and looked down at the street from the eighth-floor apartment. A people watcher in the ghetto. All the despair of a sixteen-year-old, saddened by abuse and devoid of love, arose in him as he watched his people and listened to his drunken stepfather rage at his mother.

"You just a lyin' ass ho," his stepfather spit out. Tokus' fertile young mind conjured images of the hookers he passed downtown every day. They wore outfits that stirred his imagination into hard places. They'd let you feel 'em up and everything for two dollars, but Tokus kept that to a minimum. That wasn't his mother though, and he could gladly kill his stepfather whenever that word came out his lying, drunken mouth. He looked down at the people crawling on the street far below.

The nothingness of the big city glared back at young Tokus, invading him, filling him with emptiness. I'm gonna get outta here, he thought. Education would be his rescuer, his lifeline out of the ghetto. One day he wanted to own his own business, be his own boss. Take care of his mother and help her cast off the line of losers she always seemed to reel in, present husband included, and leave this street life behind them. Soon he would enter his junior year in high school, and if he kept his grades where they were, he was sure he would be able to get a grant to attend the university. Yes, he would "learn" his way out of the projects, and nothing could stop him.

The usual suspects were hanging out on the corner. A coarse sky loomed over the drab neighborhood, spreading dreary light over the mundane existence known as the slums. There was a corner store with bars on the windows, and various colored brick buildings lined the rest of the block. Morning, noon and night the desolation was the same; poor people crammed on top of poor people with the only common denominator being pain and hunger and devising a means to get beyond and above the cycle of sleeping and waking. With no hope in between. Everything is fair when ya' living in the city, Tokus mused.

He watched through his binoculars as a Black Jesus stumbled around the corner, running down the street as if the devil were after him. He wore a tattered pair of shorts and a tiny vest a few sizes too small. On his back was a cross made of cheap wood and printed in big, white letters on a placard attached to the top of it was the word "America." His eyes bulged in fear as he pumped his fists, snatching at momentum, frantically reaching for speed to add to his cumbersome frame. Black Jesus wasn't made for running. A carload of teenagers came screeching around the corner after him with automatic weapons pointed out the windows. Tokus watched the usual suspects sprint for cover as rapid gunfire spit forth, showering the sidewalk. The first shot caught Black Jesus in the leg and spun him around as the car pulled up beside him. The second shot pierced his side and slammed him against the wall. The third bullet hit Black Jesus in the chest, and he danced, dead against the cold, brick building. He slumped to the ground, lifeless. "America" was stained with his blood.

"Why you always got to wait till you get drunk to come in here with your mess?" his mother asked the drunk. She didn't yell. "Crazed people yell," she had once told Tokus, "and I ain't crazed!" Tokus loved her for her understanding, but he just wished she would leave her husband and move on. He had long ago stopped asking his mother why she stayed, and at some point, Tokus had stopped caring. She had chosen her path and she walked it with determination. She could walk it alone as far as he was concerned, but something, somewhere had to change.

The harsh reality of his stepfather's wrath was an early lesson for Tokus. From the age of four until he was nine there were savage belts and wicked belt buckles. From ten to twelve there were stinging electrical cords and big, thick-handled straw brooms. But at fourteen, Tokus developed into a strong, muscular banger, and his stepfather resorted to using fists. He delivered solid heavyweight punches that overpowered the boy, laying him out, leaving him flat on his back, looking up at a twisted face, flared nostrils and bulging jaws that snorted air with a twisted disposition. Sweat poured angrily down the wild man's face. Yellow teeth showed unevenly as he sneered, standing over the fallen child, cursing the day of Tokus' conception. Tokus had taken many beatings, but as he grew in mental and physical strength, a lifetime of fear was replaced by a burning desire for payback. He waited. His time would come.

A piercing scream, a chorus of pain came down the hallway. Tokus winced inside and ran toward its source. He came to a stop in the bedroom doorway, catching his breath in horror. His stepfather knelt between his mother's legs. Her skirt was hiked way up over her thighs and her blouse was ripped open. Her breasts flopped out lewdly, exposed as the man reached out and pawed them. Then he slapped her in the face.

"You don't tell me 'no,' you lying slut!" he screamed. "You! Don't! Tell! Me! No!" he growled, punctuating each word with a backhand. "You just open your legs and get ready!" he finished. His chest heaved from mixing alcohol with physical exertion. He never saw Tokus charging toward him with his shoulder aimed like a battering ram.

Tokus saw his chance and hit harder than he had ever hit anyone on the football field and sent the man sprawling, face first, into the nightstand near the bedside. Tokus sprang to his feet in a defensive stance. The fading afternoon sunlight streamed through the window behind him, bathing him in ninja shadows. The stepfather rolled onto his back. The skin on his face puckered where he had been cut. The blood leaked down his face as he climbed to his feet, wobbled a bit, then threw his head back and screamed like a banshee. Tokus waited as his stepfather rushed toward him, a bulldozer with bared teeth.

Reality slowed for Tokus and he entered the "zone," a place where everything and everyone moved in surreal, slow motion. As his stepfather covered the few feet between them, Tokus realized that pound for pound, body-to-body, he would get steamrolled, so he went low, throwing his shoulders at the older man's knees. The stepfather went sailing, flailing into the curtains behind Tokus and crashing through the window. He grasped a handful of curtain and clung, pulling the fabric behind him and ripping the curtain rods out of the wall. The thin, aluminum rods wedged into the corner of the window and held for a second but the weight of the stepfather quickly snapped them in half. Tokus heard a desperate scream before the rods went clattering out the bedroom window, eight stories to the ground below.

Tokus looked at the window, shocked! For a second. Then he went over to the window to see where the creep had landed.

"Help!" came a panicked cry.

Tokus looked down, surprised to see that his stepfather was hanging on the window ledge. Shards of glass were biting into his fingers and blood leaked out onto the ledge. He was holding on with both hands, but Tokus wondered, for how long?

"Help me!" he screamed at Tokus.

"Help me, who?" Tokus asked.

"Help me, Tokus!"

"Mr. Tokus."

"Mr. Tokus! Mr. Tokus! Mr. Damn Tokus! Now pull me up! Please!" The glass bit deeper into the tender flesh of his fingers. Tokus' mother hurried over to the window, saw her husband hanging there and got frantic.

"Oh, my God!" she shrilled. "Oh! My! God! Tokus, pull him, pull him up!" she ordered and began to cry, her fingers dug deeply into the soft flesh of his shoulder.

Tokus leaned his head out the window. "You gonna die."

"Please, Tokus! Please?" The dangling stepfather kicked frantically at the building, his fingers pressed farther into the bits of glass as he fought against the fall.

"You know," Tokus began. "When you fall? Before you hit the ground? You gonna feel like I feel when you hit me. When you hit Ma."

"I won't do it no mo'!" the stepfather cried. His fingers slipped a fraction, and tiny squirts of blood shot against the windowsill. He moaned in pain and his arms tensed, tightening, gripping against the gravity that was pulling his body toward the hard concrete.

"Never no mo'! Promise! I promise! Please, Tokus!" the dying man cried for his life.

"A feelin' of nothin'," Tokus continued. "Nothin' you can do about it. As you fall. Nothin' you can hold on to. Nothin'."

"Tokus! Pull me up!" the stepfather begged.

"Tokus, help! Pull! Help him up!" his mother sobbed and collapsed to the floor, whimpering.

"Tokus, don't kill me! Don't let me die!" his stepfather yelled. Then he lost his grip.

Tokus lunged forward and caught his stepfather's hand. The momentum almost pulled Tokus out the window, but he held strongly to the wall with his free hand as the flailing, screaming man struggled against him. It took all his strength to pull the big man back up. His stepfather seemed to be fighting his efforts, twisting and turning, screaming and crying, but after a minute they both tumbled inside and sprawled on the floor, exhausted.

His mother rushed to her husband and fussed over him, ministering with a soft, gentle hand while she cried with relief and happiness. Tokus sat opposite the pair and looked into the man's eyes, surprised at the anger and fear he saw there. His stepfather was a changed man. There would be no more abuse.

The next day passed uneventfully. On the contrary, not a single word was exchanged in the strangely quiet, dysfunctional household. Hollow silence echoed ominously off the thin, plaster walls within the tenement as the three of them avoided each other in the small, two-bedroom apartment. Nothing mentioned, nothing gained.

Two days later, Tokus' mother and stepfather went away forever, leaving him alone in a man's world to fend for himself.

Tokus stood looking out the window at nothing, wondering what would happen next.

CHAPTER 1
MISTRESS OF IT

She stood, deliriously trembling, at the entrance to the park. The young girl searched frantically; her addiction screamed out for satisfaction and her flesh moved in chronic surrender. Long gone were the days when drug use was recreational fun, a fad. Times were now hardcore bouts of having and not having, getting and getting got over, even worse, acts that were once theatric drama were now hellish scenes in which she starred. Control of her life had been violently wrested from her and abused by a blizzard of white powder that enslaved her mind and spirit. Yet she loved her master. Her deeds were the proof. So she searched, following a voice only she could hear. The call of yearning.

She had to feed It. It was her habit. A greedy insatiable monster who stomped across the landscape of her soul. It talked to her often. It talked to her often. It knew where the drugs were and was well versed in all the ingenious ways in which to procure the precious substance.

The park loomed before her, threatening in the darkness of the late hour, sinister in its rolling, grassy slopes. An alarm went off somewhere in her mind, warning of danger, but that was drowned out by the thunder of It.

"Go," It said and she obediently shuffled down the man-made pathway as It grew heavy with urgency. The sights of the park held no interest to her. The beauty of nature's multicolored leaves of the tall trees, the picturesque shores on either side of the Hudson

River were a mere blur, as she set about her mission. She passed the small, outdoor amphitheater with hillside seating and the area known as The Shade, where tall trees stood with their leaves clasping together overhead, casting cool, shadowed refuge during the burning midday hours. The park was deserted—not a soul was in sight—but It guided her. She blindly obeyed. A monument saluting the Buffalo Soldiers was around the bend, hidden from her side of the path by the sloping land. The statue was huge. One soldier stood tall, rifle at the ready, while another kneeled to help a fallen comrade. This part of history meant nothing to her. It only had eyes for the three men who leaned against the tall, stone wall encrypted with the story of the all-black regiment known as the Buffalo Soldiers.

"Look!" It exclaimed as she rounded the curved pathway. She saw a light-skinned man with a big nose put a crack pipe to his lips. Reflexively, she inhaled with him and It pinpricked her brain with a glimpse of false euphoria. She put on her best sexy, crack smile and floated over to where the men stood between the soldiers and the wall.

The big-nosed smoker started rapping:
"Take two and pass,
take two and pass,
take two and pass
so the rock will last."

A dark-skinned man had the pipe. He took two hits and passed the pipe when he spotted the girl approaching.

"H-h-hold up! Waitaminute!" one of the men stuttered, looking the girl over. He recognized the type. "W-w-we got us a trick baby here. Y-y-you out here trickin', baby girl? Huh?"

The big-nosed man broke out with another rhyme:
"All men are created equal.
That's why corrupt governments
Kill innocent people.
With chemical warfare
They created crack and AIDS.
Got the public thinkin'
These are things that Black folks made."

◆ ◆ ◆

"Ask!" It commanded.
"Let me get a hit?" she asked.

"You t-t-trippin'," came the reply.

"Give me some," she said seductively.

"Yeah. You out here trickin'," the man said.

"Well," the big-nose spoke up, "I don't need no pussy, so get on, trick! I don't need no pussy."

"That's 'cause you smokin' that shit!" the dark man said. "You don't need no orgasm cause in your brain you already done got off. Skeeted ever' which-a-way!" He turned back to the girl. She could feel It agitating her. The hunger in her eyes was deepening. Her skin…her blood cried out for cocaine.

The dark man pulled a pebble-sized rock of crack cocaine out of his pocket. It's heart skipped a beat.

"You want some?" the dark man asked. She nodded her assent, mute with It.

"I give you some…if you take all your clothes off."

"No!" she shouted without consulting with It.

"What?" It said.

"No! No! Hell no!" she sang. It got angry. It was real ugly when provoked.

"Let me show you something," It said and began flashing scenes across her mind. Scenes from another time, another life. She was on her knees in the back seat of an old abandoned car with three teenaged boys. She'd spit them out the window. Then a German shepherd hunched over her, the dog's paws on her back, its hot breath on her neck. A group of men stood around watching, drinking beer and laughing at the girl who would do anything to get high.

"You will," It said and suddenly she felt the call of cocaine pulling, tearing at every fiber of her being.

"We outside," she said to the man, fighting It.

"Ain't nobody out here but us," the man and It replied in unison. Slowly, she looked around the park. In the thick stillness, she felt eyes everywhere. But there were no other people, not a one.

"Where at?" she asked.

"Here," the dark man replied, mirthfully. He leaned back against the stone wall with a knowing look.

"Go ahead," It said. "Do it. Now!" A blinding high pushed through her flesh, beamed directly into her brain that sent her mind on a spinning, flashing plateau that was miles above the cosmic reach of common thought, a teasing glimpse that quickly dissipated. She sobbed aloud and with trembling fingers, she peeled off her dirty, ripped shirt, exposing the holey, rusty bra underneath.

"Yeah!" It shouted. The three men smoked as they watched, eyeing her small pointy breasts as she removed her bra.

"The rest," said the dark man, wisps of smoke escaping from his lips. She stepped out of her pants and stood naked before them. She extended her arm, palm outward, seeking payment.

"Naw!" the dark man said. "Naw, you got to do more than that, baby!"

"You said naked," she cried.

"I know what I said!" he barked. "But let me see you crawl. Crawl to me. On your hands and knees. But sexy though! Like on TV," he finished. It brought her to her knees. She was openly crying now, and she began to crawl.

"Be sexy!" It warned.

Her sobs were alarming as she fought It. Cries of pain racked her body and she shook with the effort of trying to control herself—to lift herself from her knees, get up, get dressed and escape. She was fed up. It surged to life in response, shocking her with the overpowering need for crack, but she had reached the point of emotional saturation. She collapsed in a heap, mourning her searing desires and the pain It had wrought. The agony of living the white lie.

"She buggin' out," the big-nose said.

"Yeah," said the dark man with a mischievous grin. "Let's take her clothes." The three men gathered up her clothes and ran, laughing with chemical glee, leaving her naked and alone in the park.

◆◆◆

Tokus was taking the shortcut to Heath Street when he spotted the naked woman, shivering in the shadows of the old abandoned bridge that passed over the park. She huddled there, soaked in tears, another victim of the rock laid bare by the addiction to the altered state of mind. Her pain, her shame was something that no longer touched Tokus. He had seen her condition many times in many guises, but he attributed their plight to weak-mindedness. Some people just have addictive personalities, he reasoned.

Life had forced Tokus into a lifestyle that suited his need to survive a lifestyle just outside the word of the law. He hated the effect of drugs on people and the victims beyond the addicts. But drugs were a crutch people sought with a need, heedless of its impending, destructive effects. No matter, Tokus thought, 'cause I got dreams. Sadly, he looked at the naked girl, turned and walked away, headed back to his favorite street corner. The best drug spot in the city. He fingered the plastic-wrapped pieces of crack in his pocket and mentally prepared himself for a night of selling drugs in a world where dreams die first.